Guile of Night

Guile of Night

Dr. A. Romani

Pinion Books | Mt. Prospect, Il USA | 1 (888) 821-3271
www.PinionBooks.com

Published by **Dr. A. Romani** / Pinion Books

ISBN 979-8-9990430-8-5

"Guile of Night"

ISBN: 979-8-9990430-8-5 (print, paperback PB)

ISBN: 979-8-9990430-9-2 (EPUB)

Library of Congress Control Number 2025918595

BISAC: FIC030000 | FIC015040 | FIC022000

DEDICATION

For the ones who walk in the shadows, who find solace in the hushed corners of the world, and whose courage shines brightest when the night is at its deepest. To those who understand that the most chilling tales are often those that whisper truths we'd rather not acknowledge, and that within the darkest fears, we often find our greatest strength. May your own guile be as sharp as the night is long, and may you always find your way back to the light, even when the path is obscured. This story is woven from the threads of your silent resilience, the unspoken battles you fight, and the profound, often solitary, journey of the human spirit when confronted by the unknown. It is a tribute to the quiet observers, the keepers of forgotten stories, and the brave souls who dare to peer into the abyss, not with dread, but with a fierce, unwavering curiosity. To you, who feel the pulse of the night, this is for you. May it illuminate the hidden corners of your own extraordinary strength. May the winds blow you in the best directions.

TABLE OF CONTENT

INTRODUCTION

In the shadowy corners of Havenwood, secrets lay buried, waiting for someone to uncover them. Sarah, a historian with a passion for the past, stumbles upon a darkness that the town has fought to keep hidden. The year was 1954—a summer that should have been filled with laughter and light. Instead, it became a chapter of dread, marked by disappearances and a pact with something far more sinister than local lore suggests.

As Sarah sifts through missing council minutes and cryptic newspaper reports, she realizes that the town's silence is not merely a choice; it is a pact with a malevolent entity. Whispers echo through the empty streets, and phantom footsteps haunt her every move. She is about to learn that some histories are not just forgotten—they are erased for a reason.

Enter Silas Blackwood, a brooding artist with secrets of his own. He warns her about the dangers of digging too deep. "Some things are best left undisturbed," he says, his voice heavy with warning. But curiosity fuels Sarah, driving her to seek out the truth, even as she uncovers a diary that reveals a chilling connection to her own experiences. Eleanor Vance's words resonate with her, painting a picture of shared terror that transcends time.

With each revelation, the veil between worlds grows thinner. The entity that demands attention is no mere myth. It is alive, watching, and waiting. As the town prepares for the Founder's Day festival, a storm brews—a confrontation that will test Sarah's resolve and the very fabric of Havenwood.

What she learns will change everything. The echoes of the past are not just warnings; they are a call to action. As she becomes the reluctant guardian of Havenwood, she understands that vigilance is her only ally. The price of knowledge is high, and the stakes are higher. Will Sarah find the strength to protect her town, or will she become another whisper lost to the shadows? The battle for Havenwood is just beginning, and the darkness has a long memory.

DESCRIPTION

This is not just a story of discovery, but a gripping battle against a force that threatens to consume everything Sarah holds dear. Amidst the shadows, she must decide whether to embrace the fearful truths or fight to protect the fragile fabric separating her world from something beyond comprehension. Time races as Havenwood prepares for the Founder's Day festival — but the celebration may mark not a beginning, but an unmaking. Prepare to be drawn into a haunting narrative where every secret is weighed with consequence and every whisper echoes with warning. Moments linger long after the last page is turned, reminding us that some shadows never truly fade, and vigilance may be the only shield left.

Chapter 1: The whispers of Innocence

A Seemingly Peaceful Existence

Sarah, a librarian in her late twenties, moved through life with a quiet, almost imperceptible grace. Havenwood, the town she called home, mirrored this tranquility. Nestled beside a winding river and cradled by ancient, whispering woods, it was a place where the rhythm of life seemed to flow as gently as the water. Her apartment, a modest dwelling above a sleepy bakery, was her sanctuary, a haven of quietude built from towering stacks of books and the comforting, dry scent of old paper. Sunlight, often filtered through the leafy canopy of oak trees, dappled the worn Persian rug in her living room, illuminating dust motes dancing in the still air. Each volume on her shelves, from well-loved classics to esoteric historical texts, represented a portal to another world, a controlled escape that never demanded too much.

Her life was a testament to order and routine, a meticulously crafted symphony of predictable movements. Mornings began with the brewing of strong, black coffee, the aroma mingling with the lingering scent of yesterday's pastries from below. She'd select her attire with care, a practical yet understated elegance that suited her profession. The walk to the Havenwood Public Library, her domain, was a familiar path, past the quaint general store, the stoic town hall, and the vibrant blooms in Mrs. Gable's garden. Each step was a familiar cadence, a reassuring beat in the quiet drum of her days. The library itself was a sanctuary within a sanctuary, a hushed cathedral of knowledge where the loudest sounds were the rustle of turning pages or the gentle click of the cataloguing system. Here, Sarah thrived.

The hushed reverence of the space, the quiet concentration of the patrons, the very dust motes that danced in the sunbeams that pierced the tall, arched windows – all spoke of a deep, abiding peace.

Sarah found solace in the predictability. The predictable ebb and flow of patron requests, the satisfaction of finding the perfect book for a reader, the methodical process of shelving and archiving – these were the anchors that kept her grounded. She believed, with an almost unshakeable faith, in the inherent goodness of people and places. Havenwood, in her eyes, was a testament to this belief. It was a town where doors were rarely locked, where neighbors knew each other's routines, and where a lost child was always found with a community effort. The subtle hum of contentment that permeated the town's atmosphere was, to Sarah, a reflection of its essential purity. She felt a quiet, almost unconscious gratitude for this life, this ordered existence that shielded her from the messy, unpredictable chaos that seemed to plague the world beyond Havenwood's borders.

Yet, beneath the placid surface of her contentment, a subtle dissatisfaction stirred, like a faint tremor beneath solid ground. It wasn't a yearning for grand adventure or a desperate cry for excitement, but a more nuanced longing for something... more. A feeling, perhaps, that the edges of her existence were a little too soft, a little too unblemished. Her days were filled, but her spirit sometimes felt under-stimulated, like a well-tuned instrument left unplayed. She would sometimes catch herself staring out of the library window, her gaze drifting towards the dense, emerald mass of the woods that skirted the town, a place she rarely ventured into. There was a stillness in Havenwood that, while comforting, also felt a touch too profound, a stillness that perhaps masked a deeper, more unsettling quietude. It was a feeling akin to standing on the shore of a vast ocean, knowing its depths held mysteries, but being content to simply admire the placid surface. Her life was safe, predictable, and undeniably good, but it also felt... a little too still. The comfort she found in routine was a double-edged sword, a shield that also limited her view of what lay beyond. This subtle, unacknowledged ache, this whisper of 'what if,' was a tiny seed of dissonance in the otherwise harmonious symphony of her life, a melody that was about to be disrupted by a discordant, unforgettable note.

The Unsettling Arrival

The usual gentle hum of Havenwood seemed to falter, a subtle tremor running through its placid surface, on the day Silas Blackwood arrived. It wasn't a dramatic entrance, no fanfare or public announcement, but a quiet unfurling of a new presence that, like a stain on fine linen, began to spread. Sarah first heard his name whispered, a hushed murmur over the library counter, a hushed gossip exchanged between patrons browsing the fiction aisle. "Did you see him? The new tenant at the old Hawthorne place?" the whispers went, tinged with an undeniable curiosity that bordered on apprehension. The Hawthorne place, a sprawling, somewhat dilapidated Victorian mansion that had stood vacant for years, its darkened windows like vacant eyes staring out over the town, had always been a source of local lore and whispered warnings. Its overgrown gardens and peeling paint seemed to absorb and reflect the town's underlying unease.

Sarah, ever the observer from her quiet perch amidst the bookshelves, registered the shift in the town's emotional barometer. The usual contented murmur of daily life was now laced with a new, inquisitive thread. It was during her weekly trip to the Havenwood Farmers' Market, a vibrant tableau of local produce and friendly chatter, that she encountered him. The market, usually an oasis of wholesome familiarity, felt… different. The crisp autumn air, usually invigorating, carried a faint, almost imperceptible chill that had nothing to do with the changing season. It was here, amidst the bounty of apples and pumpkins, that Sarah's gaze fell upon a figure who seemed to command an invisible radius of stillness.

He stood by a stall laden with artisanal cheeses, his back to her initially. Tall and lean, dressed in a dark, impeccably tailored coat that seemed to absorb the sunlight rather than reflect it, he possessed an aura of profound, almost unsettling, detachment. When he turned, it was as if the world momentarily held its breath. His features were sharp, sculpted with an artist's precision, a strong jawline, an aquiline nose, and cheekbones that hinted at a lineage as ancient as the woods surrounding Havenwood. But it was his eyes that truly arrested Sarah's attention. They were the colour of storm clouds, a deep, fathomless grey, and when they met hers, there was an intensity, a piercing quality, that felt less like an observation and more like an assessment. It was a gaze that seemed to strip away the layers, to see not just the librarian in her sensible cardigan, but the woman beneath, with all her unspoken thoughts and quiet longings.

He offered a polite, almost perfunctory nod, a subtle inclination of his head, and Sarah, flustered by the unexpected directness of his gaze, managed a weak smile. The interaction was fleeting, a mere flicker of shared space, yet it lingered with an unnerving persistence. He purchased a small, pale wheel of brie, his movements economical and deliberate, and then disappeared as quietly as he had arrived, melting back into the throng of the market, yet leaving a distinct impression, like a stone dropped into still water, its ripples spreading outward.

The whispers intensified after that. Silas Blackwood, the reclusive artist. He'd purchased the Hawthorne place, people said, for its isolation, its brooding grandeur. He rarely ventured out, preferring to keep to himself, a wraith haunting the edges of their community. Some claimed he was a famous painter, others a disgraced musician, still others a man fleeing some unsavory past. The lack of concrete information only fueled the speculation, allowing the fertile imaginations of Havenwood's residents to weave elaborate narratives around him. He was an enigma, a blank canvas onto which they projected their own fears and fantasies.

Sarah found herself thinking about him, about that unsettling gaze. It was a departure from the predictable kindnesses she encountered daily. The townspeople were generally open, their lives a comfortable, well-lit panorama. Blackwood, however, felt like a shadow, a presence that hinted at depths unknown, at complexities unseen. He was an anomaly in the tapestry of Havenwood, a dark thread woven into a predominantly light pattern. Her thoughts, usually occupied with Dewey Decimal classifications and literary critiques, found themselves snagged on the image of his storm-cloud eyes. It was a subtle intrusion, a faint dissonance in the quiet symphony of her days, but it was enough to stir a nascent sense of unease, a feeling that the placid surface of her world was perhaps thinner than she had ever imagined.

The library, her sanctuary, became a subtle barometer of this shift. Conversations among patrons now frequently veered towards the new resident. "He hasn't been seen since Tuesday," Mrs. Gable, a woman whose life revolved around her prize-winning roses and town gossip, confided in Sarah, her voice a conspiratorial whisper as she checked out a gardening manual. "And the lights in Hawthorne place, they say they're never on. Or maybe they flicker, like they're fighting to stay lit."

Young Timmy Peterson, whose mother brought him in for the children's story hour, tugged on Sarah's sleeve one afternoon. "My dad said Mr. Blackwood's a vampire," he'd breathed, his eyes wide with a mixture of fear and fascination. Sarah had gently chided him, explaining that vampires were creatures of myth, but even as she spoke, a sliver of doubt, a tiny, unwelcome seed of the fantastical, took root. The idea was absurd, of course, yet the way Blackwood's presence seemed to drain the warmth from a room, the almost palpable coolness that clung to him, made the superstitious whispers gain a peculiar, unsettling traction.

It was the artistic element that truly intrigued and perturbed the townsfolk. Blackwood was rumored to be an artist, but no one had seen his work. He brought with him crates of what were described as strange, dark canvases, and hushed rumors spoke of him working at all hours, the only light emanating from his studio the eerie glow of oil lamps. Some said he painted macabre scenes, others that his art was so profound it drove viewers to madness. The very mystery surrounding his craft amplified the unease. Art, in Havenwood, was typically represented by the pleasant watercolors of local landscapes or the cheerful pottery crafted by the ladies' guild. Blackwood's art was said to be something else entirely, something that dwelled in the shadows, something that spoke of an inner world far removed from the gentle rhythms of their lives.

Sarah found herself drawn to this mystery, a silent observer of the town's collective speculation. She'd try to glean more information from patrons, subtle probes disguised as casual inquiries. "Have you heard anything more about Mr. Blackwood's art?" she'd ask, her tone carefully neutral. The responses were always vague, filled with hearsay and conjecture. "He's very private," they'd say, or, "He's a true bohemian, I suppose." The reluctance to offer concrete details only served to deepen the intrigue. It was as if Blackwood himself had cast a spell of silence around his life, a protective barrier that only amplified the whispers from beyond.

One rainy afternoon, as the scent of damp earth and decaying leaves permeated the library air, Sarah found herself staring out the tall, arched window towards the silhouette of the Hawthorne place, barely visible through the persistent drizzle. The old mansion seemed to loom, a brooding presence on the edge of town, and for the first time, Sarah felt a prickle of something akin to fear. It wasn't a rational fear, not one based on tangible evidence, but an intuitive, visceral reaction to an unknown quantity. Silas Blackwood, the artist who arrived with the turning of the leaves, had introduced a subtle, yet undeniable, element of the unsettling into her meticulously ordered world. He was a question mark, a shadow cast upon the sunlit canvas of Havenwood, and the unanswered nature of his presence began to stir a disquiet that Sarah, with all her love for predictable narratives, found increasingly difficult to ignore.

The quiet, almost imperceptible seed of dissonance she had felt before had now begun to sprout, its tendrils reaching into the carefully cultivated tranquility of her life. The whispers of innocence that had defined Havenwood were now being joined by a new, darker chorus, and Sarah, caught in its subtle resonance, felt a shiver of anticipation, a strange, unwelcome thrill, at what this new melody might portend.

Flickering Lights and Fading Memories

The subtle discord introduced by Silas Blackwood's arrival, initially a mere ripple on the placid surface of Sarah's life, began to manifest in more personal and unsettling ways. It started, as such things often do, with trifles, easily dismissed by a rational mind. The overhead light in her small, book-lined apartment, usually a steady beacon of warm illumination, began to exhibit an unnerving capriciousness. It would flicker, not in the dramatic, house-wide blackout fashion of a storm, but in short, sharp bursts, a nervous tic that seemed to mirror a growing unease within her. A quick flick, then back to normal, as if the bulb itself was catching its breath, or perhaps, catching sight of something it didn't want to see. Sarah would initially attribute it to the ancient wiring of the building, a common enough complaint in Havenwood, a town that wore its age with a certain charming, albeit sometimes inconvenient, grace. She'd tap the lampshade, wiggle the bulb, a mundane ritual performed with a sigh that was more weary acceptance than genuine concern. Yet, the flickering persisted, becoming a more frequent punctuation mark in her evenings, each burst of darkness a tiny, disorienting pause in the flow of her quiet existence.

Then came the objects. Not the grand, dramatic disappearances of the sort found in detective novels, but the subtle repositioning, the infinitesimal shifts that, upon initial observation, felt like trickery of the eye. Her favourite teacup, habitually placed precisely on the coaster by the sink, would be found a fraction of an inch to the left. A bookmark, meticulously aligned with the edge of the page before she went to bed, would be discovered lying askew, as if nudged by an unseen hand. These were not things that shouted malfeasance; they whispered doubt, inviting Sarah to question her own memory, her own meticulous habits. Had she moved the cup herself and forgotten? Was she simply tired, her usual orderliness momentarily slipping? She'd catch herself performing mental checks, retracing her steps, trying to rationalize the anomalies, each instance chipping away at her certainty. The cumulative effect was insidious, a slow erosion of her sense of a stable, predictable environment, even within the confines of her own home. The familiar, once a source of comfort, began to feel subtly alien, a stage set where the props were no longer entirely reliable.

This growing undercurrent of disquiet was amplified by a peculiar sensation, a phantom déjà vu that haunted her days. It was as if she was living moments already experienced, not in a distinct memory, but in a fleeting, visceral echo. A conversation with a patron at the library, a particular turn of phrase, a specific quality of light filtering through the windows – these would trigger a profound sense of recurrence. It was the feeling of having walked this exact path before, of having uttered these exact words, of having felt this exact sensation. The sensation was rarely pleasant; it was often tinged with a vague foreboding, an impression that this repeating moment held some unspoken significance, some hidden meaning she was desperately trying to grasp. But the recognition was always fleeting, like a half-remembered dream upon waking, leaving behind only a residue of unease. She found herself pausing mid-sentence, her mind momentarily catching on a phantom echo, her brow furrowing in a fruitless attempt to reconcile the present with the ghost of its past. This recurring disorientation chipped away at her sense of temporal continuity, making the present feel less solid, less real.

The fatigue that accompanied these minor disturbances was more than mere physical tiredness. It was a mental exhaustion, a weary draining of her reserves as she constantly battled the subtle inconsistencies that began to pepper her days. Sleep offered little respite. Instead, her nights became a canvas for fragmented dreams, vivid yet nonsensical tapestries woven from disconnected images and disembodied sensations. She'd dream of wandering through endless corridors, the walls lined with books whose titles morphed and shifted, the air thick with the scent of ozone and damp earth. She'd see fleeting glimpses of Silas Blackwood, his storm-grey eyes piercing through the darkness, not menacing, but somehow deeply, disturbingly familiar, as if he were a character from a story she'd always known but never fully understood. These dreams left her disoriented upon waking, the edges of her reality beginning to fray at the periphery. The clear lines between the waking world and the landscape of her slumber blurred, leaving her feeling adrift, struggling to anchor herself in the tangible. The familiar contours of her bedroom, the morning light painting familiar patterns on the walls, felt somehow distant, less substantial than the vivid, chaotic fragments that lingered from her sleep.

One morning, she found her keys, which she distinctly remembered placing in the ceramic bowl by the door, perched precariously on the edge of the kitchen counter. It was such a small thing, so easily explained by absentmindedness. But the cumulative weight of these minor discrepancies was beginning to press down on her. She started to feel a prickle of anxiety, a low hum of apprehension that seemed to emanate from the very air she breathed. It wasn't a fear of any specific threat, but a generalized dread, a sense that the predictable order of her world was subtly, irrevocably shifting. The whispers of Havenwood, once filled with the innocent chatter of community life, now seemed to carry an undercurrent of something darker, something that Silas Blackwood, the reclusive artist, had somehow invited into their midst.

The library, usually a bastion of calm and order, began to feel different too. The quiet murmur of patrons seemed to carry a new tension, a heightened awareness of unspoken things. Sarah found herself scanning the faces, searching for clues, for any reflection of the disquiet that had begun to bloom within her. She noticed how often the conversation would drift, almost inevitably, towards the Hawthorne place, towards its enigmatic new occupant. The hushed tones, the furtive glances exchanged, spoke of a shared, unspoken unease. Mrs. Gable, the fervent gardener, confided in Sarah with a conspiratorial whisper, "That light in his studio, Sarah. It's never a steady light. It pulses, like a dying heart. And sometimes," her voice dropped even lower, her eyes wide, "I swear I can see shapes moving behind the glass, shapes that don't look quite human."

Sarah tried to dismiss these anxieties, to reassert her rational mind. She'd remind herself that artists were often eccentric, that their lives often operated on different wavelengths. But the lingering impression of Blackwood's gaze, the unnerving stillness he exuded, coupled with the subtle disturbances in her own life, made it increasingly difficult to maintain her detachment. She began to notice a pattern, a disturbing correlation between the increasing strangeness in her apartment and the general atmosphere of hushed speculation that now permeated Havenwood.

Her dreams, in particular, became a source of growing concern. They were becoming more vivid, more intrusive. One night, she dreamt she was standing in the darkened library, the shelves stretching up into an impossible darkness, the books themselves seeming to breathe. Silas Blackwood was there, standing in the center of the room, not looking at her, but meticulously arranging an array of small, intricately carved wooden figures on a pedestal. The figures were unsettling, their forms twisted and elongated, their faces contorted in silent screams. As she watched, one of the figures seemed to twitch, its wooden limbs shifting impossibly. She'd woken with a gasp, her heart hammering against her ribs, the image of those writhing figures seared into her mind. The dream felt too real, too charged with an unspoken meaning.

The déjà vu moments intensified, becoming more frequent and more pronounced. Walking down the street one afternoon, she had a sudden, overwhelming sensation that she had already had this exact conversation, this exact exchange of glances, with the elderly Mr. Henderson walking his terrier. The feeling was so potent that she faltered, her steps faltering, a cold sweat breaking out on her brow. Mr. Henderson, oblivious, simply offered a cheerful nod, but the moment left Sarah shaken, questioning the very fabric of her reality. It was as if the world around her was repeating itself, caught in some unseen, unnatural loop.

The flickering lights in her apartment became a nightly occurrence, a silent, unnerving rhythm section to her growing anxiety. She tried to read, to lose herself in the familiar comfort of stories, but the erratic pulsing of the lamp above her head was a constant distraction. It was as if the light itself was struggling against an encroaching darkness, a losing battle against an unseen force. She found herself staring at the bulb, her mind conjuring images of an unseen hand reaching out from the shadows, manipulating the flow of electricity, toying with her sense of control.

Her memory, usually so sharp and reliable, began to betray her. She'd find herself standing in a room, a vague sense of purpose on the tip of her tongue, only for the thought to evaporate, leaving behind a frustrating blankness. She'd spend precious minutes searching for her spectacles, only to find them perched on her head. These were minor lapses, certainly, but they contributed to a pervasive sense of losing her grip, of her well-ordered mind beginning to fray. The carefully constructed narrative of her life, once so clear and linear, was becoming fragmented, punctuated by these inexplicable gaps and shifts.

The feeling of being watched, an old, dormant unease, began to resurface. It wasn't the overt, menacing gaze of a stalker, but a subtler, more pervasive sensation, as if unseen eyes were constantly observing her, cataloging her every move. She found herself instinctively checking her windows, glancing over her shoulder, a primal instinct kicking in that had no rational basis. The quiet intimacy of her apartment, once a sanctuary, began to feel exposed, vulnerable.

She noticed that the subtle changes in her surroundings seemed to coincide with Blackwood's infrequent appearances in town. When he was seen, even briefly, Sarah felt the atmospheric shift more keenly, the subtle distortions in her reality becoming more pronounced. It was as if his presence acted as a catalyst, amplifying the strange occurrences, drawing them out of the shadows and into the open, albeit in small, insidious ways. The whispers about him, once a matter of idle curiosity, now carried a weight of genuine apprehension, a sense that this outsider had brought something with him that was fundamentally at odds with the gentle spirit of Havenwood.

The dreams, too, seemed to be influenced by this growing unease. They were no longer merely fragmented; they were becoming tinged with a distinct sense of dread. She dreamt of a labyrinth, the walls made of shifting shadows, and at its center, a single, unblinking eye. The eye, when it focused on her, was the exact stormy grey of Silas Blackwood's, and in its depths, she saw not recognition, but an ancient, unfathomable emptiness. She would wake with a cry, the feeling of profound isolation and insignificance clinging to her like a shroud. The boundary between her subconscious and her waking perception was becoming porous, the anxieties of the day bleeding into the fragile landscape of her sleep, and vice versa. The world, once a place of comforting predictability, was beginning to feel like a fragile construct, easily fractured, its familiar components subtly rearranged by an unseen, unacknowledged hand. The innocence of Havenwood, once a tangible presence, felt like a memory, a distant echo, as a new, unsettling melody began to play in the quiet corners of Sarah's existence. The flickering lights were not just faulty wiring; they were signals, faint and intermittent, of a reality that was slowly, inexorably, beginning to dim.

The Shadow in the Alley

The encroaching twilight was more than a mere dimming of the sun; it was a tangible shift in the atmosphere of Havenwood. As Sarah left the hushed sanctuary of the library, the familiar cobblestone streets, usually imbued with a comforting, old-world charm, seemed to stretch out before her, imbued with a newfound menace. The quaint gas lamps that dotted the thoroughfares, their gentle glow usually a beacon of reassurance, now cast elongated, dancing shadows that played tricks on the eye, morphing familiar shapes into unsettling silhouettes. The air, cool and crisp moments before, now seemed to carry a heavy, damp chill, clinging to her skin like an unwanted embrace.

Her route home was a well-trodden path, a ribbon of normalcy she traversed almost daily. Tonight, however, each familiar landmark seemed to hold a hidden threat. The gnarled oak tree at the corner of Elm Street, its branches skeletal against the bruised sky, appeared to writhe as if in silent agony. The cheerful chime of a distant church bell, normally a comforting sound, was distorted, drawn out into a mournful, discordant toll. Sarah found herself walking faster, her sensible walking shoes clicking an anxious rhythm against the stones. The usual pleasantries exchanged with passing neighbours felt strained, their smiles seeming a little too fixed, their eyes lingering a fraction too long. A prickle of unease, a sensation she had grown increasingly accustomed to, began to bloom into a more potent, visceral fear.

It was as she neared the narrow lane that served as a shortcut between the main street and her apartment building that the incident occurred. The alley, even in daylight, was a place she instinctively avoided, a narrow chasm between two imposing brick buildings, perpetually steeped in shadow. Tonight, it was an inky void, an abyss that seemed to swallow the meagre light of the fading day. As her eyes, drawn by an instinct she couldn't quite articulate, flickered towards its entrance, she saw it. A movement. A fleeting, ephemeral glimpse of something dark and sinuous, like a thread of smoke unfurling, darting from the deeper recesses of the alley into the relative openness of the street, only to vanish again within the confines of the shadowed passage.

Sarah froze, her breath catching in her throat. For a fraction of a second, her mind struggled to process what she had seen. It was too quick, too indistinct to be anything substantial. A stray cat, perhaps? Or a stray dog, seeking refuge from the cooling air? But the impression that lingered was not of fur or flesh, but of something fluid, something impossibly agile, something that moved with a predatory grace that sent a shiver down her spine. It was a shadow detaching itself from other shadows, a fleeting disruption in the familiar pattern of the evening.

She tried to rationalize it away, to dismiss it as a trick of the fading light, a conjuration of her overwrought nerves. Havenwood, for all its idyllic facade, was a town with its share of secrets, and Silas Blackwood's arrival had seemed to stir something ancient and restless beneath its surface. But this was different. This was a primal instinct, a gut-level reaction that screamed danger. The fleeting image of that darting form, ephemeral as it was, had imprinted itself upon her consciousness with a startling clarity.

She told herself it was merely the suggestion of movement, a phantom born from the interplay of light and shadow. The alleyway was a known haunt for vagrants, for those who preferred the anonymity of the city's underbelly. But the speed, the unnatural swiftness with which it had moved, gnawed at her. It hadn't slunk or scurried; it had flowed, a silent ripple through the darkening air.

As she continued her walk, the encounter, however brief, cast a long, unsettling pall over her. The familiar streets no longer felt safe. The houses, with their warm, inviting windows, seemed to hold their breath, their silence now pregnant with unspoken possibilities. She found herself scanning every doorway, every shadowed alcove, her senses on high alert, searching for any sign of that elusive movement. The cheerful greetings of passersby now seemed like a thin veneer, a fragile shield against an encroaching darkness.

The prickling sensation on the back of her neck, the undeniable feeling of being observed, intensified. It was as if the very air had become a conscious entity, its unseen gaze fixed upon her. She imagined eyes peering from behind curtains, from darkened windows, from the very alley she had just passed. The ordinary sounds of the town – the distant rumble of a car, the chirping of unseen crickets – seemed amplified, each noise a potential signal of pursuit, each rustle of leaves a harbinger of revelation.

Her pace quickened, her stride becoming more purposeful, almost a hurried march. The perceived safety of her apartment building, a small, brick edifice that had always represented a haven of quiet solitude, now felt like a distant, desperately sought-after sanctuary. She resisted the urge to look back, the fear that she might see the shadowy form emerge from the alley, its indistinct outline solidifying, pursuing her, a tangible threat born from the ethereal.

The once-comforting familiarity of Havenwood had been subtly, yet profoundly, altered. The charming, sleepy town that had welcomed her with open arms was now layered with a disconcerting unease, a sense that beneath the placid surface, something ancient and watchful stirred. The fleeting glimpse into the alley had been more than a visual anomaly; it had been a jarring disruption of her reality, a stark reminder that even the most mundane of walks could lead to the precipice of the unknown. The very air seemed to hum with an unseen energy, a silent testament to the fact that her journey home had become a race against an unseen pursuer, a flight from a shadow that had momentarily detached itself from the fabric of the night.

The further she walked, the more convinced she became that her perception had not been deceived. The sheer speed and fluidity of the movement had defied easy explanation. It was not the clumsy scramble of an animal, nor the hurried dash of a person. It possessed a quality of motion that was both unsettling and strangely mesmerizing, a testament to something utterly alien to the ordinary rhythms of life in Havenwood.

She reached her apartment building, fumbling with her keys, her hands trembling slightly. The small, familiar lobby, usually bathed in the warm, inviting glow of a single overhead lamp, seemed dimmer tonight, the shadows pooling in the corners with a greater intensity. She ascended the creaking wooden stairs, each step a small victory against the encroaching anxiety. The lock on her apartment door seemed to resist her efforts for a moment, its tumblers stubbornly refusing to yield, amplifying her growing panic.

Finally, the click of the lock echoed through the small space, a sound of blessed release. She practically stumbled inside, closing the door behind her with a decisive thud, leaning against it, her chest heaving. Her apartment, usually a sanctuary, felt suddenly too small, too exposed. She drew the heavy velvet curtains, severing her connection with the outside world, the encroaching darkness. Even behind the drawn fabric, she could still feel it, the lingering sensation of being watched.

She walked to the window, peering through a small gap in the curtains. The street below, usually a scene of quiet domesticity, now seemed populated by an army of shadows. The gas lamps cast pools of sickly yellow light, illuminating empty patches of pavement, while the spaces between them remained in impenetrable darkness. She scanned the alleyway entrance, its maw a gaping wound in the side of the street. It was still and silent, a perfect imitation of innocence, yet she knew, with a certainty that chilled her to the bone, that something had been lurking there, something that had caught a glimpse of her, and perhaps, had even acknowledged her presence.

The encounter had fundamentally altered her perception of Havenwood. The town, which had always felt like a gentle, predictable entity, now seemed to harbor a hidden, predatory nature. The innocent whispers that had characterized its quiet charm were being replaced by a more sinister undercurrent, a silent language of apprehension that she was only now beginning to decipher. The shadow in the alley had been a stark, albeit fleeting, manifestation of this burgeoning unease, a fleeting glimpse into a reality that was far more complex, and far more menacing, than she had ever imagined.

She tried to settle herself, to return to the routine of her evening. She put on the kettle, the familiar ritual a desperate attempt to reassert control. But her thoughts kept returning to the alley, to the impossible speed of that fleeting form. It was a detail that refused to be dismissed, a sensory input that defied rationalization. Her mind, usually so adept at finding logical explanations, was struggling to accommodate this anomaly.

As she waited for the kettle to boil, her gaze fell upon a small, intricately carved wooden bird that sat on her windowsill, a gift from a long-forgotten acquaintance. It was a simple thing, meant to evoke the cheerful chirp of nature, but tonight, its smooth, polished surface seemed to gleam with an unsettling luminescence. She found herself staring at it, her mind conjuring images of its delicate wings, its poised stance, and the disturbing thought arose, unbidden, that such a creature could, in another context, possess a terrifying, unnatural agility.

The kettle whistled, a sharp, piercing sound that made her jump. She poured the hot water into her mug, the steam rising in fragrant tendrils, yet the warmth did little to dispel the chill that had settled deep within her. She sat at her small kitchen table, the book she had intended to read lying open and ignored before her. Her eyes kept drifting to the window, to the curtained void that separated her from the perceived threats lurking just beyond.

The feeling of being watched persisted, a low hum of anxiety that vibrated through her very being. It was as if the shadow she had glimpsed had left a residue of its presence, a psychic imprint upon the very air she breathed. The familiar creaks and groans of her apartment building, sounds she had long since learned to ignore, now seemed amplified, imbued with a new significance. Each settling of the timbers, each whisper of wind against the glass, felt like a furtive movement, a clandestine arrival.

She knew, with a chilling certainty, that the mundane walk home had been irrevocably altered. The perception of safety had been shattered, replaced by a gnawing vulnerability. The shadow in the alley was not just a visual disturbance; it was a symbol, a harbinger of a deeper disquiet that was beginning to take root in the heart of Havenwood, and more importantly, within the fragile architecture of her own perception. The whispers of innocence had begun to give way to a more profound, and far more terrifying, chorus of doubt. The night was no longer a time of peaceful rest, but a canvas upon which her deepest anxieties could paint their most unsettling portraits. And as she sat there, bathed in the dim, artificial light of her apartment, she knew that the shadow she had seen was merely the first whisper of a darkness that was only just beginning to reveal itself.

The familiarity of her surroundings, once a source of solace, now felt like a fragile illusion. The very walls of her apartment seemed to lean in, to press closer, as if sharing a secret that she was not yet privy to. She found herself analyzing the subtle shifts in the shadows cast by the furniture, attributing a sentience to the familiar objects that populated her small living space. The armchair in the corner, usually a comfortable haven for reading, now seemed to crouch, its upholstered form suggesting something coiled and watchful. The bookshelf, laden with stories of adventure and escape, suddenly appeared like a dense, impenetrable forest, capable of concealing any number of unseen creatures.

She stood up, pacing the confines of her living room, her movements restless, agitated. Her gaze kept returning to the drawn curtains, as if expecting them to part of their own volition, to reveal the source of her mounting dread. The memory of the alley, so brief and indistinct, was now replaying itself in her mind with an almost obsessive clarity, each iteration adding a new layer of detail, a new facet of unease. She remembered the absolute silence of the movement, the utter lack of any accompanying sound that would betray its passage. It was a silent breach of the natural order, a fleeting rupture in the expected symphony of the night.

The memory of Silas Blackwood himself, his intense, storm-grey eyes and his unnerving stillness, flickered through her thoughts. Was there a connection? Had his arrival somehow awakened something dormant within Havenwood, something that now manifested in these unsettling occurrences? The speculation, once a matter of idle curiosity, now held the weight of genuine fear. It was as if his enigmatic presence had cast a long, dark shadow, not just over the town, but over the very fabric of reality itself, allowing these more subtle, insidious disturbances to seep into the everyday.

She tried to shake off these thoughts, to anchor herself in the mundane. She remembered the library's hushed calm, the comforting scent of old paper and polished wood. But the contrast between that sanctuary and the disquiet that now gripped her was stark and unforgiving. The library, too, had begun to feel different in recent weeks, a subtle shift in its atmosphere, a growing undercurrent of hushed whispers and furtive glances that now seemed to echo the unease she felt within herself.

Her attention was drawn to the sounds from outside. A distant car door slamming shut. The mournful cry of a night bird. Each sound, once innocuous, was now imbued with a potential threat. She imagined the sound of footsteps on the pavement below, slow and deliberate, pausing beneath her window. She strained her ears, listening intently, her heart pounding a frantic rhythm against her ribs. But there was only the silence, a silence that was more unnerving than any noise.

The feeling of being watched was a tangible presence, a prickling awareness that seemed to emanate from the very air around her. It was as if the universe itself had turned its gaze upon her, scrutinizing her every move, waiting for her to falter. She instinctively lowered herself, crouching behind the sofa, as if by reducing her visibility, she could somehow become invisible. The absurdity of her action did not escape her, yet the primal instinct to hide, to seek refuge from an unseen threat, was overwhelming.

She remained there for several long minutes, the silence broken only by the ragged sound of her own breathing. When she finally dared to rise, it was with a sense of profound exhaustion, as if she had just run a marathon. The encounter in the alley, the subsequent heightened awareness of her surroundings, had taken a significant toll. The familiar comfort of her home had been replaced by a pervasive sense of vulnerability, and the once-innocent streets of Havenwood had transformed into a landscape fraught with unseen dangers. The shadow, however fleeting, had cast a long and chilling premonition, a stark reminder that the whispers of innocence were slowly, inexorably, being drowned out by a more sinister, and far more compelling, narrative. The journey home had become a prelude to a disquiet that was only just beginning to unfold.

A Community's Unease

The hushed conversations began subtly, like the first tendrils of mist creeping over the lake on a still morning. Sarah, still reeling from her own unsettling encounter the previous evening, found herself attuned to the slightest shifts in Havenwood's usually placid social current. It was in the hushed tones of Mrs. Gable, her usually robust voice reduced to a conspiratorial whisper, as she recounted a peculiar incident with her prize-winning petunias to a concerned Mrs. Albright at the bakery. "They just... withered, Eleanor. Overnight. Not a single pest to be seen, mind you. Just turned to dust, like they'd been forgotten by the sun itself." Eleanor, her flour-dusted apron a testament to years of comforting routines, nodded gravely, her eyes darting towards the shadows pooling in the corner of the shop. "It's not just the flowers, Agnes. Remember Mr. Henderson's prize bull? Went mad, they said. Broke free from his stall, charged the fence... never seen anything like it. That was... what, ten years ago? Just before that terrible storm that blew the old oak down."

Sarah, pretending to examine a display of artisanal breads, found herself leaning in, a morbid curiosity overriding her desire for normalcy. These weren't isolated complaints; they were threads, loosely woven, hinting at a pattern of disquiet that had been buried beneath Havenwood's veneer of tranquility. Later that day, while browsing the aisles of the general store for milk, she caught fragments of a conversation between old Mr. Abernathy and young Timmy Davies, who was stocking shelves with a nervous haste that belied his usual youthful exuberance. "Heard Silas Blackwood was seen out by the old quarry again last night," Mr. Abernathy rasped, his voice a dry rustle like autumn leaves.

"Just standing there, staring into the darkness. Said he looked like he was... listening to something." Timmy, his face pale, dropped a can of beans with a clatter. "My mother says he doesn't sleep. Says he's always awake, watching. And she says... she says he's got eyes like a raven."

The mention of Silas Blackwood, the reclusive newcomer whose imposing, Gothic-revival mansion now loomed on the outskirts of town like a brooding sentinel, sent a fresh wave of unease through Sarah. His arrival had coincided, she now realized with a chilling clarity, with a subtle, yet undeniable, shift in the town's atmosphere. The local newspaper, usually filled with mundane reports of bake sales and town council meetings, had recently published a brief, almost dismissive article about Blackwood purchasing the derelict Blackwood Estate, noting his singular and eccentric nature. But the whispers, the ones that slithered through back alleys and over garden fences, painted a far more disturbing portrait. They spoke of long, solitary walks under the cloak of night, of an almost preternatural stillness that unnerved even the most hardened of locals, and of an intense, unnerving gaze that seemed to pierce through polite conversation and into the very soul.

Sarah found herself piecing together these scattered narratives, each overheard snippet a brushstroke adding to a growing canvas of communal apprehension. The old fears, long dormant and dismissed as the fanciful ramblings of a bygone era, were resurfacing, drawn out from the shadows by Silas Blackwood's enigmatic presence. She recalled hushed tales from her childhood, stories her grandmother would tell with a fearful tremor in her voice, about Havenwood's darker history, about unexplained disappearances and unsettling omens that predated even the oldest families. These were stories she had always attributed to a child's overactive imagination, tales spun to add a touch of spooky allure to the sleepy town. But now, they resonated with a disturbing prescience.

The fear wasn't just in the whispers; it was in the way people looked at each other, the way their eyes darted towards darkened windows or the treeline bordering the town. It was in the hesitant way children played outdoors, their usual boisterous games muted, their games of tag frequently interrupted by anxious calls from parents. The familiar rhythm of Havenwood had been disrupted, replaced by a nervous staccato, a constant underlying hum of anxiety. Even the ever-present chirping of crickets at dusk, a sound that had always signified a peaceful end to the day, now seemed to possess a frantic, almost desperate urgency, as if the insects themselves were trying to warn of an approaching peril.

Sarah found herself drawn to the library more than ever, not for its comforting collection of stories, but for the hushed silence that allowed her to process the disjointed pieces of information swirling in her mind. She reread old town records, searching for any mention of events that might corroborate the whispered fears. She found cryptic entries about a prolonged period of blight in the late 19th century, a time when crops failed and livestock sickened without explanation, a period of unexplained disappearances that were officially attributed to harsh winters and harsh living, but whose accompanying local folklore spoke of a more sinister cause, a "shadow that fell upon the land." The language was vague, tinged with the melodrama of older times, yet the recurrence of themes – unexplained sickness, unnatural stillness, and a sense of pervasive dread – was unsettlingly familiar.

The details about Silas Blackwood continued to surface, each piece adding to the unsettling mosaic. He had arrived unannounced, purchasing the Blackwood Estate, a property that had stood vacant and decaying for decades, a place locals avoided, believing it to be haunted. His reasons for choosing Havenwood, a town so far removed from any major city or notable landmark, remained a mystery. He kept to himself, his infrequent forays into town marked by an almost unnerving intensity. He never participated in local events, never struck up conversations beyond polite, brief exchanges when absolutely necessary. His presence was a silent, gravitational force, subtly altering the orbit of Havenwood's collective consciousness.

Sarah recalled an incident from a few weeks prior, shortly after Blackwood's arrival. A freak hailstorm, of a size and ferocity entirely uncharacteristic for the season, had descended upon the town, battering homes and gardens with an almost malevolent force. It had passed as quickly as it arrived, leaving behind a trail of minor damage and a bewildered populace. At the time, it had been dismissed as a mere meteorological anomaly. But now, in the context of the growing unease, it felt different. It felt... deliberate. Like a prelude.

She overheard a conversation between two women outside the post office, their voices low and urgent. "Did you see the way he looked at the church spire?" one whispered, her eyes wide. "Like he was measuring it. Like he was... assessing it." The other woman shivered, pulling her cardigan tighter. "He's not like us, Mary. There's something ancient and cold in him. My grandmother always said that old estate held a darkness, a lingering... something. And now he's brought it back to life."

Sarah found herself increasingly preoccupied with these whispers, these fragmented narratives that seemed to weave a tapestry of dread around the town. Her rational mind fought against the rising tide of apprehension, trying to find logical explanations, to dismiss the burgeoning fears as mass hysteria, as the predictable result of a newcomer's enigmatic presence disrupting the comfortable complacency of a small town. Yet, the memory of the fleeting shadow in the alley, the impossible speed and fluidity of its movement, refused to be silenced. It was a visceral echo, a confirmation that something was indeed amiss, something that transcended the realm of ordinary explanation.

The collective unease wasn't just about Silas Blackwood, although his presence served as a potent catalyst. It was about something deeper, something woven into the very fabric of Havenwood's history, a narrative of forgotten anxieties that were now reasserting themselves. The town, once a haven of tranquil predictability, was slowly revealing a more complex, and far more unsettling, identity. The whispers of innocence were being drowned out by a growing chorus of fear, a collective intuition that the placid surface of their lives was merely a thin crust, beneath which ancient, unsettling forces were beginning to stir.

And Sarah, despite her best efforts to remain detached, found herself undeniably caught in the undertow of this deepening disquiet, a reluctant observer of a town slowly succumbing to its own buried history. The palpable shift in the air, the subtle but persistent undercurrent of dread, was no longer ignorable. It was a presence, as real and as tangible as the cobblestones beneath her feet, and it was growing stronger with each passing day, each whispered conversation, each furtive glance towards the looming silhouette of Blackwood Manor.

Chapter 2: The Unraveling Fabric

A Visit from the Artist

The midday sun, usually a cheerful presence filtering through the library's arched windows, seemed to have lost some of its warmth, casting long, distorted shadows across the polished oak tables. Sarah found solace within these hushed walls, a sanctuary where the unsettling whispers of Havenwood receded, replaced by the comforting scent of aging paper and the quiet rustle of turning pages. She had settled into her routine, a self-imposed task of research into the town's more obscure historical records, hoping to find a rational explanation for the palpable unease that had begun to permeate the air. Her fingers traced the faded ink of a local history journal, its brittle pages whispering tales of past hardships and peculiar occurrences, when a shadow fell across the page, eclipsing the faint light.

She looked up, a mild annoyance at the interruption quickly morphing into a prickle of alarm. Standing before her, impossibly silent, was Silas Blackwood. He was impeccably dressed, as always, in a dark, tailored suit that seemed to absorb the ambient light. His presence in her quiet corner of the library felt like a disruption, a discordant note in a carefully composed melody. It was as if a predatory creature had deliberately sought out the most unassuming of prey in its den. The very air around him seemed to thrum with an alien energy, a subtle distortion that made the hairs on Sarah's arms stand on end.

"Miss Davies," he said, his voice a low, resonant baritone that, despite its polite tone, carried an undeniable weight, like stones settling at the bottom of a deep well. He didn't smile, not truly. The upward curve of his lips was more a calculated arrangement of features than an expression of genuine warmth. "I hope I'm not intruding."

Sarah's mind scrambled for a response, her carefully constructed composure threatening to crumble. "Mr. Blackwood," she managed, her voice a little thinner than she would have liked. "No, not at all. I'm just... researching." She gestured vaguely at the book, feeling a desperate need to anchor herself to something familiar, something mundane.

"Researching," he repeated, his gaze sweeping over the shelf behind her, then settling back on her face with an unnerving intensity. His eyes, a shade of dark, unsettlingly deep grey, seemed to hold an ancient knowledge, a disconcerting depth that made her feel as though he could see right through her carefully constructed facade. "A noble pursuit. The pursuit of knowledge. Though, I confess, the limited collection here seems... rather provincial." He spoke with a mild, almost detached amusement, as if he were discussing a child's crude drawings.

Sarah bristled inwardly. The library, small as it was, was her haven. "It has its gems," she replied, her voice regaining some of its steadiness. "If one knows where to look." She couldn't resist the urge to subtly challenge him, to push back against his condescending assessment.

"Indeed," he murmured, his gaze lingering on a particular section of shelves. "I was hoping you might be able to assist me. I'm in search of a rather specific volume. An obscure treatise on

Renaissance portraiture. 'The Alchemy of the Gaze,' by a Maestro Bellini. Have you perhaps seen it?"

Sarah blinked, surprised. It was a rather specialized request, and not one she'd expected from Silas Blackwood. She knew the library's collection intimately, every spine, every misplaced volume. "Maestro Bellini," she repeated slowly, trying to recall. "I don't believe we have anything by that title. Or by a Maestro Bellini, for that matter. We have a few books on Renaissance art, but nothing quite that... specific."

Blackwood's expression remained unreadable, a mask of polite interest. "A pity," he said, a subtle shift in his posture indicating he wasn't entirely convinced. "I was told by a... local acquaintance that this establishment housed a surprisingly comprehensive collection for its size. Particularly in the more esoteric arts."

The mention of a "local acquaintance" sent a fresh wave of unease through Sarah. Who would have directed Silas Blackwood to the library, and more importantly, to her? Her mind immediately flashed to the hushed conversations, the fragmented whispers that had become the soundtrack to her life in Havenwood. Had someone pointed her out as the resident know-it-all, the one who could unearth any obscure fact?

"I'm afraid I can't help you with that particular title, Mr. Blackwood," she reiterated, her gaze flicking back to the book in her hands, a silent plea for him to leave. But he didn't move. Instead, he leaned in, his voice dropping to a more intimate, almost conspiratorial tone.

"Tell me, Miss Davies," he began, his dark eyes locking with hers, and in that instant, Sarah felt a profound, disorienting pull, a strange magnetism that was both terrifying and inexplicably compelling. It was as if his gaze was a physical force, drawing her in, her instincts screaming a primal warning to flee, to break eye contact, to put as much distance between them as possible. Yet, her body remained rooted to the spot, caught in the strange gravitational field of his presence. "You seem... unusually perceptive. You notice things others miss. What do you truly see when you look at the people of Havenwood?"

The question hung in the air, heavy and loaded. It wasn't a casual inquiry; it was a probe, a deliberate attempt to gauge her awareness, her understanding of the town and its inhabitants. Sarah felt a flush creep up her neck, a mixture of indignation and fear. His calm demeanor, his unsettlingly direct questions, felt like a performance, a carefully choreographed dance designed to unsettle her.

"I... I see people, Mr. Blackwood," she replied, choosing her words carefully. "They're like any other people. They have their routines, their worries, their joys." She avoided his eyes, focusing on a dust mote dancing in a shaft of light.

"Do they?" he countered, his voice soft, but with an undercurrent of something sharp, something that hinted at a hidden cynicism. "Or do you see the layers beneath? The anxieties they try to mask? The unspoken histories that cling to them like old cobwebs?" He paused, letting his words sink in. "You spend your days surrounded by stories, Miss Davies. You must surely understand that every person carries their own narrative, often one far more complex and terrifying than the one they present to the world."

Sarah's heart hammered against her ribs. He was articulating her own burgeoning fears, the very thoughts she'd been trying to suppress. His understanding, his almost preternatural insight into her own internal landscape, was profoundly disturbing. It felt less like conversation and more like an interrogation, conducted with unnerving politeness.

"I believe everyone has their own inner life, Mr. Blackwood," she said, her voice trembling slightly. "But it's not my place to pry into it." She finally met his gaze, a flicker of defiance in her eyes.

A ghost of a smile touched his lips, a fleeting, almost imperceptible twitch. "No," he conceded. "Of course not. But sometimes, one cannot help but notice the patterns, can one? The subtle shifts in the collective mood. Havenwood, for instance, seems to be experiencing a particular... disquiet of late. A nervousness, perhaps?"

He was pressing, pushing her to articulate the very anxieties she'd been trying to analyze. The way he spoke, so calmly, so detachedly, made it sound as though he were discussing a mild weather phenomenon, rather than the palpable fear that was slowly gripping the town.

"The weather's been a bit unusual," Sarah offered, grasping at the most innocuous explanation she could find. "That hailstorm a few weeks ago was quite something."

Blackwood's gaze sharpened, a flicker of something unreadable in its depths. "Ah, yes. The... precipitation. A rather violent disruption, wasn't it? Almost as if the sky itself had decided to vent its displeasure."

He turned his head slightly, as if listening to something far beyond the quiet confines of the library. "Tell me, Miss Davies, have you ever felt the presence of something... ancient? Something that predates memory, yet still exerts an influence?"

His questions were becoming increasingly abstract, yet they resonated with the hushed tales she'd overheard, the vague pronouncements about Havenwood's hidden history. She felt a cold dread begin to creep into her bones. His calm demeanor was a chilling contrast to the unnerving nature of his inquiries. It was as if he were deliberately trying to evoke a specific reaction, to test her boundaries, to see how much she could absorb before succumbing to fear.

"I'm not sure I understand what you mean, Mr. Blackwood," she said, her voice barely a whisper. She felt a desperate urge to flee, to escape the suffocating atmosphere he seemed to carry with him. The magnetism, the pull she felt towards him, warred with every survival instinct screaming at her to run. It was a dangerous dance, a flirtation with something unknown and deeply unsettling.

He leaned a fraction closer, his dark eyes seeming to bore into her very soul. "You feel it too, don't you, Miss Davies?" he murmured, his voice a low, persuasive caress. "The subtle shift. The unraveling of the fabric. Havenwood is not as... stable as it appears. And you, with your keen intellect, must surely be sensing the fissures opening beneath the surface."

Sarah swallowed, her throat dry. He was articulating her deepest fears, her most unsettling observations. He knew. Or at least, he suspected she knew more than she let on. The realization was both terrifying and strangely validating. She wasn't imagining things; the unease was real, and perhaps, just perhaps, he understood its origins better than anyone.

"I... I just feel that things are a little different lately," she admitted, her voice barely audible. "But I don't attribute it to anything... out of the ordinary."

Blackwood's lips curved into a slow, knowing smile, a chillingly predatory expression that sent a shiver down her spine. "And yet," he said, his gaze sweeping over her, lingering on her flushed cheeks, her slightly trembling hands, "you are here, in this quiet sanctuary, poring over books about the past. Perhaps you are searching for answers, Miss Davies. Answers that the present cannot provide." He paused, his eyes holding hers captive. "Perhaps you are looking for a way to understand what is happening, before it is too late."

He reached into the breast pocket of his suit jacket, and Sarah tensed, expecting some sort of threat, some overt display of power. Instead, he produced a small, leather-bound notebook. "I must apologize again for disturbing your research," he said, his tone shifting back to one of polite civility, as if their intense, unnerving exchange had never happened. "But if you do happen upon that Bellini volume, or anything else that might shed light on the peculiar nature of artistic influence, do let me know. I find such matters… fascinating."

He gave a slight, almost imperceptible nod, and then, as silently as he had arrived, he turned and walked away, his presence a lingering disturbance in the otherwise tranquil air of the library. Sarah watched him go, her heart still pounding a frantic rhythm against her ribs. The unnerving magnetism, the unsettling questions, the chillingly accurate observations – they all coalesced into a profound sense of dread. He had invaded her sanctuary, probed her mind, and left her with a terrifying certainty: Silas Blackwood was not just a recluse; he was a force, a dark, intriguing, and utterly dangerous enigma, and he had just made it clear that he was aware of her. The carefully constructed walls she had built around herself were beginning to crumble, and the unraveling fabric of Havenwood was starting to pull her in. She was no longer an observer; she was becoming involved, drawn into a vortex of mystery and fear by the man who held its unseen center. The library, once her refuge, now felt like the edge of a precipice, and Silas Blackwood had just given her a terrifying glimpse into the abyss. She knew, with a certainty that chilled her to the bone, that this was only the beginning. His visit was a deliberate signal, a calculated overture that promised further, more significant encounters. The quiet solitude she craved was shattered, replaced by the unnerving awareness of his attention, a scrutiny that felt both predatory and strangely intoxicating. The subtle, disquieting magnetism he exuded was a dangerous lure, and she found herself grappling with an unfamiliar conflict within herself – a primal urge to flee warring with a growing, morbid fascination, a desire to understand the unsettling depths of the man who had so effortlessly disrupted her world. The quiet hum of the library now seemed to amplify the frantic beat of her own heart, a constant reminder of the invisible threads Silas Blackwood had begun to weave around her.

Echoes in the Silence

The residual unease from Silas Blackwood's visit lingered like a phantom limb, an ache in the quiet spaces of Sarah's mind. She had returned to her small, rented cottage on the outskirts of Havenwood, seeking the familiar comfort of solitude. Yet, the silence there felt different now. It was no longer a peaceful void but a palpable presence, a heavy blanket woven from unspoken anxieties and the echo of Blackwood's unnerving questions. He had left her with a kind of a sense of profound disquiet, an awareness that the carefully constructed normalcy of her life was a fragile veneer, easily pierced.

The first true crack in her composure appeared that evening. As she sat at her kitchen table, attempting to lose herself in a mundane task—sorting through a pile of old photographs—a sound, barely audible, snaked through the stillness. It was a whisper, faint and sibilant, like dry leaves skittering across pavement. Sarah froze, her hand hovering over a faded image of her childhood home. She strained to listen, her breath held captive in her chest. The sound came again, a breathy exhalation that seemed to coalesce into a single syllable: "Sarah…"

Her heart gave a violent lurch. She was alone. Utterly, undeniably alone. The cottage was small, a single story with no upstairs, no adjoining rooms that could harbor an unseen presence. She stood slowly, her chair scraping against the wooden floor, the sound unnaturally loud in the charged silence. Her eyes scanned the dimly lit kitchen, then darted to the hallway leading to the bedroom and bathroom. Nothing. The air was still, heavy with the scent of old wood and the faint, lingering aroma of the herbal tea she'd brewed earlier.

"Hello?" she called out, her voice a thin, reedy sound that seemed to mock her attempt at bravery. Only silence answered. She told herself it was the wind, a trick of the old house settling, a product of her own overwrought nerves, frayed by Blackwood's spectral appearance. But the whisper had been too distinct, too deliberate. It had felt personal, an intimate intrusion into her solitude.

She spent the rest of the evening in a state of hypervigilance, jumping at every creak of the floorboards, every rustle of leaves against the windowpanes. Sleep offered little respite. Her dreams were a disorienting blur of shadowed figures and disembodied voices, all swirling around the unnerving clarity of Silas Blackwood's dark eyes.

The next morning, the unsettling occurrences continued, each one a subtle erosion of her carefully maintained calm. As she prepared breakfast, the faint whisper returned, this time seeming to emanate from the empty living room. It was the same soft, almost seductive hiss of her name. She walked into the room, her movements deliberate, her gaze sweeping across the worn armchair, the small bookshelf, the empty fireplace. The room was bathed in the pale morning light, serene and undisturbed. Yet, the impression of a voice, a presence just beyond the veil of perception, remained.

Later, as she sat by the window, nursing a cup of lukewarm coffee, she heard it: the distinct sound of footsteps. They were light, deliberate, and seemed to be approaching her front door. Her pulse quickened. Was it Blackwood again? Or perhaps a neighbor? She peered through the sheer curtains, her eyes fixed on the narrow path leading from the overgrown lane to her cottage. The footsteps grew louder, closer. They paused. Right outside her door.

Sarah's breath hitched. She waited, her muscles tensed, ready to confront whoever stood there. But the silence that followed was absolute. No knock, no ring of the doorbell. Nothing. Hesitantly, she pushed the door open, her heart hammering against her ribs. The porch was empty. The path was empty. The only movement was the gentle sway of the overgrown weeds lining the walkway, disturbed by a breeze that seemed to have sprung from nowhere.

The escalating events began to chip away at her resolve, at the rational core that had always anchored her. Was she imagining things? Had the stress of her research, coupled with Blackwood's unsettling visit, finally fractured her perception of reality? The whispers, the phantom footsteps – they were insidious, subtle enough to be dismissed as auditory hallucinations, yet persistent enough to sow seeds of doubt. Her solitude, once a source of strength, now felt like a cage, amplifying her fears, making her question her own sanity. The silence of the cottage, once a comforting balm, had transformed into an oppressive entity, pregnant with unseen presences that seemed to feed her burgeoning paranoia.

She tried to focus on her work, on the historical records that had initially drawn her to Havenwood. She pored over brittle newspaper clippings, local histories, and dusty town ledgers, searching for any mention of peculiar occurrences, of unexplained phenomena that might corroborate her own unsettling experiences. But the written word offered no immediate solace. The past, when she forced herself to engage with it, seemed to whisper its own disquieting tales, fragmented accounts of lost children, unexplained disappearances, and hushed rumors of things that dwelled in the shadows of the surrounding woods.

One afternoon, while sifting through a box of assorted documents from the Havenwood Historical Society, she found a small, leather-bound diary, its pages brittle and yellowed with age. The handwriting was elegant, though faded, and the entries, dated from the late 19th century, spoke of a woman named Eleanor Vance. Eleanor's words painted a picture of a quiet, isolated life in Havenwood, punctuated by a growing sense of dread.

October 14th, 1888. Eleanor wrote. *The nights grow longer, and with them, the whispers. They call my name from the empty rooms, a siren song that draws me to the precipice of fear. I hear footsteps outside my door, always when I am alone, always when the world outside has surrendered to sleep. Yet, when I dare to look, there is nothing. Only the vast, indifferent darkness.*

Sarah's blood ran cold. Eleanor Vance. Her words were a chillingly accurate mirror of Sarah's own experiences. The whispers, the phantom footsteps, the oppressive silence—they were not new to Havenwood. They were echoes from the past, a testament to a shared, disquieting experience that transcended time.

November 3rd, 1888. Another entry read. *The silence... it is the worst. It is a living thing, a watchful entity that presses in, suffocating reason. I find myself straining to hear anything, any proof that I am not alone, that this unease is not a figment of my own unraveling mind. But the silence holds its secrets, mocking my attempts to break its hold. I fear I am losing my grip.*

Sarah closed the diary, her hands trembling. Eleanor's descent into paranoia, her struggle to distinguish reality from delusion, mirrored Sarah's own growing fears. The diary was a testament to the insidious nature of whatever haunted Havenwood, a force that preyed on isolation and amplified internal anxieties. It wasn't just the physical manifestations—the whispers and footsteps—but the psychological toll they took, the slow erosion of certainty, the insidious creep of self-doubt.

She tried to rationalize it. Perhaps Eleanor Vance had suffered from a mental illness, a common affliction in times when understanding of such conditions was limited. Perhaps her "whispers" were simply the ramblings of a troubled mind, amplified by isolation and a vivid imagination. But the uncanny parallel to Sarah's own experiences made such explanations feel hollow, insufficient. It felt less like coincidence and more like a shared inheritance of dread, a psychic resonance with a past trauma that had imprinted itself upon the very fabric of the town.

Sarah found herself scrutinizing her surroundings with a new intensity. The creaks and groans of the cottage were no longer benign sounds of an old structure; they were potential harbingers of the unseen. The shadows that stretched across the floorboards seemed to deepen, to coalesce into more defined shapes. Even the familiar landscape outside her windows — the gnarled trees, the winding paths — took on a menacing aspect, as if they too held a dormant awareness, a silent complicity.

The whispers became more frequent, more insistent. Sometimes, they seemed to swirl around her, a chorus of indistinct murmurs that faded the moment she tried to focus on them. Other times, it was a single, chillingly clear utterance of her name, seeming to come from just around a corner, or from behind a closed door. She began to develop rituals to ward off the encroaching dread. She would leave lights on in every room, even during the day, creating a defiant blaze against the encroaching shadows. She played music constantly, a cacophony of classical melodies and folk songs, anything to drown out the silence and the whispers it concealed.

One evening, as a storm gathered force outside, lashing rain against the windows and wind howling through the eaves, Sarah was in her study, attempting to transcribe a particularly difficult passage from an old parish record. The storm's fury seemed to amplify the internal turmoil within the cottage. Amidst the tempest's roar, she heard a distinct sound, separate from the wind and rain. A soft, rhythmic thudding. *Thump... thump... thump...* It was coming from the attic, a small, rarely accessed space above the study.

Her breath caught in her throat. The attic door was firmly shut, secured with a heavy bolt. She had never even been inside it. The thudding continued, steady and unnerving. It wasn't the frantic scrabbling of a trapped animal, but something more deliberate, more measured. It sounded almost like a slow, patient knocking.

Sarah's resolve faltered. She was no longer just observing the unsettling phenomena; she was becoming a participant, drawn into a narrative of fear that stretched back through generations. The isolation of Havenwood, the peculiar atmosphere Blackwood had alluded to, Eleanor Vance's diary—they were all threads in a tapestry of unease that was slowly but surely entangling her. She felt a profound sense of vulnerability, a gnawing fear that her grip on reality was slipping, that the whispers and footsteps were not external intrusions but manifestations of something breaking within her own mind. The silence was no longer just an absence of sound; it was a void, a canvas upon which her deepest fears were being painted, and the brushstrokes were becoming ever more vivid, ever more terrifying. She was unraveling, just as Blackwood had subtly implied. The fabric of her composure was fraying, and the whispers in the silence were the threads being pulled loose, one by one. The oppressive weight of the unseen pressed down, making her question every sound, every shadow, every fleeting thought. The cottage, once a haven, now felt like a trap, and the silence within it was the most terrifying predator of all. She was trapped in a cycle of heightened awareness and creeping paranoia, each event reinforcing the last, creating a feedback loop of dread that threatened to consume her entirely. Her sanity, once a steadfast anchor, now felt like a ship adrift in a churning, tempestuous sea, battered by waves of inexplicable phenomena. The very air she breathed seemed charged with a malevolent energy, a palpable tension that kept her on edge, perpetually waiting for the next unsettling manifestation. The world outside, with its ordinary routines and predictable rhythms, felt impossibly distant, a faded memory from a life that no longer seemed to belong to her. She was caught in the tightening grip of Havenwood's secrets, and the whispers in the silence were her only, terrifying companions. The rational explanations she clung to were growing weaker with each passing hour, replaced by a growing, chilling acceptance of the inexplicable. This was not merely research anymore; it was survival, a desperate attempt to navigate a reality that was rapidly becoming alien and hostile. Her focus narrowed, becoming solely centered on the immediate threat, the next sound, the next shadow, the next whisper that chipped away at the edifice of her composure.

The thudding from the attic ceased as abruptly as it had begun, leaving behind a silence that was somehow more terrifying than the noise. Sarah remained frozen, her ears straining, waiting for its return. But it didn't come. The storm outside continued its assault, a furious symphony that seemed to mock her fragile state. She huddled in her study, the yellowed diary clutched tightly in her hand, the words of Eleanor Vance echoing in her mind like a prophecy fulfilled. She was no longer just an observer of Havenwood's disquiet; she was a participant, caught in its suffocating embrace, her sanity fraying like the ancient pages of the diary itself. The realization was a cold, hard stone settling in her gut: she was not alone in her distress, but the company she kept was a testament to a darkness that had plagued this town for generations, and it was now her turn to face its chilling whispers.

The Missing Pages

The musty scent of aged paper and binding glue, usually a comforting balm to Sarah's investigative spirit, now carried a faint undertone of disquiet. She was deep within the labyrinthine stacks of the Havenwood Public Library, a place that, until recently, had represented a sanctuary of quiet research. Silas Blackwood's unnerving visit and the escalating whispers in her cottage had pushed her to seek tangible answers, to ground herself in the factual accounts of the town's past. She had focused her attention on the town's administrative records, specifically those pertaining to the mid-20th century, a period that had been conspicuously vague in the initial historical overviews she'd consulted.

Her fingers, stained faintly with the ink of forgotten scribes, traced the spines of ledger books, each one a potential repository of the town's hidden narratives. She had been meticulously working her way through the county clerk's records, a dry but essential account of land deeds, council meetings, and local ordinances. It was in a collection of bound volumes labeled "Town Council Minutes, 1950-1959" that she first encountered the anomaly.

The initial entries were unremarkable, detailing mundane discussions about road repairs, school board appointments, and local festivals. Sarah worked systematically, her brow furrowed in concentration, making notes of any pertinent information that might shed light on the peculiar atmosphere she'd detected in Havenwood. She was particularly interested in any records pertaining to unexplained events, disappearances, or unusual occurrences that might have been downplayed or omitted from official town histories.

It was during her examination of the 1954 volume that she noticed the first break in the narrative. A specific meeting, dated June 17th, 1954, seemed to abruptly conclude its agenda with a general statement about "ongoing town matters." Yet, the subsequent entry, dated July 15th, 1954, referred back to decisions made at the previous meeting, implying a continuity that was, in fact, missing. A quick flipping through the pages revealed that the entries for the intervening month were simply… gone. Not torn out crudely, but meticulously removed, leaving behind the faint, ghost-like impressions of where the pages had once been. The edges were unnaturally smooth, suggesting a surgical precision that sent a shiver down Sarah's spine.

Her heart began to pound an anxious rhythm against her ribs. This was no accident. The deliberate excision of these pages screamed of intent, of a conscious effort to erase a specific period of time. She carefully turned back to the preceding pages, her eyes scanning for any annotations or indications of why this section might have been removed. There was nothing. The removal had been thorough, almost surgical, leaving no trace of foul play beyond the undeniable void itself.

Driven by a rising sense of urgency, Sarah broadened her search. She moved to the collections of local newspapers from the same era, painstakingly sifting through microfiche reels of the *Havenwood Chronicle*. The headlines spoke of the usual small-town affairs – harvest festivals, the opening of a new general store, the local high school football team's successes. But as she delved into the summer of 1954, a disturbing pattern began to emerge.

There were reports of missing persons, initially treated as isolated incidents. A teenage boy, Johnny Miller, had vanished from his family's farm on the outskirts of town in late May. A week later, a young woman, Eleanor Vance – the same name as the diarist Sarah had found – a seamstress working in the town's small textile mill, failed to return home after an evening walk. Then, in July, a retired schoolteacher, Mr. Abernathy, disappeared from his home, leaving behind a half-eaten meal on his kitchen table.

What was most chilling was how these disappearances were reported, or rather, how they *stopped* being reported. The initial articles, filled with concern and appeals for information, gradually gave way to shorter, more perfunctory mentions, and then, abruptly, to silence. The *Chronicle*'s coverage of Johnny Miller's disappearance, which had initially spanned several front-page articles, dwindled to a single, brief mention that he was still missing. Eleanor Vance's story was similar, her missing person posters fading from community notice boards, her name eventually disappearing from the news. Mr. Abernathy's disappearance was barely acknowledged, a brief note tucked away on an inside page.

Sarah felt a growing dread, a visceral connection to these forgotten lives. It wasn't just a historical curiosity; it was a profound resonance. The methodical erasure of the town council minutes, coupled with the abrupt cessation of reporting on these disappearances, painted a disturbing picture of a deliberate cover-up. Someone, or some entity, had gone to great lengths to ensure that whatever happened in the summer of 1954 was buried, forgotten, and most importantly, never explained.

She returned to the town council minutes, her focus now sharper, her movements more agitated. She examined other volumes, particularly those immediately preceding and following the missing section. Were there any discussions, any hints, that might explain the sudden silence? The minutes from June 1954 spoke of a town council meeting where the primary agenda item was the upcoming Fourth of July celebration. There was a brief mention of a "growing unease" among the populace, attributed to "rumors and gossip concerning the recent disappearances," but the council seemed intent on downplaying it, urging citizens to remain calm and avoid speculation.

The following council meeting in August 1954, however, took a decidedly different tone. While the minutes still omitted any direct mention of the missing individuals, there was a palpable shift in the discussions. The council seemed preoccupied with "community safety measures" and "strengthening local security."

There were references to increased patrols, although the specific reasons for this heightened vigilance remained unstated. One entry noted a unanimous vote to establish a "special committee to investigate matters affecting public welfare," but the committee's findings, if they ever existed, were nowhere to be found in the subsequent records. It was as if the council, having removed the evidence of a problem, was now feverishly trying to implement solutions without acknowledging the source of the threat.

Sarah's mind raced. This wasn't just about missing people; it was about a deliberate manipulation of information, a systematic suppression of truth. The very fabric of Havenwood's history, the documented reality of its past, had been tampered with. And the more she uncovered, the more she felt a chilling kinship with the vanished individuals, a sense that their fate was somehow intertwined with her own present predicament. The whispers in her cottage, the phantom footsteps – they felt like distant echoes of a past trauma that was now bleeding into her reality.

She spent hours in the library, her focus unwavering, her exhaustion ignored. She cross-referenced newspaper articles with town records, searching for any discrepancies, any hints of what might have been deliberately omitted. She found a brief, almost cryptic mention in the *Chronicle* from late July *1954*, referring to "unsubstantiated reports of unusual activity in the western woods," but the article quickly pivoted to more mundane local news, dismissing these reports as the product of overwrought imaginations.

The sheer deliberateness of the missing pages gnawed at her. It wasn't a case of records being lost to time or fire; these were pages that had been physically removed with precision. Who would do such a thing? And why? Was it to protect the town's reputation?

Or was it to conceal something far more sinister, something that still held sway over Havenwood?

She remembered Silas Blackwood's veiled warnings, his oblique references to the town's "unfortunate history" and the "secrets it kept." He had spoken of a darkness that permeated Havenwood, a pervasive unease that clung to its very foundations. Now, Sarah felt she was finally beginning to understand the depth of what he had alluded to. The missing pages were not just a historical curiosity; they were a symptom of a deeper malaise, a deliberate obfuscation of a truth that was too terrible to be recorded.

The weight of this discovery pressed down on her, a heavy, suffocating blanket. She felt like an intruder, unearthing secrets that had been buried for a reason. The library, once a place of solace, now felt charged with a hidden tension, as if the very air around her was aware of her intrusion. She glanced around, half-expecting to see a watchful librarian, a concerned citizen, anyone who might know what she was uncovering. But the library remained a quiet, unassuming space, its silence a stark contrast to the turmoil raging within her.

Her thoughts drifted back to Eleanor Vance, the diarist. Eleanor had written of whispers, of phantom footsteps, of a suffocating silence. Could Eleanor have been one of the individuals who disappeared in the summer of 1954? Sarah desperately scanned the newspaper microfiche again, her eyes darting across the grainy images of headlines and articles. She found a brief notice from early August 1954, stating that Eleanor Vance, a resident of Willow Creek Lane, was still missing. The notice was short, almost dismissive, and offered no further details.

The connection was undeniable. Eleanor Vance, the woman whose intimate fears had mirrored Sarah's own, had vanished during the very period that had been systematically purged from the town records. The missing pages weren't just empty space; they were the silent testament to her fate, and the fate of others like her.

Sarah's hands trembled as she carefully replaced the town council minutes. She knew she couldn't stop here. The missing pages were a gaping wound in the town's historical narrative, a wound that festered with unanswered questions. She felt a responsibility, not just to her own research, but to the memory of those who had been silenced, erased from existence. The historical dread was no longer a vague, abstract concept; it was a tangible reality, a chilling confirmation that Havenwood's darkness was not a mere figment of imagination but a deeply ingrained, deliberately perpetuated darkness. The whispers she heard in her cottage no longer felt like isolated occurrences; they felt like the faint, desperate cries of the past, reaching out to her across the years, pleading for their story to be told. The unraveling fabric Blackwood had spoken of was not just her own composure; it was the very historical record of Havenwood, meticulously torn apart, leaving behind only the terrifying, unspoken truth. She left the library that evening with a new resolve, a grim determination to piece together the fragments of the past, no matter how dangerous it might be. The silence of the missing pages was deafening, and Sarah was compelled to break it.

Blackwood's Cryptic Warning

The chill of the late afternoon had begun to seep into Sarah's bones, a damp, clinging cold that had nothing to do with the dropping temperature. She'd left the comforting, albeit unsettling, embrace of the library hours ago, the weight of the missing town council minutes and the chilling newspaper accounts of vanished residents a heavy burden. The silence of her cottage, usually a welcome respite, now felt charged with the phantom echoes of Eleanor Vance's fears, a constant reminder of the deliberate void she had uncovered. Blackwood's cryptic words, the unnerving feeling of being watched, had driven her out again, seeking a different kind of grounding, a tangible anchor in the growing tide of unease.

She found herself drawn, almost against her will, towards the decaying husk of the old Havenwood textile mill. It stood on the edge of town, a skeletal silhouette against the bruised twilight sky, its broken windows like vacant eyes staring out at the desolate landscape. The air around it was thick with the scent of decay and rust, a melancholic perfume of industry long since abandoned. It was a place steeped in history, a history that, like so much in Havenwood, felt tainted. She remembered the brief newspaper mention of Eleanor Vance, the seamstress who had vanished. Had she worked here? The thought sent a fresh tremor of apprehension through her.

As she approached the looming structure, a figure detached itself from the deepening shadows near a collapsed section of the outer wall. Sarah's breath hitched. It was Silas Blackwood. He stood unnervingly still, a silhouette of stillness against the chaotic decay, his presence as unsettling and out of place as a perfectly preserved antique in a heap of rubble. He hadn't called out, hadn't made any movement to indicate he was expecting her, yet his presence felt deliberate, almost orchestrated.

"Still digging, are we?" His voice, low and raspy, carried on the faint breeze, devoid of any warmth. It was a voice that suggested secrets held for too long, a voice that had seen things the daylight never touched.

Sarah stopped, her hand instinctively tightening around the strap of her satchel. She hadn't seen him since his unsettling visit to her cottage, and the intervening time had done little to assuage the disquiet he evoked. "Mr. Blackwood," she managed, her voice betraying a slight tremor she couldn't quite suppress. "What are you doing out here?"

He didn't answer directly, his gaze sweeping over the derelict mill, then settling on her. There was an unnerving intensity in his eyes, a knowing glint that made her feel as if he could see the very thoughts churning within her mind. "Some places... they hold onto things," he said, his voice barely above a whisper, as if sharing a confidence with the crumbling bricks and mortar. "Memories. Echoes. Especially places where lives were... unravelled."

The word "unravelled" struck a chord, echoing the very metaphor Blackwood himself had used to describe her own state of mind, and now, it seemed, the state of the town's history. Sarah felt a prickle of fear. Was he referring to the mill? To Eleanor Vance? Or to something far more pervasive?

"I've been looking into the town's past," she stated, keeping her tone carefully neutral, betraying none of the frantic energy that had consumed her in the library. "Some parts of it seem... deliberately obscured."

Blackwood offered a faint, almost imperceptible smile that didn't reach his eyes. It was the kind of smile that promised nothing but implied everything. "Ah, yes. Obscured. A kind word for it. Some truths, you see, are like fragile threads. Pull too hard, and the whole tapestry can come undone." He took a slow, deliberate step towards her, his gait unnervingly smooth, as if he glided rather than walked. "You have a knack for finding the loose ends, don't you? For seeing what others miss, or perhaps, what they choose to ignore."

His words were a riddle, veiled in ambiguity. Was he complimenting her, or warning her? The unnerving balance between the two was characteristic of their brief encounters, each conversation leaving her more perplexed than the last. She felt a rising suspicion, a gnawing unease that Blackwood wasn't just an observer of Havenwood's secrets, but somehow intrinsically linked to them. His very presence here, at this abandoned mill, felt like a deliberate convergence, a staged encounter.

"The town council minutes from the summer of 1954 are incomplete," Sarah stated, her voice firmer now, a sliver of defiance piercing through her fear. "Pages are missing. And the newspaper reports of disappearances stopped abruptly." She met his gaze, searching for a flicker of surprise, of denial, anything that might exonerate him. But his expression remained a carefully constructed mask.

Blackwood tilted his head, his eyes narrowing slightly as if considering a complex puzzle. "Missing pages," he mused, the words rolling off his tongue as if tasting them. "A common enough occurrence in old records. Dust, damp, careless hands." He let the statement hang in the air, a deliberately dismissive gesture. Then, his gaze sharpened, pinning her in place. "But you, you see more than dust, don't you? You see the intentionality. The *why* behind the emptiness."

He was acknowledging her discovery, yet his acknowledgment was laced with a subtle menace. He knew she was uncovering something, and his reaction wasn't one of alarm, but of a detached, almost academic interest. It was as if he were observing her in a sort of detached, intellectual experiment.

"It suggests a deliberate cover-up," Sarah pressed, her heart hammering against her ribs. "A suppression of information."

Blackwood took another step closer, and Sarah resisted the urge to step back. The air between them crackled with an unspoken tension. "Or," he corrected, his voice dropping to a near whisper, each syllable carrying an unnerving weight, "a necessary preservation. Some things are best left undisturbed, Miss Vance. Some dogs are best left sleeping. Waking them can have… unpredictable consequences."

The hairs on the back of Sarah's neck prickled. "Sleeping dogs?" she echoed, her voice barely audible. "Are you threatening me, Mr. Blackwood?"

A slow, chilling smile spread across his lips. It was a predatory smile, a smile that promised teeth. "Threatening? My dear, I am merely offering a word of caution. Havenwood has a long memory. It remembers what it chooses to remember. And it forgets what it must." He gestured vaguely towards the darkened maw of the mill. "This place… it remembers a great deal. And what it remembers is not always pleasant. Sometimes, ignorance is a more comfortable blanket than truth."

He then turned his back to her, a stark and definitive gesture of dismissal. "Do be careful, Miss Vance," he called over his shoulder, his voice already fading as he melted back into the encroaching gloom. "The past is a treacherous landscape. And you, it seems, have wandered into its most shadowed valleys."

Sarah stood frozen for a long moment, the echo of his words reverberating in the desolate air. He hadn't threatened her directly, but the implication was chillingly clear. He knew what she was investigating. He knew about the missing pages, the vanished people. And he seemed to believe that her pursuit of the truth was a dangerous act, an act that would stir up forces best left dormant. His warning about "sleeping dogs" and "unpredictable consequences" was a veiled threat, a thinly disguised intimation that her actions could have severe repercussions.

The old mill loomed behind him, a silent, decaying monument to secrets long buried. As Sarah looked at its broken facade, she felt a profound sense of dread. Blackwood's cryptic pronouncements, his unsettling presence, his connection to this place – it all coalesced into a disturbing picture. He was a gatekeeper of sorts, a guardian of Havenwood's hidden history, and he clearly did not want her to pry further. The unraveling fabric Blackwood had spoken of was not just her own mental state; it was the very fabric of the town's carefully constructed facade, and he seemed determined to mend it by any means necessary, even if it meant silencing those who sought to expose its flaws.

The encounter left her more unnerved than ever, the sinister ambiguity of his words a heavy weight settling upon her shoulders. She had the distinct and terrifying impression that Silas Blackwood knew far more about the missing pages, and the people who disappeared, than he was ever willing to reveal, and that his cryptic warnings were not just about the past, but a stark foreshadowing of her own immediate future. The scent of decay from the mill seemed to cling to her, a reminder of the rot that lay beneath Havenwood's surface, a rot that Blackwood, in his own enigmatic way, seemed to be actively protecting.

The late afternoon sun, now a sickly, attenuated glow, cast long, distorted shadows that stretched and writhed like spectral fingers across the library's polished floor. Sarah's breath hitched, the echo of Silas Blackwood's parting words - "the past is a treacherous landscape" - still a cold knot in her stomach. His cryptic pronouncements, the unnerving way he'd seemed to anticipate her thoughts, had left her more disoriented than ever. He was a phantom himself, a harbinger of dread, and his connection to the decaying mill, to the very secrets she was trying to unearth, felt like a silken cord tightening around her throat. She needed to anchor herself, to find something tangible, something real, in the swirling mist of suspicion and fear that was Havenwood.

The library, usually her sanctuary, now felt like a repository of the town's hushed anxieties. She'd spent hours poring over the scant records, the missing minutes, the fragmented newspaper clippings. It was a painstaking, often fruitless, endeavor, but Sarah possessed a stubborn resilience, a refusal to be deterred by the deliberate obscurities. It was during one such relentless delve, in a seldom-used alcove tucked away in the dusty rear archives, that her fingers brushed against something unexpected.

Beneath a stack of brittle, yellowed town ledgers, a book lay half-concealed. It was old, bound in a dark, cracked leather that felt strangely supple beneath her touch, as if the years had only deepened its peculiar character. There was no title on the spine, no identifying mark to betray its contents or origin. It simply *was*, an anomaly in the ordered chaos of the archives, a silent invitation to a forgotten narrative.

Curiosity, a double-edged sword in Havenwood, urged her to pull it free. The pages were thick and creamy, a stark contrast to the brittle paper of the town records. As she opened it, a faint, musty scent, mingled with something else – a metallic tang, like dried blood – pricked at her senses. The handwriting, penned in a flowing, elegant script, was immediately recognizable as belonging to a bygone era. It was a journal, she realized, a personal chronicle of a life lived within the quiet, yet somehow charged, atmosphere of Havenwood. The first entry was dated July 14th, 1954, the very summer that seemed to hold the key to the town's unraveling. The name inscribed at the beginning of the first page sent a jolt of recognition through her: Eleanor Vance.

Sarah's heart hammered against her ribs. Eleanor Vance. The seamstress who had vanished. The same name mentioned in the brief newspaper clipping she'd found, the one that had alluded to her disappearance with a chilling lack of detail. This was not just a journal; it was a direct link, a voice from the past speaking from the very heart of the mystery. With trembling hands, she turned the pages, her eyes devouring the elegant script.

The initial entries were mundane, detailing the quiet routines of a librarian's life: the changing seasons, the patrons who frequented the library, the small joys and frustrations of her work. Eleanor Vance wrote of the comfort she found in the hushed halls, the intellectual stimulation of her profession, the quiet rhythm of Havenwood life. But even in these early passages, Sarah detected a subtle undercurrent of unease, a nascent awareness of something lurking just beyond the periphery of Eleanor's perception.

"August 3rd, 1954. The silence in the library today was... different. Not the usual comforting hush, but a heavy, expectant quiet, as if the very air was holding its breath. I keep feeling a prickling sensation on my skin, as if unseen eyes are watching my every move. I dismissed it as nerves, the

consequence of too many late nights cataloging new acquisitions. Yet, the feeling persists, an unwelcome guest in the quiet corners of my mind."

Sarah's breath caught. This was it. The very paranoia she had begun to experience, the chilling sensation of being observed, was mirrored in Eleanor Vance's words, penned over seventy years ago. The uncanny resonance between their experiences sent a fresh wave of apprehension through her. It wasn't just her imagination. Something in Havenwood had the power to sow these seeds of dread, to foster this pervasive sense of being watched.

The entries grew more frequent, the tone gradually shifting from quiet observation to palpable apprehension. Eleanor's meticulous prose began to fray at the edges, her sentences becoming shorter, more clipped, as if the act of writing itself was becoming a struggle against an encroaching darkness.

"August 19th, 1954. I saw him again today. Or rather, I felt him. A presence. Not human, not entirely. A flicker at the edge of my vision, a disturbance in the air, a cold breath on my neck when no windows were open. It's as if this town is a vast, intricate tapestry, and I've accidentally pulled a thread, and now the whole thing is beginning to unravel. I find myself checking the locks multiple times, jumping at every creak of the floorboards. My concentration is shot. It's all I can do to focus on the Dewey Decimal system without imagining a... shadow... looming behind the shelves."

Sarah felt a visceral connection to Eleanor's words. The "shadow" she spoke of, the feeling of an encroaching presence, resonated deeply with the unsettling encounters Sarah herself had been experiencing, with the unnerving stillness of Silas Blackwood, with the lingering dread that clung to the very air of Havenwood. Eleanor's diary was a testament to the fact that these feelings were not new, that this fear had a history in this town, a history that had been deliberately erased.

The next few entries painted a picture of increasing isolation and terror. Eleanor began to document strange occurrences within the library itself – books found out of place, whispers heard in empty rooms, a pervasive chill that no amount of heating could dispel. She spoke of a growing conviction that the disappearances, the missing council minutes, were not isolated incidents, but part of a larger, more sinister pattern.

"September 5th, 1954. The whispers are louder now. They seem to emanate from the walls themselves, from the very dust motes dancing in the shafts of light. They speak of forgotten things, of darkness that sleeps but never truly dies. I tried to discuss my anxieties with Mrs. Gable at the post office, but she merely smiled thinly and spoke of the harvest moon and the overactive imagination of a woman alone. They don't understand. Or perhaps they do, and choose not to. Perhaps they are all complicit in this... this conspiracy of silence."

Sarah's hands trembled as she read. Complicit. The word hung in the air, heavy with implication. Were the townsfolk aware of what was happening, and had they chosen to turn a blind eye, to protect themselves by maintaining the silence? Or was there something more insidious at play, something that compelled their cooperation? Silas Blackwood's words about "sleeping dogs" and "unpredictable consequences" echoed in her mind. He had implied that some truths were better left buried, that disturbing them would have repercussions. Was this what Eleanor Vance had uncovered? Had she seen too much, or too deeply, into the heart of Havenwood's secrets?

The journal entries became more desperate, the handwriting more erratic, scrawled with a frantic urgency that bled through the page.

Eleanor's descriptions of the "presence" grew more vivid, more terrifying. She wrote of a malevolent entity, a shadow that fed on fear, growing stronger with every tremor of her terror.

"September 20th, 1954. It's no longer just a feeling. I saw it. A shadow, impossibly tall, detaching itself from the corner of the reading room. It had no distinct features, yet I felt its gaze, cold and piercing. It exuded a palpable aura of despair, a suffocating dread that threatened to crush me. It's drawing strength from my fear, I know it. The more I tremble, the more solid it becomes. I lock myself in my small apartment above the library each night, but I know it can slip through the cracks, through the very walls. It's always there, waiting."

Sarah shivered, the chill in the air of the library suddenly feeling far more profound. Eleanor Vance wasn't just experiencing paranoia; she was describing a tangible, supernatural threat, a dark force that was inextricably linked to the disappearances, to the silence. The metallic tang on the pages suddenly seemed more sinister, less like old ink and more like a grim harbinger of the horrors Eleanor was facing.

"October 2nd, 1954. I haven't slept properly in weeks. The whispers are constant now, a cacophony of dread. They speak to me, promising oblivion, promising an end to this terror, if only I would surrender. I fear I am losing myself. The journal is the only thing that keeps me tethered, the only proof that I am still here, that these things are happening. I've tried to gather more information, to find patterns in the missing records, in the names of those who have vanished before me. There is a pattern, a chilling regularity, but it's obscured, like a half-erased inscription on a tombstone."

Sarah's gaze flickered to the dates. October 2nd, 1954. She remembered the newspaper clipping, the one that had mentioned Eleanor Vance's disappearance. It had been vague, uninformative, simply stating that she had not been seen since the beginning of October. This journal entry was from mere days before her vanishing. The weight of it settled upon her, a suffocating blanket of premonition. Eleanor Vance had been documenting her own descent into the very abyss that Sarah was now staring into.

The final entries were almost illegible, the ink smeared in places as if from tears or frantic movements. The words were fragmented, broken, a desperate testament to a mind under unimaginable duress.

"October 7th, 1954. It's here. Inside the library. It's... inside me. The fear... it's a parasite. It wants... it wants to feed. I can't... can't write anymore. Must hide this. For... if anyone... if anyone else..."

The final words trailed off, smudged into an unintelligible blur. The last page was blank, save for a single, dark, fingerprint smudged near the bottom edge, as if Eleanor had pressed her hand down in a final, desperate act of farewell.

Sarah closed the journal, her hands shaking uncontrollably. The silence of the library pressed in on her, no longer a comforting hush, but a vast, echoing void filled with the unspoken horrors documented within the leather-bound pages. Eleanor Vance's journal was not just a historical curiosity; it was a chilling echo of her own burgeoning fears, a confirmation that the unease she felt was not a figment of her imagination but a tangible force at play in Havenwood. The town wasn't just hiding secrets; it was actively harboring a darkness that preyed on the very essence of its inhabitants, a darkness that Silas Blackwood seemed to understand all too well, perhaps even to serve. He had spoken of the past as a treacherous landscape, and Eleanor Vance had stumbled into its most shadowed valleys, her journal a desperate map left behind for anyone brave, or foolish, enough to follow.

Sarah clutched the journal tighter, its weight a grim comfort, a tangible link to the truth that lay buried beneath Havenwood's placid surface. The unraveling fabric was indeed pulling tighter, and Sarah knew, with a certainty that chilled her to the bone, that she was now inextricably caught within its threads. The journey into the forgotten fears of Havenwood had just begun, and the journal of Eleanor Vance was its first, terrifying chapter.

Chapter 3: The Shifting Veil

A Night of Terrors

The weight of Eleanor Vance's journal felt like a physical anchor, a solid reality in the increasingly insubstantial world Sarah was inhabiting. Clutching it to her chest, she left the hushed sanctuary of the library, the deepening twilight casting long, skeletal shadows that seemed to writhe with a life of their own. The walk back to her small apartment above the old mill felt like traversing a familiar landscape that had been subtly, malevolently altered.

Every creak of the weathered wood underfoot, every rustle of leaves in the unseen wind, seemed to carry a whispered accusation, a silent acknowledgement of her intrusion into Havenwood's festering secrets. Silas Blackwood's words, "the past is a treacherous landscape," replayed in her mind, no longer a metaphor but a stark, present reality.

She fumbled with her keys, the metallic click echoing unnervingly in the sudden stillness that had fallen over the street.

The apartment, usually a refuge, felt exposed, vulnerable. As she stepped inside, the air seemed to thicken, to press in on her, carrying with it the same faint, metallic tang she'd detected on Eleanor's journal pages. The weak glow of the single overhead bulb seemed insufficient, swallowed by the encroaching gloom that clung to the corners of the room like cobwebs spun from dread. Sarah dropped her bag, the thud jarring in the oppressive quiet, and made her way to the small kitchenette, a desperate need for warmth, for normalcy, driving her.

As she filled the kettle, a flicker at the edge of her vision caught her attention. A shadow, impossibly elongated, seemed to detach itself from the wall, elongating and contorting before snapping back into the mundane plane of reality. Sarah's heart leaped into her throat, a visceral jolt of pure terror. She spun around, her eyes wide, scanning the empty room. Nothing. Just the familiar, albeit now menacing, contours of her living space. "Just nerves," she whispered, her voice trembling, echoing Eleanor's own attempts to rationalize the inexplicable. But the conviction was already draining from her words, replaced by a gnawing certainty that she was not alone.

The kettle whistled, a piercing shriek that seemed to cut through the thick silence, but the sound offered no comfort. It was too shrill, too frantic, like a trapped animal's cry. As she poured the hot water into a mug, her hand shook so violently that a splash escaped, scalding her fingers. She gasped, the brief pain a distraction, a sharp counterpoint to the deeper, more insidious dread that was now coiling in her gut. She glanced down at her hand, the angry red mark blooming on her skin, and for a terrifying instant, the shadows in the room seemed to coalesce around her, to reach out, to mock her vulnerability.

She sank onto the worn sofa, cradling the mug of tea, its warmth a fragile barrier against the chilling atmosphere. Eleanor Vance's journal lay open on the coffee table, its pages still bearing the ghostly imprint of a life consumed by fear. Sarah's eyes traced the elegant, then frantic, script, the words of October 7th, *1954,* burning themselves into her mind: *"It's here. Inside the library. It's... inside me. The fear... it's a parasite. It wants... it wants to feed."* The fear. It was a tangible entity, a presence that fed on her own growing terror. She could feel it now, a creeping cold that had nothing to do with the autumn chill outside. It was an internal frost, seeping from her very bones.

The apartment began to warp, its familiar dimensions twisting and distorting in the dim light. The walls seemed to recede, then advance, creating a disorienting sense of claustrophobia and agoraphobia simultaneously. The shadows lengthened, not with the natural progression of dusk, but with an unnerving, predatory slowness. They pooled in the corners, grew, and shifted, coalescing into fleeting, indistinct shapes. Sarah found herself mesmerized, horrified, by the silent ballet of darkness playing out before her. She saw a figure standing in the doorway of her bedroom, impossibly tall and gaunt, its form indistinct, a smudge against the deeper darkness. She squeezed her eyes shut, then forced them open again. It was gone. But the impression lingered, a chilling afterimage burned onto her retinas.

Then came the whispers. Faint at first, like the rustling of dry leaves, they seemed to emanate from the very fabric of the apartment. They were indistinct, unintelligible, a murmur of voices just beyond the threshold of comprehension. Yet, Sarah felt their intent, their malevolence. They spoke of secrets, of forgotten names, of things that should have remained buried. They seemed to probe her mind, seeking out her deepest fears, her most profound anxieties. They were Eleanor Vance's whispers, echoing from the past, amplified by the oppressive atmosphere of Havenwood.

Sarah pressed her hands to her ears, trying to block out the insidious murmur, but it was no use. The whispers seemed to penetrate her very skull, to resonate within the hollow spaces of her own anxieties. She imagined them to be the voices of all those who had vanished, trapped in a perpetual loop of terror, their final moments replaying in an endless, spectral chorus. A cold sweat broke out across her forehead, her breath coming in ragged gasps. She felt a desperate urge to flee, to escape this suffocating cage of dread, but where could she go? The whispers were everywhere, and the shadows... the shadows were always watching.

She glanced at the journal again, her gaze falling on the final, smudged words. *"Must hide this. For... if anyone... if anyone else..."* Eleanor had been trying to warn her. She had known. She had understood that this encroaching darkness, this consuming fear, was not an isolated incident but a continuation of a terrible cycle. Sarah felt a kinship with the long-dead librarian, a shared understanding forged in the crucible of supernatural terror. They were both women who had dared to look too closely into the shadowed heart of Havenwood, and Havenwood, it seemed, did not suffer such curiosity gladly.

The feeling of being watched intensified, becoming a palpable pressure, a suffocating embrace. Sarah had felt an unseen gaze, cold and piercing, fixed upon her. It was a gaze that stripped away all pretense of safety, all illusion of solitude. She imagined it to be the gaze of the shadow she had glimpsed, of the entity Eleanor had described. It was a gaze that promised not mere observation, but possession, a consuming hunger that sought to drain her of her very essence.

She stood up, the urge to move, to fight against this encroaching dread, overwhelming her. She paced the small living room, her footsteps echoing hollowly on the wooden floor. The shadows danced around her, taunting her, growing bolder. They no longer remained at the periphery; they seeped into the center of the room, blurring the edges of the furniture, distorting the familiar into the grotesque. The armchair in the corner seemed to sprout gaunt limbs, the bookshelf loomed like a skeletal ribcage, and the very air around her pulsed with a malevolent energy.

The whispers coalesced, and for a terrifying moment, Sarah thought she heard her own name being spoken, drawn out and distorted, laced with a chilling mockery. She flinched, a choked sob escaping her lips. This was more than psychological torment; it was an assault on her sanity, a deliberate attempt to break her. She felt her resolve begin to crumble, the carefully constructed edifice of her resilience beginning to buckle under the relentless pressure.

Then, a new sensation, one that sent a fresh wave of icy terror through her. A distinct feeling of coldness, not just in the air, but on her skin, as if an invisible hand were tracing its chilling path along her arm, up her neck, towards her face. She recoiled, stumbling backward, her breath catching in her throat. It was the presence, Eleanor's presence, no longer just a feeling or a whisper, but a tangible, spectral caress that promised oblivion. She could almost feel the icy breath on her cheek, the vacant void where eyes should have been, staring into her very soul.

Sarah found herself caught in a terrifying loop. She would try to focus on something real – the chipped ceramic of her teacup, the rough weave of the sofa, the single, persistent stain on the ceiling – but the distortions would invariably overwhelm her senses. The boundaries between reality and the hallucination blurred, then dissolved entirely. Was the shadow in the corner a trick of the light, or was it the manifestation of a deeper, more terrifying truth? Were the whispers the wind, or the disembodied voices of the lost? The uncertainty was a torment in itself, a fertile ground for the encroaching dread to take root and flourish.

She stumbled into the bedroom, seeking the perceived safety of its small confines, only to find it offered no respite. The darkness within the room was even more profound, more absolute. The shadows here seemed to pulse with a more concentrated malevolence, gathering in the corners, around the foot of the bed, coalescing into a formless, oppressive mass. She could feel it pressing in, its unseen weight threatening to crush her. She sank onto the edge of the bed, her body trembling uncontrollably, the journal clutched tightly in her hand. It was her only tether to reality, her only proof that she was not yet entirely lost.

The whispers intensified, becoming more distinct, more insidious. They spoke of surrender, of release, of an end to the fear if she would only embrace the encroaching darkness. They promised an escape from the struggle, a peace found only in oblivion. Sarah felt a seductive pull, a dangerous allure to their whispered invitations, a primal weariness that yearned for an end to the terror. But then she saw it, in the fleeting darkness of her peripheral vision, a brief, almost imperceptible movement. A shadow detaching itself from the shadows, impossibly tall, impossibly thin, and in its formless emptiness, she felt a chilling recognition, a sense of ancient, predatory hunger. It was the parasite Eleanor had written about, and it was here, in her room, in her apartment, in her mind.

The night stretched on, an eternity of psychological torment. Sarah found herself caught in a waking nightmare, the apartment transforming into a labyrinth of shifting shadows and disembodied voices. The boundaries between her conscious thoughts and the invasive intrusions of the unknown blurred, leaving her in a state of profound exhaustion and terror. She saw fleeting figures darting at the edges of her vision, heard whispers that seemed to carry the weight of forgotten sorrows, and felt a palpable, cold presence moving through the rooms, a constant, chilling reminder that she was not alone. By the time the first hint of dawn began to paint the sky a sickly grey, Sarah was utterly spent, deeply shaken, the chilling echo of Eleanor Vance's final, desperate words reverberating in the hollow spaces of her mind. The veil had indeed shifted, and what lay beyond was a darkness that threatened to consume her whole.

The Artists Obsession

The whispers from the previous night had receded with the encroaching dawn, leaving Sarah in a state of bone-deep exhaustion, her mind a battlefield where fear and reality had waged a brutal war. Yet, even in the fragile light of morning, the oppressive atmosphere of Havenwood clung to her like a shroud. The journal, Eleanor Vance's testament to a similar descent into terror, lay on the coffee table, its pages now seeming to vibrate with a latent energy, a silent witness to the horrors she had endured. Sarah felt a profound, unsettling connection to the woman, a shared burden of knowledge that had become an unbearable weight.

Her initial instinct was to barricade herself within the perceived safety of her apartment, to deny the encroaching dread, to pretend that the shadows and whispers were merely figments of an overstressed imagination. But the memory of Eleanor's desperate plea – "Must hide this. For… if anyone… if anyone else…" – echoed relentlessly, a stark reminder that isolation was a luxury she could no longer afford. The secrets of Havenwood, it seemed, demanded to be unearthed, and Sarah was increasingly certain that she was the unwilling inheritor of that perilous task.

The need for answers, for confirmation that her terror was not a solitary delusion, gnawed at her. She decided to venture out, to seek any crumb of information that might shed light on the events unfolding around her. The local diner, a relic of a bygone era with its checkered floors and worn vinyl booths, was her first destination. It was a place where the town's inhabitants, or what remained of them, often gathered, their hushed conversations a potential source of the gossip Sarah desperately sought.

She sat at the counter, ordering a black coffee, the bitter liquid a small comfort against the chill that had settled deep within her. The diner was sparsely populated, a handful of locals nursing their own cups, their faces etched with the weariness that seemed to permeate Havenwood. Sarah tried to appear nonchalant, her senses on high alert, straining to catch any stray snippet of conversation that might offer a clue.

It was a hushed exchange between two elderly women at a nearby table that finally snagged her attention. Their voices, barely above a whisper, carried the distinctive cadence of small-town secrets being passed like contraband. Sarah leaned in, her heart thudding against her ribs.

"…seen him again, Martha. Over by the old mill path, just watching."

"Him? Silas Blackwood?"

"Who else? Always with that sketchbook, isn't he? Like a vulture, just circling."

"And what was he sketching this time, Agnes?"

"Couldn't quite make it out from where I was. But I swear, Martha, it looked like... well, it looked like that new girl. The one in Eleanor Vance's old apartment."

Sarah froze, her hand tightening around the ceramic mug. Her blood ran cold. Silas Blackwood. The enigmatic man she had encountered at the library, whose gaze had felt unnervingly intense, had been watching her. Sketching her. The realization hit her with the force of a physical blow, a fresh wave of dread washing over her, far more potent than the lingering phantoms of the night.

The nonchalant facade she had attempted to maintain crumbled. She felt a visceral, primal fear prickle her skin. She was not merely an observer of Havenwood's secrets; she was becoming a subject. The notion that Blackwood, the man who seemed to embody the town's oppressive history, had turned his artistic gaze upon her was profoundly disturbing. Eleanor Vance's journal entries, filled with paranoia and the feeling of being relentlessly observed, suddenly took on a chillingly personal resonance.

Agnes continued, her voice dropping even lower, "He's got a peculiar interest in this town, that one. Almost too peculiar. Ever since he arrived, things just feel... off."

Martha huffed, a low, dismissive sound. "Well, he's an artist, Agnes. They're all a bit... eccentric."

"Eccentricity doesn't explain what I saw. The way he was hunched over, concentrating... and the way he looked up, directly at the windows of her building. It wasn't just casual observation, Martha. It was... possession."

Possession. The word sent a fresh shiver down Sarah's spine. Blackwood's artistic obsession wasn't a benign eccentricity; it was a manifestation of something far more sinister. She felt a prickling sensation, as if his eyes were still upon her, even now, miles away from the mill path. The sense of being watched, a low hum of anxiety that had been a constant companion since her arrival in Havenwood, intensified dramatically.

She paid for her coffee, her movements jerky, her mind a whirlwind of fear and suspicion. The walk back to her apartment felt different now. The familiar path, once merely a route home, was now a potential vantage point for Blackwood's unnerving scrutiny. Every rustle of leaves, every distant sound, seemed to carry a hidden threat. She found herself glancing over her shoulder, her gaze darting to the shadowed windows of the surrounding buildings, imagining his presence behind them, his charcoal sketching her every move.

The illusion of solitude, already fragile, shattered completely. Her apartment, once a sanctuary, now felt like a glass house, her life laid bare for any passerby to observe, to document, to covet. The creak of the wooden stairs under her feet, the groan of the old building settling, no longer sounded like the natural accompaniments of an aging structure. They were the subtle sounds of surveillance, the creaks of a watchman moving on his rounds, the groans of a structure that knew it was being observed.

She reached her apartment door, her hand trembling as she inserted the key. The metallic click echoed with a new, terrifying significance – the sound of a lock that could only offer a temporary, and perhaps illusory, barrier. Inside, the familiar space felt alien, violated. She could almost feel Blackwood's gaze lingering on the worn armchair, on the stack of books, on her very presence. The air felt heavy, charged with an unseen energy, the lingering residue of his focused attention.

She walked to the window, her movements hesitant, as if expecting to be met by a tangible presence. The street below was quiet, bathed in the pale morning light. Yet, she imagined him there, perhaps disguised, perhaps lurking in the shadows of the adjacent buildings, his sketchbook open, his eyes fixed on her window. The intimacy of his supposed artistic pursuit felt like a profound violation. He was capturing her likeness, her form, perhaps even her vulnerability, without her consent, without her knowledge.

Eleanor Vance's journal lay open on the table, a silent companion in her growing terror. Sarah picked it up, her fingers tracing the elegant script that had devolved into frantic scribbles. She remembered Eleanor's words: *"He watches me. Always watching. I feel his eyes even when he is not there. He knows..."* Knows what? Sarah wondered, her own fear mirroring Eleanor's. What did Blackwood know? And how had his obsessive gaze become intertwined with the unsettling phenomena she was experiencing?

The sense of being watched was no longer a vague unease; it was a palpable weight, a constant pressure on her senses. Every shadow seemed to deepen, every sound seemed to carry a hidden meaning. She found herself analyzing the smallest details of her surroundings, searching for any sign of Blackwood's continued observation. Had that curtain moved? Was that a glint of light reflecting off a lens? The paranoia was a suffocating blanket, suffocating her reason, feeding the very dread she was trying to combat.

She moved through her apartment, her movements stiff and unnatural, as if under a spotlight. She felt exposed, vulnerable, her privacy an invaded territory. The realization that an individual, a specific person, was actively monitoring her existence amplified the horror. It was no longer a faceless, formless dread; it was the focused intent of an artist whose obsession had crossed the boundary into something predatory.

The mundane actions of daily life became fraught with anxiety. Making tea, reading a book, even sitting still felt like drawing attention to herself, like offering a more detailed subject for Blackwood's gaze. She found herself avoiding the windows, drawing the curtains tight, attempting to create a physical barrier against his imagined scrutiny. But the knowledge that he *could* see her, that he *had* been watching, rendered these attempts at concealment futile.

She remembered the fleeting shadow she had seen the previous night, the way it had detached itself from the darkness. Could that have been an echo of Blackwood's presence, a spectral manifestation of his obsessive attention? The thought was chilling, suggesting a connection between his artistic focus and the more supernatural elements plaguing Havenwood. Perhaps his art was not merely a depiction, but a form of conduit, a way to draw closer to the town's hidden truths, and by extension, to her.

The isolation deepened. She felt cut off from the world, trapped within the confines of her own paranoia and the watchful eye of Silas Blackwood. The hushed gossip at the diner had confirmed her deepest fears, stripping away any remaining comfort she might have found in the possibility of delusion. She was seen, she was documented, and the implications of that artistic obsession sent a cold wave of dread through her veins, a dread that mirrored the terror captured in Eleanor Vance's desperate, fading ink. The veil had indeed shifted, revealing not only the town's dark secrets, but the unsettling proximity of a man who seemed determined to paint himself into the very fabric of her unraveling reality. The artist's obsession had found its subject, and Sarah was its unwilling muse, trapped in a canvas of growing terror. The world outside her small apartment, once a source of potential escape, now felt like a stage upon which Blackwood's disturbing performance was unfolding, with her as the central, terrified character. The quiet unease that had initially drawn her to Havenwood had blossomed into a full-blown phobia, a constant, gnawing awareness of being perpetually under surveillance. Every creak of the floorboards, every distant car horn, every murmur of the wind through the skeletal branches of the ancient oak outside her window, was now imbued with the sinister implication of a keen observer, a hidden artist documenting her descent into fear. It was as if Blackwood's gaze had rendered her transparent, her inner turmoil laid bare for his artistic interpretation.

The gossip, though unsettling, had also provided a peculiar kind of validation. It confirmed that her heightened sense of unease was not entirely unfounded. Others noticed Blackwood, his peculiar habits, his almost predatory focus. Agnes's description of him as a "vulture" and his gaze as "possession" resonated deeply, tapping into the primal fear of being consumed, of being rendered into an object, stripped of agency and self. The artistic process, usually associated with creation and beauty, had been twisted into something sinister, a mechanism of surveillance and perhaps something more.

Sarah found herself scrutinizing the very architecture of her apartment, the way the light fell, the way the shadows played. She imagined Blackwood's keen artist's eye dissecting these elements, finding compositional harmony in her growing distress. Was he sketching the way her shoulders tensed as she passed the window? The way her hand trembled as she reached for a glass of water? The intimacy of this imagined artistic observation felt more violating than any physical intrusion. It was an invasion of her inner landscape, a dissection of her fear for the sake of a morbid creation.

The knowledge that he was sketching her from a distance, unseen, unacknowledged, made the previous night's spectral visitations seem almost... less terrifying. Those had felt external, beyond human control. This was the deliberate, focused intent of another human being, a chilling manifestation of a human obsession. It was the fear of the unknown amplified by the fear of the known, the spectral dread now anchored to a tangible, albeit elusive, perpetrator.

She reread Eleanor Vance's journal, seeking solace or guidance, but finding only further confirmation of her escalating dread. Eleanor's paranoia about being watched, her sense of an unseen observer, felt like a direct premonition, a script written for Sarah's own unfolding nightmare. "He is in the periphery," Eleanor had written, "always just beyond the edge of sight, but I feel him. I feel the weight of his attention like a physical thing. It drains me." Sarah understood that feeling with a terrifying clarity. The weight of Blackwood's attention was a tangible force, pressing down on her, sapping her strength, her resolve.

She tried to reason with herself, to cling to logic. He was an artist, perhaps a sensitive soul drawn to the melancholic beauty of Havenwood, and she, by virtue of her dwelling in a place of historical tragedy, had inadvertently become part of his artistic inspiration. But the gossip, the descriptions of his intensity, belied such a simple explanation. There was a darkness in his observed behavior, a possessiveness that transcended mere artistic appreciation. It was the same darkness that seemed to seep from the very foundations of Havenwood, the same predatory hunger that had whispered to her in the shadows.

The isolation became a crushing burden. Without friends or family nearby, with her days consumed by the gnawing fear of Blackwood's unseen gaze, Sarah felt her grip on reality loosening. The world outside her apartment was no longer a place of potential comfort or connection; it was a landscape populated by unseen observers, by hidden threats. The simple act of stepping outside felt like an invitation to be captured, to be documented, to be consumed by the insatiable appetite of Silas Blackwood's artistic obsession.

She found herself constantly scanning her surroundings, her eyes darting to every corner, every shadow, every window. The fear had become a sixth sense, a hyper-awareness that made her jump at every sudden noise, every unexpected movement. The creaks and groans of her building were no longer just ambient sounds; they were coded messages, signals of proximity, of observation. She was trapped in a constant state of alert, her nervous system frayed, her sanity hanging by a thread.

The journal, clutched tightly in her hand, felt less like a historical document and more like a prophecy, a chilling premonition of her own fate. Eleanor Vance had been consumed by this town, by its secrets, and by the men who seemed to prey upon its vulnerabilities. Sarah was beginning to suspect that Silas Blackwood was not merely an observer, but an active participant in Havenwood's dark legacy, his art a means of drawing closer to the very forces that had driven Eleanor to her desperate final entries. The artist's obsession was not just a personal eccentricity; it was a symptom of Havenwood itself, a manifestation of the town's pervasive, suffocating dread, and Sarah was its unwilling subject, her life becoming the canvas for a tragedy she was only just beginning to understand. Her vulnerability, her fear, the very unraveling of her mind – these were the raw materials of Blackwood's art, and he was, she suspected, a very patient artist. The silence of her apartment was no longer a comfort; it was a pregnant pause, a moment of stillness before the next brushstroke of terror. The artist's obsession had become Sarah's reality, and the lines between observation and possession had blurred into a terrifying, indistinguishable whole.

Deciphering the Past

The weight of Silas Blackwood's gaze, so vividly confirmed by the hushed whispers in the diner, had settled upon Sarah like a physical burden. It was a constant, unnerving presence that amplified the already suffocating atmosphere of Havenwood. The initial shock of being watched had begun to recede, replaced by a more insidious dread, a creeping paranoia that began to seep into the very fabric of her thoughts. She found herself scrutinizing every reflection, every shadow, searching for confirmation of the artist's unseen observation. Her apartment, once a refuge, now felt like a stage, the worn furniture and peeling wallpaper mere props in a silent, terrifying play where she was the sole, unwilling protagonist. The journal of Eleanor Vance, still open on her coffee table, felt less like a historical account and more like a personal diary, its pages filled with the same fear and isolation that Sarah was now experiencing. Eleanor's frantic scrawls about being watched, about a pervasive sense of unease that clung to her like the damp Havenwood air, were no longer just echoes from the past; they were a terrifying premonition of her own future.

The confirmation that Silas Blackwood was indeed observing her, and not just casually, but with an artist's discerning, almost predatory eye, propelled Sarah into a new phase of desperate investigation. Her initial desire to flee Havenwood, to escape the oppressive grip of its history and its inhabitants, had been supplanted by an unyielding need to understand. To understand why she was being watched, why this town seemed to prey on the vulnerable, and why Eleanor Vance's fate felt so inextricably linked to her own. The fragmented clues from the missing library documents and the cryptic entries in Eleanor's journal were the only tangible leads she possessed. She knew she couldn't afford to remain a passive observer, a mere subject in Blackwood's morbid artistic study. She had to actively delve into Havenwood's past, to excavate the secrets buried beneath its veneer of quiet decay.

Her research began tentatively, at first, a cautious probing of the town's archives. The local historical society, housed in a drafty old building that smelled of dust and forgotten memories, became her new haunt. The librarian, a stooped woman with spectacles perched precariously on her nose and a perpetually bewildered expression, seemed as much a part of the town's history as the artifacts she curated. Sarah approached her with a carefully constructed story of academic research, a vague interest in local folklore and its impact on community development. The librarian, thankfully, seemed more intrigued by the prospect of a visitor than suspicious of her intentions.

As Sarah sifted through brittle newspaper clippings and faded town records, a pattern began to emerge, a recurring motif of unease and inexplicable events that mirrored her own experiences with chilling accuracy. Early newspaper articles from the late 19th century spoke of "unsettling occurrences" and a "palpable sense of dread" that had descended upon Havenwood. There were mentions of strange lights in the woods, disembodied whispers carried on the wind, and a pervasive feeling of being watched that drove several early settlers to abandon their homes. One article, dated 1887, recounted the disappearance of a young woman named Abigail Thorne, whose belongings were found meticulously arranged in her empty cottage, as if she had simply vanished into thin air, leaving no trace but an overwhelming sense of her presence. The accompanying illustration, a crudely drawn sketch of a desolate cottage, sent a shiver down Sarah's spine, a faint, unsettling resemblance to the stillness of her own apartment after a night of unseen torment.

The further back she delved, the more pronounced the similarities became. There were accounts of unexplained phenomena, of objects moving on their own, of shadows that seemed to possess a life of their own. But it was the recurring theme of a watchful presence that truly captivated and terrified her. Time and again, the records spoke of individuals who felt they were being observed, scrutinized, their every move cataloged by an unseen entity. This wasn't just vague paranoia; it was a consistent, documented experience that spanned generations. The whispers that had tormented Sarah in her sleep, the feeling of eyes upon her even in the deepest darkness, were not new to Havenwood. They were a legacy, a shared burden passed down through the town's hushed history.

Then there were the artists. Not just Silas Blackwood, but others, historical figures who had been drawn to Havenwood, often leaving behind a trail of unsettling works and equally unsettling rumors. A painter named Elias Croft, who had lived in

Havenwood for a brief period in the early 1920s, was known for his disturbing portraits of local residents. His canvases were said to capture not just their likeness, but their deepest fears, their hidden anxieties, as if he were peering directly into their souls. His later works, according to a local historian's blog Sarah stumbled upon, became increasingly abstract, filled with swirling patterns and distorted figures that many interpreted as expressions of his own descent into madness, fueled by the oppressive atmosphere of Havenwood. Croft had disappeared as suddenly as he had arrived, leaving behind a studio filled with unfinished canvases, many of them depicting scenes of isolation and an all-seeing, shadowed eye. Sarah felt a prickle of recognition; the shadowed eye was a motif that now seemed to haunt her waking hours as well.

She found references to a sculptor, a reclusive man named Thomas Ashton, who had attempted to capture the "essence of Havenwood" in his work. His sculptures, carved from the dark, gnarled wood of the surrounding forests, were described as embodying a profound sense of melancholy and unease. They were said to emanate a strange energy, a palpable sense of foreboding that unnerved those who viewed them. One local legend claimed that Ashton's most prized sculpture, a depiction of a cloaked figure with its face obscured by shadow, seemed to follow viewers with its unseen gaze. Sarah shivered, imagining the artist's intent, the deliberate act of imbuing his creations with the very dread that seemed to permeate the town. She could almost see Silas Blackwood's charcoal lines mirroring Ashton's shadowed carvings, his sketches of her becoming a modern iteration of this unsettling artistic tradition.

The missing documents from the library, the ones Sarah had been trying to locate, were mentioned in several accounts as being part of a collection belonging to a former town historian, a man named

Reverend Silas Blackwood – not the artist, but perhaps an ancestor, whose meticulous records detailed the town's more peculiar history. The librarian confirmed that such a collection had indeed existed, but it had been "misplaced" years ago, during a period of significant staff turnover. The irony was not lost on Sarah; a Blackwood had been diligently chronicling Havenwood's strangeness long before Silas, the artist, had appeared. Was the artist's name a coincidence, or was there a lineage of obsession, a hereditary connection to the town's darker currents?

As Sarah pieced together these fragments, a chilling narrative began to solidify. Havenwood wasn't just a town with a few isolated incidents; it was a place steeped in a history of paranoia, of inexplicable phenomena, and of artists who seemed to be drawn to its darkness like moths to a flame. The common thread was the overwhelming sense of being watched, a collective hallucination that had plagued its inhabitants for centuries. But Sarah couldn't shake the feeling that this was more than mere folklore or mass hysteria. The tangible manifestations of her own terror – the whispers, the shadows, the feeling of being stalked by Silas Blackwood – suggested a far more insidious reality.

She found an old newspaper clipping detailing a series of "mass delusions" that had gripped Havenwood in the early 1950s. During this period, numerous residents reported seeing spectral figures and experiencing vivid hallucinations, all seemingly triggered by a series of unusual atmospheric conditions and localized seismic activity. The article dismissed these events as a product of shared anxiety and the isolation of rural life, but Sarah saw a familiar pattern. Eleanor Vance's journal entries spoke of similar unsettling atmospheric shifts, of an oppressive stillness that preceded moments of intense terror. Was there a cyclical nature to these events, a recurring manifestation of the town's inherent malevolence that ebbed and flowed like a dark tide?

The librarian, sensing Sarah's genuine interest, confided in her about certain local legends, tales that never made it into the official records. She spoke of the "Whispering Woods" that bordered the town, a place where people were said to get lost, not by losing their way, but by being lured deeper by phantom voices. She mentioned old rituals and forgotten protective charms that some of the older residents still practiced, remnants of a time when the townspeople believed they were living in constant battle against unseen forces. These whispered tales, dismissed by the librarian as fanciful notions, resonated deeply with Sarah. They spoke of a community that had long understood the pervasive nature of the darkness that clung to Havenwood.

The more Sarah researched, the more she realized that her current predicament was not an anomaly, but a continuation of a long, dark tradition. The fear she felt was not unique to her; it was a sentiment that had been shared by generations of Havenwood's inhabitants. The question that gnawed at her was not *if* something was wrong with Havenwood, but *what* it was, and why it seemed to manifest itself so consistently, so cyclically. The town's past was a dark mirror, reflecting her present terror, suggesting that the veil between the mundane and the malevolent was not a singular tear, but a persistent, thinning membrane, worn down by the weight of centuries of fear and unspoken horrors. Silas Blackwood, she suspected, was not merely an artist capitalizing on the town's atmosphere; he was a product of it, perhaps even a conduit for it, his obsession with her a morbid continuation of Havenwood's enduring legacy of watchful dread. The historical record was no longer just a source of information; it was a chilling roadmap, charting the course of a darkness that had been patiently waiting, and now seemed to have found a new subject in Sarah. She felt a grim resolve hardening within her. To understand Havenwood, she had to understand its past, to decipher the language of its fear, for only then could she hope to break the cycle, to escape the shadow that Silas Blackwood and the town itself seemed intent on casting over her life. The fragmented pieces of history were slowly coalescing, forming a picture both terrifying and strangely familiar, a testament to the enduring power of a place that seemed to feed on the anxieties of its inhabitants, perpetuating a cycle of paranoia and dread that had now ensnared her.

A Cryptic Message

The morning after her deep dive into Havenwood's archives, Sarah woke with a start, the residual echoes of Eleanor Vance's journal still clinging to her consciousness. The oppressive stillness of the previous day had been replaced by an unnerving quiet, a silence that felt less like peace and more like anticipation. As she brewed her morning coffee, her gaze fell upon the worn wooden bird, nestled amongst the scattered pages of historical accounts on her coffee table. It was a small thing, no larger than her thumb, intricately carved from what appeared to be dark, aged oak. Its wings were poised in mid-flight, its tiny eyes rendered with a surprising degree of detail, and its beak, though delicate, seemed to possess an almost defiant sharpness. Sarah had initially dismissed it as a curious, if slightly unsettling, find from the antique shop, a piece of local kitsch that had somehow found its way into her possession. But the librarian's hushed recounting of a similar artifact, a token left by the town's unseen 'presence,' had irrevocably altered her perception.

The librarian, Mrs. Gable, had spoken in a low, almost conspiratorial tone, her voice barely rising above a whisper as she'd recounted the old tales. "They say," she'd begun, her eyes darting nervously towards the dusty shelves, "that sometimes, the… the *thing* that watches, it leaves little gifts. Small things. Things that look like they belong, but with a… a wrongness about them. Like this little bird," she'd gestured vaguely towards a glass display case that held a collection of faded photographs and miscellaneous trinkets. Sarah hadn't paid it much mind then, attributing it to the whimsical folklore of a small, isolated town. But now, staring at the very same type of wooden bird, a cold knot of dread began to tighten in her stomach. She remembered finding it on her doorstep the previous evening, a solitary object placed with an almost ceremonial care, its smooth, cool surface a stark contrast to the rough wood of her front door. She had brought it inside, a fleeting curiosity, and left it amidst the detritus of her research.

Now, she picked it up, turning it over in her fingers. It felt unnervingly familiar, its weight oddly significant. The librarian had described it as a token, a calling card left by whatever malevolent entity haunted Havenwood, a subtle yet undeniable mark of its attention. And Sarah had a chilling certainty that this little bird was no different. She ran her thumb along the smooth curve of its belly, her touch almost reverent. There was a faint scent of something earthy and ancient emanating from it, a whisper of the surrounding woods, perhaps, or something older, something deeper. It was then that she noticed it – a subtle seam, almost imperceptible, running along the underside of the bird's body.

Her heart began to pound a frantic rhythm against her ribs. This was no mere trinket. This was a vessel, a deliberate concealment. With trembling fingers, she worked at the seam, the wood yielding slightly under her persistent pressure. A tiny click, barely audible, echoed in the sudden silence of her apartment.

The base of the bird separated from the body, revealing a hollow cavity within. Nestled inside, no bigger than a grain of rice, was a minuscule, rolled-up piece of parchment.

Sarah's breath hitched. She carefully extracted the parchment, its texture rough and brittle, like ancient paper that had been exposed to the elements for far too long. Unrolling it with painstaking slowness, her eyes fixed on the single word scrawled across its surface in faded, spidery ink: 'Soon.'

The word landed with the force of a physical blow. It wasn't a greeting, nor a threat, not directly. It was a promise. A chilling, undeniable affirmation that the unseen observer, the presence that had haunted Eleanor Vance and now seemed to have fixated on her, was not only aware of her but was actively engaging with her. The deliberate placement of the bird, the hidden message, the single, resonant word – it all coalesced into a terrifying confirmation of her worst fears. This was not a random act of curiosity or an artistic fascination from Silas Blackwood. This was something far older, far more insidious, and it was reaching out to her. The 'presence' the librarian spoke of, the force that had left similar tokens, had found her. And it was announcing its impending arrival.

The implication of the word 'Soon' hung in the air, heavy and suffocating. Soon for what? Soon for what event was this cryptic message a prelude? The chilling specificity of the discovery, the realization that she was not merely being observed but was being directly communicated with, sent a fresh wave of terror through her. This wasn't the detached scrutiny of an artist, however unsettling that might have been. This was a deliberate, intimate intrusion, a sign that the veil between her reality and whatever lurked beyond was thinning, not just metaphorically, but tangibly. The intricately carved bird, a symbol of innocence and freedom, had become a harbinger of dread, a silent testament to the escalating danger she was in.

Sarah carefully placed the two halves of the bird back together, the seam almost disappearing once more. She couldn't bring herself to discard it, nor could she bear to keep it openly displayed. It was a tangible link to the encroaching darkness, a constant reminder of the sinister game she had unknowingly become a part of. She tucked it into the pocket of her jeans, the cool wood a constant, unsettling presence against her thigh. The single word, 'Soon,' echoed in her mind, a persistent, unnerving mantra. It spoke of a planned convergence, a culmination of unseen forces that were drawing closer.

Her research had confirmed that Havenwood was a town steeped in a history of unease, of unexplained occurrences that spanned generations. The whispers, the feeling of being watched, the inexplicable events – they were not figments of her imagination or the product of a town simply steeped in folklore. They were recurring patterns, deeply woven into the fabric of Havenwood's existence. And now, she had a direct, undeniable piece of evidence that this history was not merely a collection of stories but a living, breathing entity, one that was actively reaching out, leaving its mark.

The realization that the 'presence' was capable of such deliberate communication was a profound and terrifying escalation. It suggested a level of consciousness, an intent, that went far beyond what she had previously considered. The anonymous artist, Silas Blackwood, with his watchful gaze and unsettling sketches, now seemed almost secondary, a more visible, albeit disturbing, manifestation of a deeper, more ancient dread. The wooden bird, with its hidden message, was a direct communication from the source, a chilling confirmation that she was not alone in her perception of being watched.

Sarah found herself scanning her surroundings with renewed intensity, every shadow seeming to deepen, every creak of the old building a potential harbinger of something more. The meticulously arranged wooden bird, a sign of careful, deliberate action, underscored the meticulous nature of the observer. It wasn't chaos or random chance; it was a calculated approach. The 'presence' was methodical, patient, and now, it was making its intentions known.

The word 'Soon' was a temporal marker, a sign that the waiting was nearly over. But what was it waiting for? Was it waiting for her to be fully ensnared, to be completely immersed in its influence? Or was it waiting for a specific moment, a confluence of astrological or atmospheric conditions that would signal the perfect time for its full manifestation? The ambiguity was almost more terrifying than a direct threat. It left her mind to conjure the most horrific possibilities, to fill in the blanks with the darkest fears imaginable.

She thought back to Eleanor Vance's journal. Eleanor had written of a similar sense of impending doom, of a feeling that something was drawing nearer, something inevitable. Her entries had become increasingly frantic in the weeks leading up to her disappearance, filled with a growing terror that she was being targeted, that the watchful presence was no longer content with mere observation. Sarah's own experience, from the initial unsettling awareness of being watched to the tangible evidence of the carved bird and its cryptic message, was mirroring Eleanor's descent with an alarming accuracy.

The small, wooden bird had become a focal point, a tangible piece of evidence that tied her directly to the town's dark history. It was proof that the whispers weren't just echoes, and the shadows weren't just tricks of the light. They were manifestations of a sentient force, a force that was now directly acknowledging her existence. The word 'Soon' was not a warning to flee, but an invitation to witness, a promise of revelation. And Sarah, despite the paralyzing fear, felt a strange, morbid curiosity beginning to take root. She had stumbled into a hidden world, a tapestry woven with threads of dread and ancient secrets, and now, the threads were tightening around her. The arrival of the wooden bird and its chilling message was a turning point, a clear signal that the quiet phase of observation was over, and something far more active, far more dangerous, was about to begin. She was no longer just a researcher delving into the past; she was an active participant, a chosen subject in a drama that had been unfolding in Havenwood for centuries. The weight of that realization settled upon her, heavy and inescapable, as she stood in the quiet of her apartment, the small, silent bird a potent symbol of the approaching storm.

The Town's Collective Amnesia

The unsettling quiet of the previous night had not dissipated with the dawn. If anything, it had deepened, settling over Sarah like a shroud. The single word, "Soon," from the hidden parchment felt less like a cryptic message and more like a prophecy etched onto her soul. It was a tangible threat, delivered with the chilling precision of a whisper in a crowded room. The small wooden bird, now tucked away in her pocket, felt like a lead weight, a constant reminder of her untenable position. She was no longer an observer; she was a participant, and the game, whatever it was, had just moved into its next, more dangerous phase.

Driven by a desperate need for answers, and a gnawing fear that she was spiraling into a solitary madness, Sarah decided to reach out. She needed to gauge the town's awareness, to see if anyone else felt the oppressive weight of Havenwood's history, if anyone else perceived the subtle wrongness that had begun to permeate her own reality. Her thoughts turned to the few people she had spoken to during her initial days in town, individuals who had seemed more open, less guarded. There was Martha, the kindly owner of the local diner, whose eyes held a perpetual hint of sadness, and old Mr. Henderson, a retired history teacher who had offered a few cryptic remarks about the town's "peculiar nature."

Her first stop was Martha's Diner. The familiar scent of brewing coffee and frying bacon usually offered a measure of comfort, a semblance of normalcy. But today, as Sarah pushed open the door, the warmth seemed to recoil from her. Martha, wiping down the counter with a practiced, almost automatic motion, looked up. Her smile, usually a genuine crinkle around her eyes, seemed to falter for a split second before snapping back into place.

"Morning, dear," Martha said, her voice a little too bright, a little too strained. "Just the usual for you?"

Sarah slid onto a stool at the counter, the worn vinyl cool against her back. "Martha," she began, her voice low, "I... I found something yesterday.

Something in the archives. It was about... well, it was about some of the older stories. The disappearances." She hesitated, searching Martha's face for any flicker of recognition, any sign that her anxieties were not entirely unfounded.

Martha's smile tightened. She busied herself with Sarah's coffee, her movements jerky. "Oh, the archives," she said, her gaze fixed on the steaming mug. "Such dusty old things. So much history, you know. Some of it best left undisturbed." She placed the coffee in front of Sarah, her fingers brushing the mug a little too forcefully.

Sarah watched her, a cold dread coiling in her stomach. "But Martha, some of it feels… real. Like it's still happening. I heard stories, about strange occurrences, about people feeling watched. And I've felt it too." She lowered her voice further. "I found this yesterday." She reached into her pocket, her fingers closing around the smooth wood of the bird. She hesitated, then pulled it out, placing it on the counter between them. "Have you ever seen anything like this?"

Martha's eyes flickered towards the small carving. Her hand, which had been resting on the counter, recoiled as if burned. Her face drained of color, her breath catching in her throat. For a fleeting moment, Sarah saw it – a raw, unadulterated fear that mirrored her own. But then, just as quickly, it was gone, replaced by a practiced mask of indifference.

"A little bird," Martha said, her voice a near whisper, her gaze now fixed on a point somewhere beyond Sarah's shoulder. "A nice little trinket. Probably made by one of the local craftsmen years ago." She picked up a damp cloth and began vigorously wiping the counter near Sarah's hand, her movements agitated. "Don't worry yourself too much about old tales, dear. This town… it has its share of spooky stories, but you know, they're just stories to keep the tourists entertained."

Sarah's heart sank. The fear in Martha's eyes had been genuine, but her denial was equally absolute. It was as if she had been slapped with a physical barrier, an invisible wall erected between them. "But the feeling…" Sarah pressed, her voice laced with desperation. "The feeling that something is watching us?"

Martha finally met her gaze, and Sarah was met with a chilling blankness. There was no recognition, no shared unease. It was as if Sarah was speaking a foreign language. "I don't know what you're talking about, dear," Martha said, her tone polite but firm, a polite dismissal that felt more damning than any outright accusation. "Perhaps you're just tired. You've been working hard in those archives. Why don't you have a nice, hearty breakfast? Build you right up."

Sarah felt a profound sense of isolation wash over her. Martha, whom she had considered a potential ally, had retreated into a fortress of denial. The collective amnesia was not just an abstract concept; it was a tangible force, actively repelling any attempt to breach its walls. She paid for her coffee, the small wooden bird feeling heavier than ever in her pocket. As she left the diner, the cheerful chime of the bell above the door sounded hollow, mocking her fruitless attempt at connection.

Her next attempt was with Mr. Henderson. She found him in his small, cluttered study, surrounded by stacks of books and the lingering scent of pipe tobacco. He greeted her with a kindly nod, his eyes, magnified by thick spectacles, holding a spark of intellectual curiosity.

"Sarah, my dear," he said, gesturing to a worn armchair. "Back from your historical explorations, I see. Found anything to pique your interest?"

Sarah sat down, the silence of the house amplifying the thrumming anxiety in her chest. "Mr. Henderson," she began, carefully choosing her words. "I've been looking through the town records, and I've come across... well, I've come across some disturbing patterns. Stories that seem to repeat themselves, generations apart. And I've also been experiencing some rather unsettling things myself."

She explained her feelings of being watched, the strange coincidences, and finally, she produced the wooden bird. "I found this," she said, her voice trembling slightly. "And I was told that sometimes... that certain 'presences' leave tokens like this. It feels significant."

Mr. Henderson took the bird, turning it over in his gnarled fingers. A faint frown creased his brow, a flicker of something unreadable in his eyes. He held it for a long moment, the silence stretching between them, taut and expectant. Sarah leaned forward, her hopes rising with each passing second.

Then, with a sigh that seemed to carry the weight of years, he placed the bird back on the table. "A charming piece of folk art," he said, his voice regaining its academic tone. "These old towns are full of such things, you know. Echoes of the past, embellished by time and imagination. People have always projected their fears and anxieties onto the unknown, and Havenwood, with its isolation and long history, is a fertile ground for such projections."

He gestured around his study. "I've dedicated my life to understanding history, Sarah. And what I've learned is that the past is often far more mundane than the stories we tell about it. We tend to romanticize or demonize events, to imbue them with a significance they never truly possessed. This town... it's no different at all."

Sarah stared at him, dumbfounded. The flicker of recognition, the almost imperceptible pause before he spoke, had convinced her he knew something. But his words were a complete negation of her experience, a polite dismissal that felt like another door slamming shut.

"But the feeling, Mr. Henderson," she pleaded, her voice cracking. "The feeling of unease? The shadows…?"

Mr. Henderson patted her hand gently, his touch cool and dry. "The mind is a powerful thing, my dear. It can play tricks on us, especially in unfamiliar surroundings. Havenwood has a certain… atmosphere. It's easy to get caught up in it, to let your imagination run wild. My advice? Focus on the tangible facts, the documented history. Don't let the whispers of the past consume you."

He smiled, a thin, reedy smile. "Why don't you tell me about your research? Perhaps I can help you find some more concrete information. Facts, not feelings."

Sarah felt a profound sense of despair. Mr. Henderson, the retired history teacher, the man who had once spoken of the town's "peculiar nature," was now acting as if he had never uttered those words. His denial was as complete and as unnerving as Martha's. It was as if a collective switch had been flipped, silencing any hint of awareness, any acknowledgement of the town's darker undercurrents.

She managed a weak smile. "Yes, of course. Facts." But the word tasted like ash in her mouth. The tangible evidence of the wooden bird, the undeniable message – these were facts, yet they were being dismissed as figments of her overactive imagination. The shared amnesia of Havenwood was not a passive forgetting; it was an active, enforced silence, a collective agreement to ignore the truth, to bury it so deeply that no one, not even those who had experienced it firsthand, could acknowledge its existence.

Leaving Mr. Henderson's house, Sarah felt more alone than ever. The weight of the wooden bird in her pocket seemed to grow heavier with each step. The town, which had initially seemed quaint and charming, now felt like a place of deep, unsettling secrets, a community bound together not by shared history, but by a shared, terrified silence. The more she tried to pry open the past, the more it seemed to snap shut, pushing her further into an isolated dread.

She realized then that her attempts to find answers among the townsfolk were futile. They were not just unaware; they were actively, perhaps unconsciously, policing the boundaries of memory. Any deviation, any attempt to reawaken the dormant terrors, was met with swift, practiced deflection. It was a defense mechanism, a way to survive in a town that seemed to exist in a perpetual state of unspoken dread.

The collective amnesia of Havenwood was a powerful, suffocating force. It wasn't just a lack of memory; it was a deliberate, ingrained suppression. It was as if the very air in the town was imbued with a potent opiate, dulling the senses, clouding the minds, ensuring that the dark heart of Havenwood remained undisturbed. Sarah understood now that the "presence" wasn't just a singular entity that was just haunting the town; it had woven itself into the very fabric of the community, its influence so pervasive that it had shaped their collective consciousness, forcing them into a state of willful ignorance.

This realization left Sarah adrift. The carefully constructed edifice of her research had crumbled around her. The archival documents, Eleanor Vance's journal, the cryptic message on the parchment –

all of it pointed to a horrifying truth, a truth that the very people who should have been her guides were actively denying. The isolation was crushing. She was the only one who seemed to see the cracks in Havenwood's placid facade, the only one who felt the chilling hand of something ancient and malevolent reaching out from the shadows.

The "Soon" taunted her from the confines of her pocket. Soon for what? Soon for the truth to break through the dam of collective denial? Or soon for the darkness to finally claim her, just as it had claimed Eleanor Vance, and countless others before her? The silence of the townsfolk, their averted gazes and strained smiles, was more terrifying than any overt threat. It was the silence of complicity, the silence of those who knew, but dared not speak, lest they awaken the slumbering horror that lay at the heart of Havenwood. Sarah was left with only the echoes of her own fears, and the chilling certainty that she was utterly, terrifyingly alone.

Chapter 4: The Hunter and the Hunted

Blackwood's Confession

The air outside Blackwood's studio was thick with the scent of pine and damp earth, a stark contrast to the sterile silence Sarah had left behind in town. The cabin, perched precariously on the very edge of Havenwood, felt less like a dwelling and more like an outpost, a solitary sentinel against the encroaching wilderness. As she approached, a single light bled from the grimy windowpanes, a beacon in the gathering dusk. She'd debated this encounter for hours, the futility of her conversations with Martha and Mr. Henderson still a raw wound. They had offered no solace, only a chilling testament to the town's collective amnesia. Blackwood, however, was an unknown quantity. His name had surfaced in hushed tones at the archives, a recluse with an obsessive interest in Havenwood's peculiar history, a history that Sarah was increasingly convinced was not merely history at all, but a present, malevolent force.

She hesitated at the weathered wooden door, the rough-hewn planks cool beneath her hesitant touch. A faint scratching sound emanated from within, a rhythmic, almost frantic rhythm that snagged her attention. Taking a deep breath, she knocked. The scratching stopped abruptly, followed by the sound of heavy footsteps approaching the door. A bolt slid back with a resonant thud that echoed in the stillness.

The door creaked open, revealing a man silhouetted against the dim interior light. He was tall, gaunt, his face etched with a weariness that went beyond mere physical fatigue. His eyes, however, were sharp, unnervingly alert, and fixed upon her with an intensity that made her skin prickle. He wore a thick, woollen jumper, stained with what looked like paint or ink, and his hands, large and calloused, were splayed against the doorframe.

"You're Sarah, aren't you?" His voice was a low rumble, surprisingly steady, devoid of the strained brightness or dismissive politeness she had encountered earlier.

Sarah nodded, clutching the small wooden bird in her pocket, its familiar shape a small anchor in the churning sea of her anxiety. "Yes. And you're Mr. Blackwood?"

He offered a curt nod, stepping back to allow her entry. "Arthur Blackwood. Please, come in." His gaze never left her, and as she stepped across the threshold, she felt a subtle shift in the atmosphere, as if the air itself had thickened, charged with an unseen energy. The studio was a chaotic symphony of artistic endeavor and obsessive research. Canvases, some finished, some starkly blank, were stacked against the walls, interspersed with shelves overflowing with books, ancient maps, and what looked like scientific equipment. The scratching sound had returned; it was a pencil, she realized, sketching furiously on a large pad resting on an easel.

The room was illuminated by a single, bare bulb dangling from the ceiling, casting long, dancing shadows that distorted the already disarrayed space. The scent of turpentine mingled with the earthy aroma of the surrounding woods, creating a peculiar, almost intoxicating perfume. On a workbench, scattered amongst tubes of paint and brushes, were several more of the small wooden birds, identical to the one Sarah carried.

"I assume you're not here for a landscape painting," Blackwood said, gesturing to a worn armchair near a crackling fireplace. "Though I dabble. I've seen you at the archives. You have an… inquisitive nature."

Sarah sank into the chair, the worn fabric surprisingly comfortable. "I've been trying to understand what's happening in Havenwood," she began, her voice betraying a tremor she couldn't quite suppress. "The disappearances, the… the feeling.

The silence of the people."

Blackwood walked over to the easel, picking up his pencil. He didn't resume sketching immediately but held it poised, his attention still on her. "The silence is the loudest part, isn't it?" he murmured, almost to himself. "A collective breath held, a shared secret whispered in the dark." He finally returned to his sketching, the graphite scratching across the paper with a renewed urgency. "You found something, I presume. Something that the good people of Havenwood would prefer to remain buried."

"I found a parchment," Sarah said, her eyes drawn to the wooden birds on his workbench. "And I found this." She drew the bird from her pocket, its smooth, worn surface a stark contrast to the rough textures of the studio. She placed it on the small table between them.

Blackwood's hand paused in its movement. His gaze dropped to the carving, and Sarah watched as a subtle, almost imperceptible shift occurred within him. The weary resignation in his eyes seemed to recede, replaced by a flicker of intense, almost predatory interest. He picked up one of his own carvings, turning it over in his fingers, his thumb tracing its delicate lines.

"The Wood Carver's Mark," he stated, his voice barely a whisper. "They say it's a ward. Others say it's a calling card. I've always suspected it's something far more… resonant." He looked at Sarah, a faint, almost amused smile touching his lips. "You're not the first to come looking for answers, Sarah. And you won't be the last. This town… it draws them in. Those who are sensitive to the currents, those who can feel the fraying at the edges of reality."

"You feel it too?" Sarah pressed, leaning forward. "You understand what I'm talking about?"

Blackwood finally set his pencil down. He turned fully towards her, his gaze unwavering. "Feel it?" He chuckled, a dry, rustling sound. "My dear, I've been trying to understand it for years. This place, Havenwood, it's a nexus. A point where the veil between worlds is... thin. Thinner than anywhere else I've ever encountered."

He gestured around the studio, his gaze sweeping over the canvases, the books, the jumble of artifacts. "I'm not the source of the malevolence, Sarah. Far from it. I'm a chronicler. A documentarian. I try to capture it, to understand its patterns, its motivations, before it consumes everything." He picked up another wooden bird, its detail exquisite, a small, perfectly rendered avian form. "These are my attempts. My observations rendered tangible."

"But... what is it?" Sarah asked, her voice barely audible. "What is this 'veil'? What happens when it thins?"

Blackwood walked over to a large, cluttered desk, pulling out a thick ledger bound in faded leather. He flipped through its pages, his movements deliberate. "It's difficult to articulate, to put into words that make sense to those who haven't experienced it. Imagine... imagine reality as a solid surface. Most of the time, it's impenetrable. But here, in Havenwood, there are fissures. Cracks. Through these cracks, things... seep. Influences. Presences. Sometimes, echoes of what once was, or what could be."

He stopped at a particular page, his finger tracing a series of intricate symbols that seemed to pulse with a subtle, inner light. "I first encountered *it* – this... phenomenon – over twenty years ago. It was in a place far from here, a place that felt equally... charged. I was young, foolish, arrogant. I thought I could control it, understand it through pure intellect. It nearly broke me."

His voice dropped, a note of raw pain surfacing. "It left scars. Not physical ones, but deeper. A constant awareness of the unseen, the lurking possibilities that lie just beyond our perception."

He looked up, his eyes meeting Sarah's, and for the first time, she saw not just an eccentric artist, but a man who had walked through fire and emerged, however scarred, still standing. "That experience... it drove me to seek out other such places. Places where the veil was thin. And Havenwood... Havenwood is the most potent I've ever found. It's a magnet for it. And for those who are drawn to it, whether to exploit it, to understand it, or simply to survive it."

"So you came here to study it?" Sarah clarified, the pieces beginning to form a terrifying, yet coherent, picture.

"To study, yes," Blackwood confirmed. "And to document. To try and leave a record, a warning, perhaps. The disappearances you mentioned... they are not isolated incidents. They are the natural consequence of the veil thinning too severely, of something... crossing over. The people of Havenwood, they know this on some primal level. Their silence is not ignorance, Sarah. It's a desperate, ingrained defense mechanism. A pact of mutual forgetting, born out of sheer terror."

He gestured to a large canvas on the wall, a dark, brooding depiction of the Havenwood woods, rendered in shades of deep indigo and midnight blue. Within the tangled branches, barely visible, were subtle, unsettling forms, distorted faces peering from the shadows. "I try to paint what I sense. The weight of it, the suffocating pressure. The feeling of being watched, not by eyes, but by something far more ancient, far more alien."

Sarah felt a chill that had nothing to do with the draft from the door. "But... the parchment. The word 'Soon.' It felt like a direct message. A threat."

Blackwood nodded slowly, his gaze distant, as if he were seeing beyond the confines of the studio, beyond the present moment. "The energies here are... complex. They can manifest in subtle ways. The parchment, the bird, whispers in the dark, shadows that move when you're not looking. These are all manifestations. Attempts to communicate, or perhaps, to manipulate. The entity, or entities, that reside here are ancient. Their motives are beyond our comprehension. They may be curious, hungry, territorial. Or perhaps, they simply exist, and we are merely caught in their wake."

He walked over to a small, intricate carving of a bird, so finely detailed that it seemed to possess a life of its own. "I believe these carvings are more than just art. They are anchors. Ways to focus the inherent energies of this place, to create a semblance of order, of control, in the face of overwhelming chaos. They are my attempts to hold the line, to understand what is on the other side without being pulled through myself."

Sarah thought of Martha's averted gaze, Mr. Henderson's carefully constructed denial. Their fear was palpable, a tangible entity that had forced them into a shared conspiracy of silence. They weren't just afraid of what Blackwood described; they were afraid of acknowledging it, of giving it power by speaking its name.

"What about Eleanor Vance?" Sarah asked, her voice tight with dread. "She wrote about these things in her journal. She tried to warn people."

Blackwood's expression darkened. He turned back to his desk, running a hand through his already dishevelled hair. "Eleanor Vance," he repeated, the name a heavy sigh. "She was one of the few who truly understood. And because she understood, she was a threat. Not to the townspeople, but to the *presence* itself. She tried to fight it, to expose it. And it... dealt with her. Swiftly and brutally." He looked at Sarah, his eyes filled with a profound sadness. "The parchment you found, the message, it's a continuation of a pattern. A deliberate attempt to draw you in, to make you the next focus of its attention. Just as it was with Eleanor."

Sarah's hand instinctively went to her pocket, her fingers closing around the small wooden bird. It no longer felt like a mere object, but a conduit, a fragile link to something vast and terrifying. "Why me?" she whispered, the question hanging heavy in the charged air.

"Perhaps you have a particular resonance," Blackwood mused, his gaze sharp. "Or perhaps it's simply random. A fly caught in a spider's web. But now that you've been touched, Sarah, now that you've found the parchment and the bird, you cannot simply unknow it. You are marked, in a way. And the longer you stay, the more you investigate, the more you will attract its attention."

He paused, his gaze returning to the dark woods depicted on his canvas. "My own encounter, all those years ago, it wasn't as direct as yours seems to be becoming. It was more... insidious. A gradual erosion of sanity. I saw things in the periphery, heard whispers that felt like my own thoughts. It was a slow descent, and it took me years to claw my way back to something resembling clarity. But the awareness never truly leaves. It's like a phantom limb, a constant ache reminding you of what you brushed against."

He looked at Sarah again, his expression grave. "The woods are not just trees and earth, Sarah. They are a living, breathing entity, and they are aware of you. Every step you take, every thought you have, it's all being observed. And they are patient. They have all the time in the world."

Sarah's breath hitched. The carefully constructed denial of the townsfolk, the unsettling quiet, Blackwood's frank confession – it all coalesced into a terrifying panorama. She wasn't just chasing a historical mystery; she was walking into a predatory landscape, a hunter who had unknowingly become the hunted. The subtle wrongness she had sensed in Havenwood wasn't a figment of her imagination; it was the oppressive weight of something ancient and terrible, a force that had ensnared the entire town in its silent, suffocating grip. And now, it had its sights set on her. The word "Soon" echoed in her mind, no longer a vague prediction, but a chilling certainty. The game had indeed moved into its next, far more dangerous phase, and Blackwood, the solitary chronicler, was the only one who seemed willing to acknowledge the terrifying truth of the hunt.

The Whispering Woods

The air outside Blackwood's studio was thick with the scent of pine and damp earth, a stark contrast to the sterile silence Sarah had left behind in town. The cabin, perched precariously on the very edge of Havenwood, felt less like a dwelling and more like an outpost, a solitary sentinel against the encroaching wilderness. As she approached, a single light bled from the grimy windowpanes, a beacon in the gathering dusk. She'd debated this encounter for hours, the futility of her conversations with Martha and Mr. Henderson still a raw wound. They had offered no solace, only a chilling testament to the town's collective amnesia. Blackwood, however, was an unknown quantity. His name had surfaced in hushed tones at the archives, a recluse with an obsessive interest in Havenwood's peculiar history, a history that Sarah was increasingly convinced was not merely history at all, but a present, malevolent force.

She hesitated at the weathered wooden door, the rough-hewn planks cool beneath her hesitant touch. A faint scratching sound emanated from within, a rhythmic, almost frantic rhythm that snagged her attention. Taking a deep breath, she knocked. The scratching stopped abruptly, followed by the sound of heavy footsteps approaching the door. A bolt slid back with a resonant thud that echoed in the stillness.

The door creaked open, revealing a man silhouetted against the dim interior light. He was tall, gaunt, his face etched with a weariness that went beyond mere physical fatigue. His eyes, however, were sharp, unnervingly alert, and fixed upon her with an intensity that made her skin prickle. He wore a thick, woollen jumper, stained with what looked like paint or ink, and his hands, large and calloused, were splayed against the doorframe.

"You're Sarah, aren't you?" His voice was a low rumble, surprisingly steady, devoid of the strained brightness or dismissive politeness she had encountered earlier.

Sarah nodded, clutching the small wooden bird in her pocket, its familiar shape a small anchor in the churning sea of her anxiety. "Yes. And you're Mr. Blackwood?"

He offered a curt nod, stepping back to allow her entry. "Arthur Blackwood. Please, come in." His gaze never left her, and as she stepped across the threshold, she felt a subtle shift in the atmosphere, as if the air itself had thickened, charged with an unseen energy. The studio was a chaotic symphony of artistic endeavor and obsessive research. Canvases, some finished, some starkly blank, were stacked against the walls, interspersed with shelves overflowing with books, ancient maps, and what looked like scientific equipment. The scratching sound had returned; it was a pencil, she realized, sketching furiously on a large pad resting on an easel.

The room was illuminated by a single, bare bulb dangling from the ceiling, casting long, dancing shadows that distorted the already disarrayed space. The scent of turpentine mingled with the earthy aroma of the surrounding woods, creating a peculiar, almost intoxicating perfume. On a workbench, scattered amongst tubes of paint and brushes, were several more of the small wooden birds, identical to the one Sarah carried.

"I assume you're not here for a landscape painting," Blackwood said, gesturing to a worn armchair near a crackling fireplace. "Though I dabble. I've seen you at the archives. You have an... inquisitive nature."

Sarah sank into the chair, the worn fabric surprisingly comfortable. "I've been trying to understand what's happening in Havenwood," she began, her voice betraying a tremor she couldn't quite suppress. "The disappearances, the... the feeling. The silence of the people."

Blackwood walked over to the easel, picking up his pencil. He didn't resume sketching immediately but held it poised, his attention still on her. "The silence is the loudest part, isn't it?" he murmured, almost to himself. "A collective breath held, a shared secret whispered in the dark." He finally returned to his sketching, the graphite scratching across the paper with a renewed urgency. "You found something, I presume. Something that the good people of Havenwood would prefer to remain buried."

"I found a parchment," Sarah said, her eyes drawn to the wooden birds on his workbench. "And I found this." She drew the bird from her pocket, its smooth, worn surface a stark contrast to the rough textures of the studio. She placed it on the small table between them.

Blackwood's hand paused in its movement. His gaze dropped to the carving, and Sarah watched as a subtle, almost imperceptible shift occurred within him. The weary resignation in his eyes seemed to recede, replaced by a flicker of intense, almost predatory interest. He picked up one of his own carvings, turning it over in his fingers, his thumb tracing its delicate lines.

"The Wood Carver's Mark," he stated, his voice barely a whisper. "They say it's a ward. Others say it's a calling card. I've always suspected it's something far more… resonant." He looked at Sarah, a faint, almost amused smile touching his lips. "You're not the first to come looking for answers, Sarah. And you won't be the last. This town… it draws them in. Those who are sensitive to the currents, those who can feel the fraying at the edges of reality."

"You feel it too?" Sarah pressed, leaning forward. "You understand what I'm talking about?"

Blackwood finally set his pencil down. He turned fully towards her, his gaze unwavering. "Feel it?" He chuckled, a dry, rustling sound. "My dear, I've been trying to understand it for years. This place, Havenwood, it's a nexus. A point where the veil between worlds is… thin. Thinner than anywhere else I've ever encountered."

He gestured around the studio, his gaze sweeping over the canvases, the books, the jumble of artifacts. "I'm not the source of the malevolence, Sarah. Far from it. I'm a chronicler. A documentarian. I try to capture it, to understand its patterns, its motivations, before it consumes everything." He picked up another wooden bird, its detail exquisite, a small, perfectly rendered avian form. "These are my attempts. My observations rendered tangible."

"But… what is it?" Sarah asked, her voice barely audible. "What is this 'veil'? What happens when it thins?"

Blackwood walked over to a large, cluttered desk, pulling out a thick ledger bound in faded leather. He flipped through its pages, his movements deliberate. "It's difficult to articulate, to put into words that make sense to those who haven't experienced it. Imagine… imagine reality as a solid surface. Most of the time, it's impenetrable. But here, in Havenwood, there are fissures. Cracks. Through these cracks, things… seep. Influences. Presences. Sometimes, echoes of what once was, or what could be."

He stopped at a particular page, his finger tracing a series of intricate symbols that seemed to pulse with a subtle, inner light. "I first encountered *it* – this… phenomenon – over twenty years ago. It was in a place far from here, a place that felt equally… charged. I was young, foolish, arrogant. I thought I could control it, understand it through pure intellect. It nearly broke me." His voice dropped, a note of raw pain surfacing. "It left scars. Not physical ones, but deeper. A constant awareness of the unseen, the lurking possibilities that lie just beyond our perception."

He looked up, his eyes meeting Sarah's, and for the first time, she saw not just an eccentric artist, but a man who had walked through fire and emerged, however scarred, still standing. "That experience... it drove me to seek out other such places. Places where the veil was thin. And Havenwood... Havenwood is the most potent I've ever found. It's a magnet for it. And for those who are drawn to it, whether to exploit it, to understand it, or simply to survive it."

"So you came here to study it?" Sarah clarified, the pieces beginning to form a terrifying, yet coherent, picture.

"To study, yes," Blackwood confirmed. "And to document. To try and leave a record, a warning, perhaps. The disappearances you mentioned... they are not isolated incidents. They are the natural consequence of the veil thinning too severely, of something... crossing over. The people of Havenwood, they know this on some primal level. Their silence is not ignorance, Sarah. It's a desperate, ingrained defense mechanism. A pact of mutual forgetting, born out of sheer terror."

He gestured to a large canvas on the wall, a dark, brooding depiction of the Havenwood woods, rendered in shades of deep indigo and midnight blue. Within the tangled branches, barely visible, were subtle, unsettling forms, distorted faces peering from the shadows. "I try to paint what I sense. The weight of it, the suffocating pressure. The feeling of being watched, not by eyes, but by something far more ancient, far more alien."

Sarah felt a chill that had nothing to do with the draft from the door. "But... the parchment. The word 'Soon.' It felt like a direct message. A threat."

Blackwood nodded slowly, his gaze distant, as if he were seeing beyond the confines of the studio, beyond the present moment. "The energies here are... complex. They can manifest in subtle ways. The parchment, the bird, whispers in the dark, shadows that move when you're not looking. These are all manifestations. Attempts to communicate, or perhaps, to manipulate. The entity, or entities, that reside here are ancient. Their motives are beyond our comprehension. They may be curious, hungry, territorial. Or perhaps, they simply exist, and we are merely caught in their wake."

He walked over to a small, intricate carving of a bird, so finely detailed that it seemed to possess a life of its own. "I believe these carvings are more than just art. They are anchors. Ways to focus the inherent energies of this place, to create a semblance of order, of control, in the face of overwhelming chaos. They are my attempts to hold the line, to understand what is on the other side without being pulled through myself."

Sarah thought of Martha's averted gaze, Mr. Henderson's carefully constructed denial. Their fear was palpable, a tangible entity that had forced them into a shared conspiracy of silence. They weren't just afraid of what Blackwood described; they were afraid of acknowledging it, of giving it power by speaking its name.

"What about Eleanor Vance?" Sarah asked, her voice tight with dread. "She wrote about these things in her journal. She tried to warn people."

Blackwood's expression darkened. He turned back to his desk, running a hand through his already dishevelled hair. "Eleanor Vance," he repeated, the name a heavy sigh. "She was one of the few who truly understood. And because she understood, she was a threat. Not to the townspeople, but to the *presence* itself.

She tried to fight it, to expose it. And it... dealt with her. Swiftly and brutally." He looked at Sarah, his eyes filled with a profound sadness. "The parchment you found, the message, it's a continuation of a pattern. A deliberate attempt to draw you in, to make you the next focus of its attention. Just as it was with Eleanor."

Sarah's hand instinctively went to her pocket, her fingers closing around the small wooden bird. It no longer felt like a mere object, but a conduit, a fragile link to something vast and terrifying. "Why me?" she whispered, the question hanging heavy in the charged air.

"Perhaps you have a particular resonance," Blackwood mused, his gaze sharp. "Or perhaps it's simply random. A fly caught in a spider's web. But now that you've been touched, Sarah, now that you've found the parchment and the bird, you cannot simply unknow it. You are marked, in a way. And the longer you stay, the more you investigate, the more you will attract its attention."

He paused, his gaze returning to the dark woods depicted on his canvas. "My own encounter, all those years ago, it wasn't as direct as yours seems to be becoming. It was more... insidious. A gradual erosion of sanity. I saw things in the periphery, heard whispers that felt like my own thoughts. It was a slow descent, and it took me years to claw my way back to something resembling clarity. But the awareness never truly leaves. It's like a phantom limb, a constant ache reminding you of what you brushed against."

He looked at Sarah again, his expression grave. "The woods are not just trees and earth, Sarah. They are a living, breathing entity, and they are aware of you. Every step you take, every thought you have, it's all being observed. And they are patient. They have all the time in the world."

Sarah's breath hitched. The carefully constructed denial of the townsfolk, the unsettling quiet, Blackwood's frank confession – it all coalesced into a terrifying panorama. She wasn't just chasing a historical mystery; she was walking into a predatory landscape, a hunter who had unknowingly become the hunted. The subtle wrongness she had sensed in Havenwood wasn't a figment of her imagination; it was the oppressive weight of something ancient and terrible, a force that had ensnared the entire town in its silent, suffocating grip. And now, it had its sights set on her. The word "Soon" echoed in her mind, no longer a vague prediction, but a chilling certainty. The game had indeed moved into its next, far more dangerous phase, and Blackwood, the solitary chronicler, was the only one who seemed willing to acknowledge the terrifying truth of the hunt.

The following morning, armed with Blackwood's dire pronouncements and a gnawing unease, Sarah found herself standing at the edge of the woods that bordered Havenwood. The previous day's rain had left the earth saturated, the air heavy with the scent of decay and damp foliage. Blackwood had pointed her towards a specific area, a section of the woods locals referred to with a superstitious dread, a place where the trees grew closer, their branches interwoven like skeletal fingers clawing at the sky. This was where Eleanor Vance's journal indicated the earliest disappearances had occurred, long before the town itself had a documented history.

As Sarah stepped beneath the dense canopy, the world transformed. The soft, diffused light of the morning was instantly swallowed by the thick foliage, plunging the forest into a perpetual twilight. The vibrant greens and browns she'd seen from the outside were muted, the colours leached away, leaving behind a palette of somber greys and deep, oppressive shadows. It was as if the woods themselves held their breath, an unnerving stillness that Sarah hadn't anticipated. There were no birdsong, no scurrying of small animals, not even the rustle of leaves underfoot that should have accompanied her every step. Her own breathing seemed unnaturally loud, a coarse intrusion into the pervasive silence.

The trees here were ancient, their trunks thick and gnarled, covered in a tapestry of moss and lichen that clung like a second skin. They seemed to lean in towards her, their massive forms creating claustrophobic aisles that twisted and turned, disorienting her sense of direction. Eleanor Vance's journal had spoken of these woods as being "alive," not in a metaphorical sense, but in a way that suggested a sentience, a consciousness that permeated the very soil and bark. Sarah had dismissed it as poetic license, the ravings of a mind perhaps unhinged by isolation. Now, however, she couldn't shake the feeling that the woods were indeed observing her.

A faint, almost imperceptible whisper brushed against her ear. Sarah stopped, straining to hear. It wasn't the sound of wind; the air was utterly still. It was more like a sibilant hiss, a collection of low, breathy sounds that seemed to coil and uncoil just at the edge of her hearing. She spun around, her heart hammering against her ribs, but saw nothing but the endless, silent sentinels of the forest. The whispers seemed to come from everywhere and nowhere at once, like phantom voices woven into the fabric of the trees. They weren't distinct words, more like the murmur of a crowd heard from a great distance, or the hiss of static on a radio tuned between stations.

She pressed on, guided by the vague markings Eleanor had described – an unusually twisted oak, a cluster of oddly smooth stones. Each step felt like a transgression, an intrusion into a place that did not welcome her. The whispers intensified, seeming to coalesce, to form fleeting patterns of sound that suggested language, but always just out of reach. They tugged at her senses, drawing her attention to the periphery, to the shadows that seemed to shift and deepen even as she watched. She caught herself glancing repeatedly into the dense undergrowth, half-expecting to see something emerge, something that moved with a predatory grace that belonged to neither animal nor human.

The feeling of being watched was overwhelming. It wasn't the casual observation of a curious creature; it was a heavy, sustained scrutiny, as if the very air held an innumerable, unseen gaze. It prickled the back of her neck, making her skin crawl. She felt a strange dissociation from her own body, as if she were observing herself from a distance, a fragile intruder in a vast, ancient domain.

Her mind began to play tricks on her. A branch that swayed without wind, a patch of shadow that seemed to detach itself from a tree and slink away. The whispers grew louder, more insistent, and now, they seemed to carry a hint of malice, a taunting quality. They seemed to mimic familiar sounds, the creak of a floorboard, a soft sigh, a child's giggle – sounds that twisted and warped into something deeply unsettling, something that spoke of a warped reality. Sarah's grip tightened on the wooden bird in her pocket. It felt less like an anchor now and more like a fragile charm against an encroaching darkness.

She found the clearing Eleanor Vance had described. It was small, oddly barren, with no undergrowth, only a scattering of dark, iron-rich soil. In the centre of the clearing stood a single, colossal oak, its branches reaching towards the sky like grasping hands. The whispers here were almost deafening, a constant, low hum that vibrated in Sarah's bones. It was as if the clearing was the epicentre of the forest's awareness, a place where its consciousness was most concentrated.

Eleanor's journal had mentioned a specific mark on this tree, a symbol carved deep into its bark. Sarah approached the oak, her boots crunching softly on the dry earth. The bark was rough and deeply fissured, a testament to centuries of growth. She ran her hand over it, searching. The whispers seemed to intensify around her, swirling like an invisible current. She felt a dizzying sensation, a sense of profound disorientation, as if the very ground beneath her was unstable.

Then her fingers brushed against something unnaturally smooth, something deeply incised into the rough bark. It was a symbol, an intricate pattern that seemed both familiar and alien. It was similar to the markings Blackwood had in his ledger, but more complex, imbued with a strange, almost hypnotic power. As she traced the lines of the carving, a cold dread washed over her, a primal fear that spoke of things best left undisturbed. The whispers around her seemed to pause, as if in anticipation, then surged with renewed intensity, taking on a chorus-like quality, an ethereal symphony of incoherent dread.

Sarah felt a wave of nausea, her vision blurring at the edges. The trees seemed to press in closer, their shadowy forms elongating, twisting into grotesque shapes. She heard a faint, rhythmic scraping sound, like fingernails dragging across wood, coming from directly above her. Her breath caught in her throat. She dared not look up. The whispers were now coalescing into a single, undeniable word, repeated over and over, like a chilling mantra: *Soon. Soon. Soon.*

The journal spoke of a specific time, a convergence, when the veil was at its thinnest, when the forest was most receptive. Sarah checked her watch. The sun, what little of it pierced the canopy, was beginning its slow descent. The shadows were lengthening, deepening, bleeding into the already dim light. The air grew colder, the whispers taking on an almost physical pressure against her skin. She felt a terrible certainty that she had stumbled into something far older and more dangerous than she had ever imagined, a predatory consciousness that had been waiting, patiently, for the right moment, for the right victim. She was not just in the woods; she was *in* them, and they were aware. The hunting season, it seemed, had truly begun.

A Glimpse of the Entity

The oppressive silence of the woods pressed in on Sarah, a physical weight that amplified the frantic thumping of her heart. She had followed Eleanor Vance's cryptic directions, tracing a path through the ancient trees that seemed to actively resist her presence, their branches a tangled web designed to ensnare and disorient. The clearing, stark and unsettling, had felt like a stage set for something ancient and terrible. The colossal oak, bearing Eleanor's mark, stood as a sentinel, its presence radiating a palpable malevolence. As Sarah traced the symbol, the woods had erupted in a symphony of whispers, a chorus of disembodied sounds that seemed to coil and writhe around her, hinting at a language she couldn't comprehend but instinctively feared.

The feeling of being watched had intensified, no longer a vague unease but a focused, consuming scrutiny.

And then, it happened. It wasn't a sound, not precisely, but a distortion in the very fabric of reality. In the deepest shadow cast by the ancient oak, where the light seemed to falter and die, a shape began to coalesce. It was formless, yet possessed a definite presence, a void that seemed to suck in the surrounding light and sound. Sarah's breath hitched, her eyes widening in disbelief and terror. It was a manifestation of pure dread, a silhouette etched not with lines, but with the absence of them. It pulsed, not with a heartbeat, but with a malevolent thrum that resonated deep within her bones.

This was no trick of the light, no figment of an overactive imagination. This was *it*. The entity that had whispered through the trees, the presence that had driven a town to collective amnesia, the power that had claimed Eleanor Vance. It was a patch of negative space, a tear in the world's tapestry. It seemed to writhe, to shift without discernible movement, like oil on water, but imbued with an awareness that was utterly alien and terrifying. The air around it crackled with an unseen energy, a tangible force that made Sarah's hair stand on end. She could feel the sheer *wrongness* of it, a violation of every natural law she understood.

For a fleeting, agonizing moment, it seemed to turn its attention towards her. There were no eyes, no discernible features, yet Sarah felt an immense, crushing awareness fixated upon her. It was the gaze of something ancient, something that perceived her not as a living being, but as an anomaly, an intrusion. A wave of primal fear, cold and absolute, washed over her, rendering her limbs useless, her mind a frozen tableau of terror. The whispers, which had been a cacophony of indistinct sounds, suddenly seemed to

117

converge, to form a single, chillingly coherent thought that echoed not in her ears, but directly in the core of her being: *Mine.*

The sheer intensity of the encounter was overwhelming. It felt as though the entity was not merely observing her, but *ingesting* her, its very presence a draining force that leached the warmth and vitality from her surroundings. The shadows deepened, coalescing around the amorphous form, making it seem like a hole torn in the very fabric of the forest. Sarah could feel a phantom chill, a preternatural cold that seeped into her very marrow, despite the clammy sweat that now plastered her clothes to her skin.

Then, as abruptly as it had appeared, it was gone. It didn't retreat, it didn't fade; it simply ceased to be. The void winked out of existence, leaving behind only the deepening twilight of the woods and the deafening echo of its passage. The whispers receded, as if chastened, leaving behind a vacuum that Sarah's own ragged breaths struggled to fill. Her knees buckled, and she sank to the damp earth, her body trembling uncontrollably. The wooden bird in her pocket felt strangely warm against her palm, a tiny point of familiar texture in the face of the unfathomable.

The glimpse had been terrifyingly brief, a mere fragment of a second, but it had irrevocably shattered any remaining skepticism. Blackwood had been right. This was not merely a localized phenomenon, not a mass delusion or a series of unfortunate accidents. This was something tangible, something actively malevolent, something that existed beyond the realm of human understanding. Eleanor Vance hadn't been delusional; she had been a witness, a victim of a power that defied explanation.

Sarah's mind raced, trying to process what she had seen. It had been a shape, yet shapeless. It had absorbed light and sound, yet pulsed with an undeniable energy. It radiated dread, a primal fear that had paralyzed her more effectively than any physical restraint. It had communicated, not with words, but with a pure, unadulterated sense of possession. *Mine.* The implication was chilling. Was she the object of this possessiveness? Had her intrusion into this ancient place, her touching of Eleanor's mark, declared her as such?

She forced herself to look around. The clearing was just a clearing again, the oak just a tree, albeit a disturbing one. Yet, the memory of the void, the tangible impression of its presence, lingered like a residue. The woods still felt watchful, but the intense focus of the manifestation had shifted, diffused back into the general atmosphere of unease. It was as if the entity had made its point, a terrifying, unambiguous declaration of its nature and its claim.

The immediate urge was to flee, to run blindly back the way she came, to escape the suffocating embrace of these ancient, sentient woods. But another part of her, the part that had driven her to seek out Blackwood, the part that refused to be silenced by the town's collective amnesia, held her rooted. She had seen it. She had confirmed its existence. Now, she had to understand it. And understanding it meant pushing forward, not retreating.

With a supreme effort, Sarah pushed herself to her feet. Her legs were shaky, her hands still trembling, but a new resolve had settled over her, born of sheer, unadulterated terror and a desperate need to comprehend. She still had Eleanor Vance's journal. She remembered the subsequent entries, the growing desperation, the cryptic references to "the thinning," and the increasing frequency of the "whispers." Blackwood had spoken of the entity's attempts to communicate, to manipulate. What had Eleanor been trying to convey in her final days? What had she learned before she was silenced?

She opened the journal, her fingers still slick with sweat. The ink on the pages seemed darker, more ominous in the failing light. Eleanor's handwriting, once precise and almost scientific, had become increasingly erratic, the words blurring into panicked scrawls. Sarah scanned the later entries, her eyes darting over the desperate attempts to document the inexplicable.

"It watches. Not with eyes, but with a hunger. A deep, hollow hunger that consumes existence itself. The forest is its skin, its voice the rustle of leaves, its breath the stillness between breaths. I feel its awareness expanding, pressing in. It knows I know. It knows I write."

Sarah shivered, a fresh wave of dread washing over her. The entity's manifestation had been precisely this – a hunger, a void. Eleanor had seen it, felt it, understood its pervasive nature long before Sarah's own chilling glimpse.

"The carvings are anchors. Blackwood was right. They channel the energy, but they also attract it. A beacon. My mistake. The mark on the oak… it's a gateway. A thinning point. It's more than just a symbol; it's an invitation."

An invitation. Sarah's hand instinctively tightened around the wooden bird. Was her own carving, her familiar little bird, also a beacon? Blackwood had called them resonance points, anchors. But perhaps, as Eleanor suggested, they were also lures. The implication was terrifying: had her attempt to understand, to seek out Blackwood, to follow Eleanor's path, inadvertently drawn the entity's attention directly to her?

The journal entries grew more fragmented, the fear palpable.

"The whispers… they're not just sounds. They are thoughts. Imposed. Corrupting. They twist memory, sow doubt. I see shadows move. I hear…

laughter. Not human laughter. It's ancient. Mocking. It promises oblivion. Soon... it whispers... soon."

The word. *Soon.* It was a constant thread, a chilling refrain that echoed the parchment Sarah had found. It wasn't just a word; it was a temporal anchor, a marker of an approaching culmination. The entity was counting down. But to what? And why?

Sarah felt a profound sense of isolation, a crushing weight of knowledge that no one else in Havenwood seemed willing or able to share. Blackwood was a recluse, a man haunted by his past encounters, a chronicler who kept his observations locked away in his studio. The townsfolk were terrified into silence, their fear a collective shield against a horror they could not name. And Eleanor Vance was gone, her warnings ultimately failing to save her.

The lingering vision of the void, of that silent, hungry presence, replayed in her mind. It was not a creature in the conventional sense, not something that hunted with fang and claw. Its method of predation was far more insidious, a slow erosion of reality, a psychological assault that preyed on the mind and spirit. It was an entity of absence, of negation, a force that sought to unmake rather than to destroy.

As the last vestiges of daylight faded, the woods seemed to shift and stir around her. The whispers returned, softer now, more insidious, weaving through the trees like tendrils of mist. They brushed against Sarah's mind, probing, testing, attempting to insinuate their corrupting influence. She focused on the wooden bird in her hand, its smooth, familiar shape a grounding sensation. She tried to recall Blackwood's words: "These are my attempts. My observations rendered tangible." Perhaps the carvings were not just passive beacons, but active wards, tools that could be used to push back against the encroaching darkness.

She thought of the raw, unadulterated terror she had felt when the entity manifested. It was a primal fear, one that bypassed rational thought and struck at the very core of her being. This was the entity's power – to evoke such profound terror that it immobilized its victims, rendering them helpless and vulnerable. It was a hunter that didn't need to chase; it simply had to make its prey too afraid to move.

The silence that followed the brief, terrifying manifestation was almost worse than the event itself. It was a pregnant silence, a pause filled with the unspoken threat of recurrence. Sarah knew, with a certainty that chilled her to the bone, that she had merely glimpsed the surface of something vast and ancient. The entity was aware of her, its attention captured, its patience perhaps wearing thin. The encounter had confirmed the supernatural nature of the threat, but it had also amplified the urgency of her task. She was no longer just investigating a mystery; she was actively involved in a dangerous game, a dance with a predatory consciousness that seemed to operate on scales of time and motive far beyond her comprehension. The woods held their secrets, and the entity was its ultimate guardian, its manifestation a terrifying glimpse into the abyss that lay just beyond the veil. Sarah's purpose had narrowed, sharpening into a singular focus: survival, and the desperate need to understand what it was she was surviving against, before "Soon" became an irreversible, all-consuming reality. She was the quarry now, and the hunt had only just begun.

The Archivists Legacy

Sarah's gaze fell upon the librarian's desk, a sturdy, unassuming piece of furniture that seemed to have weathered the decades with a quiet stoicism. It was here, amidst the scent of aged paper and a lingering hint of lavender, that Eleanor Vance had spent countless hours cataloging the town's history, meticulously preserving its memories. The desk itself felt like an extension of her, a repository of a life dedicated to understanding and safeguarding the past. As Sarah ran a gloved hand over its polished surface, a faint tremor coursed through her. She had witnessed firsthand the entity's terrifying power, its ability to warp reality and instill an existential dread that went beyond mere fear. The whispers that had slithered into her mind, the amorphous manifestation in the clearing – these were not figments of a disturbed imagination, but tangible evidence of a force that defied conventional understanding. Eleanor Vance, the quiet archivist, had been the first to truly confront it, not with physical strength, but with the tools of her trade: knowledge, research, and a desperate, unyielding curiosity.

Her attention was drawn to a subtle anomaly in the desk's construction. A slight misalignment of a decorative inlay, a grain pattern that seemed to break its natural flow. It was the kind of detail an archivist, trained to spot the minute deviations that could signify a hidden truth, would naturally gravitate towards. With a gentle pressure, Sarah explored the area. A faint click, almost imperceptible against the lingering echoes of the woods, rewarded her efforts. A hidden drawer, seamlessly integrated into the desk's façade, slid open with a soft sigh.

Inside, nestled amongst meticulously organized papers, lay a collection of Eleanor Vance's personal notes. These weren't the dry, factual entries of a librarian's log; these were the frantic, deeply personal chronicles of a woman grappling with the unimaginable. The ink was darker here, the handwriting tighter, more urgent, a stark contrast to the earlier, more measured script Sarah had seen in the journal found within the clearing. This was the raw, unedited outpouring of Eleanor's struggle, her descent into the heart of the encroaching darkness, and her desperate attempts to find a way to fight back.

Sarah's heart pounded with a mixture of dread and anticipation as she lifted the first sheaf of papers. Eleanor's initial entries in this hidden cache detailed her growing unease, the subtle shifts in the town's atmosphere that had preceded the more overt manifestations. She wrote of a pervasive malaise, a collective sigh of forgotten memories that settled over Havenwood like a shroud. The entity, Eleanor hypothesized, wasn't a sudden invasion, but a slow seep, a gradual erosion of reality that began by consuming the town's collective consciousness. She documented instances of inexplicable forgetfulness among the residents, gaps in their personal histories that mirrored the larger amnesia that had befallen Havenwood's past.

"It's not just about forgetting," Eleanor had written, her script trembling on the page. *"It's about a rewriting. A subtle, insidious alteration of truth. The 'thinning' I've observed isn't just a metaphor for its increasing presence; it's an actual thinning of the veil between what is and what should be. And the whispers... they are its architects, nudging minds, twisting perceptions, preparing the ground for its full manifestation."*

Sarah traced the words, a chilling resonance echoing the whispers she herself had heard. Eleanor's meticulous research had led her to believe that the entity communicated not through spoken words, but through a form of psychic resonance, implanting thoughts and emotions that felt alien yet deeply personal. This was its method of propagation, its way of slowly integrating itself into the fabric of human perception.

The next set of notes detailed Eleanor's pivot from passive observation to active investigation. She had realized that understanding the entity's nature was the first step towards countering it. She had delved into ancient texts, folklore, and forgotten scientific theories, searching for any parallel to the phenomenon plaguing Havenwood. Her research led her to a fascination with sonic frequencies and their potential impact on consciousness, a field that had been largely dismissed by mainstream science.

"The resonance is key," one entry stated, accompanied by complex diagrams and mathematical equations. *"The entity operates on a frequency of absence, a void that disrupts existing patterns. If we can find a counter-frequency, a specific vibration that is antithetical to its nature, we might be able to disrupt its coherence, even repel it."*

Sarah pored over the pages, her librarian's instinct kicking in, guiding her through the dense technical jargon and esoteric symbols. Eleanor had painstakingly cataloged a series of sonic frequencies, along with specific geometric patterns and glyphs that she believed acted as amplifiers or disruptors. She had dedicated months to testing these theories, using makeshift equipment in the quiet solitude of the archives. The old library, with its soundproofed rooms and access to antique audio equipment, had become her laboratory.

"Initial tests with a pure sine wave at 13.7 kHz produced a noticeable attenuation in the ambient whispers," another note revealed. *"But it was fleeting, a mere ripple. The true breakthrough came when I combined the frequency with the 'Sigil of Sundering' – an ancient Babylonian*

symbol of cosmic disruption. The resulting resonance created a localized distortion, a brief but palpable pushback against the encroaching dread. It felt… like a shield."

The 'Sigil of Sundering' was drawn with a bold, decisive stroke on the parchment, a complex arrangement of interconnected lines and sharp angles. Sarah felt a prickle of recognition; she had seen similar symbols in Blackwood's studio, the ones he had dismissed as mere doodles. Now, they held a terrifying significance. These weren't random markings; they were weapons, painstakingly researched and tested by Eleanor Vance.

Eleanor's notes became increasingly focused on practical applications. She described constructing a device, a rudimentary sonic emitter, that could generate the specific frequencies and project the sigils through modulated light. Her objective was not to destroy the entity – she recognized its fundamental nature as an absence, something that couldn't be annihilated – but to create zones of safety, pockets of reality where its influence was diminished.

"The desk itself has proven to be an unexpected asset," Eleanor wrote. *"The older wood seems to possess a natural resonance, a harmonic quality that enhances the emitter's output. I've managed to integrate a modified version of the device into the desk's drawer mechanism. It activates when the drawer is opened, creating a temporary buffer, a brief sanctuary from its gaze. It was here, within my own sanctuary, that I felt safest to document my findings. This compartment… it is my final testament, a desperate message in a bottle for whoever might follow."*

Sarah's eyes widened as she understood the full implication of Eleanor's words. The hidden compartment wasn't just a hiding place for her notes; it was an active defense mechanism, a testament to her foresight and ingenuity. The entity had not been able to breach this small sanctuary, this pocket of engineered resistance.

The final sections of the hidden notes were a desperate plea, a set of instructions for the next person brave enough to confront the darkness. Eleanor detailed the construction of the sonic emitter, providing schematics and a list of components, some of which were incredibly rare and difficult to procure. She explained how to calibrate the frequencies, how to etch the sigils onto various materials, and how to create 'resonance points' – safe zones that could be established to push back the entity's influence.

"The symbols are anchors," she wrote, her tone now urgent, bordering on frantic. *"They ground reality, disrupt its unmaking. Combine them with the frequencies. Project them. Create barriers. Do not underestimate their power, but do not overestimate your own resilience. It learns. It adapts. Its hunger is eternal."*

She had also included a small, carefully wrapped package. Inside, Sarah found a collection of small, intricately carved wooden discs, each bearing a different sigil. They were not as finely crafted as the carvings she had found previously, but they pulsed with a similar subtle energy. These were Eleanor's personal arsenal, her legacy of resistance.

"These are my final offerings," the last entry read, the ink smudged as if from a tear or a sudden tremor. *"My research, my tools, my hope. I could not hold it back indefinitely. The pressure... it's too great. But perhaps, with these, someone else can. Someone who understands the weight of memory, the fragility of truth. Someone who will not be silenced. The entity is a predator of the mind, but it is also vulnerable to order, to intention. Remember the frequencies. Remember the symbols. Remember that even in the deepest shadow, light can find a way."*

Sarah closed her eyes, the weight of Eleanor's legacy settling upon her. The archivist, the quiet guardian of Havenwood's past, had become its unlikely savior, a warrior fighting a war on a plane of existence most people couldn't even comprehend. She had not just observed the horror; she had dissected it, understood its mechanics, and forged weapons against it. Her research, her desperate attempts to fight back, were laid out before Sarah, a roadmap through the encroaching madness.

The entity's manifestation in the clearing had been a terrifying confirmation of Eleanor's fears, but it had also galvanized Sarah. She understood now that her own small wooden bird, the one she carried in her pocket, was more than just a sentimental trinket; it was a resonant object, a potential tool, a tangible piece of Eleanor's own desperate defense. The very act of holding it, of tracing its familiar contours, felt like an echo of Eleanor's own struggle.

She carefully placed Eleanor's notes and the carved discs back into the hidden compartment, securing them with the gentle click of the drawer. The oppressive silence of the woods outside seemed less daunting now, replaced by the hum of purpose that vibrated within her. She had seen the entity, felt its chilling hunger, and now she possessed the knowledge, the tools, and the desperate courage of a woman who had faced it before and refused to yield. Eleanor Vance's legacy was not merely a collection of forgotten research; it was a living testament, a call to arms, a final, defiant act of preservation in the face of an unmaking force. The hunt was far from over, but now, Sarah had a chance. She had the archivist's desperate, brilliant legacy.

A Race Against Time

The hum of the library, once a comforting symphony of hushed whispers and turning pages, now felt like a prelude to something far more sinister. Sarah's fingers still tingled with the phantom touch of Eleanor Vance's legacy, the weight of her research a palpable burden in her hands, even after the notes had been carefully returned to their hidden sanctuary. The archival desk, a silent witness to a desperate battle waged with ink and intellect, seemed to hold its breath. Outside, the ordinary cadence of a small town day continued – the distant chime of the ice cream truck, the rumble of a passing car, the murmur of unseen lives. But Sarah knew, with a chilling certainty, that the veneer of normalcy was as thin and fragile as old parchment.

Eleanor's final, frantic scribblings had painted a terrifying picture: the entity wasn't merely a passive observer or a lurking predator. It was a parasitic consciousness, feeding on the very fabric of memory and emotion that bound Havenwood together. And the town, in its blissful ignorance, was unknowingly preparing a feast. The upcoming Founder's Day festival, a yearly ritual of communal nostalgia and civic pride, loomed like a dark omen. It was meant to be a celebration of Havenwood's history, a testament to its enduring spirit. But Sarah now understood it as something far more potent – a massive, unfocused outpouring of collective memory, a potent cocktail of joy, melancholy, regret, and suppressed longing, all of which could serve as fuel for the encroaching darkness.

She recalled snippets from Eleanor's research, the archivist's desperate attempts to quantify the entity's growth.

Eleanor had theorized about 'resonance points,' moments or places where the entity's influence was amplified, often correlating with periods of intense emotional or historical significance for the town. Founder's Day, with its parades, its historical reenactments, its shared meals, and its potent blend of remembered triumphs and forgotten sorrows, was shaping up to be the ultimate resonance point. The collective energy, normally diffused and benign, could be weaponized, directed, and magnified by the entity, transforming it into an overwhelming force.

This realization struck Sarah with the force of a physical blow. It wasn't just about the whispers anymore, or the fleeting glimpses of impossible geometry. It was about an active escalation, a strategic maneuver by the entity that dovetailed alarmingly with another piece of information she'd uncovered in Eleanor's notes: the cryptic references to Silas Blackwood. Eleanor had written of him not as a threat, but as an unwitting pawn, a man whose own delving into the town's hidden history, his own attempts to unearth its secrets, were inadvertently drawing the entity's attention, creating localized ripples that allowed it to probe and test. Blackwood's obsession, his almost manic pursuit of certain historical anomalies, was acting as a beacon, drawing the entity closer, preparing the ground for its eventual, devastating manifestation. Eleanor had written, with a tone of profound regret, that Blackwood's relentless curiosity was like throwing a stone into a pond – the ripples spread, attracting attention from the murky depths. His investigation was creating a more concentrated area of psychic disturbance, a point of focus that the entity could exploit.

The more Sarah pieced together Eleanor's fragmented insights, the clearer the timeline became. The entity's activity wasn't random; it was escalating, sharpening its focus, drawn by the confluence of Blackwood's probing and the looming promise of the Founder's

Day festival. The archivist had painstakingly documented a correlation between Blackwood's research breakthroughs and subtle increases in the 'ambient psychic static' she had been measuring. It was as if Blackwood's focused mental energy, coupled with his subconscious engagement with the town's buried truths, acted like a tuning fork, vibrating at a frequency that resonated with the entity, drawing it nearer.

Sarah felt a cold dread seep into her bones, a stark counterpoint to the determined resolve she'd felt moments before. The festival was less than a week away. A week. A week to decipher the complex schematics for Eleanor's sonic emitter, to source the impossibly rare components, and to somehow build a device capable of disrupting a reality-bending entity. A week to warn the town, or at least, to prepare some form of defense. A week to contend with the fact that Silas Blackwood, the man she had dismissed as a harmless eccentric, was actively, albeit unknowingly, accelerating the very apocalypse she was trying to prevent. His digging into the town's past, his fascination with its darker, more forgotten corners, was directly feeding the force that threatened to consume it. Eleanor had described it as a "symbiotic decay," where the entity fed on the suppression of truth, and those who sought to uncover that truth inadvertently provided the very nourishment it craved. Blackwood's relentless pursuit of what was hidden was, in essence, a feeding frenzy for the entity.

She imagined the town square, usually a place of community gathering, transformed. The cheerful banners, the scent of fried dough, the laughter of children – all of it a backdrop to an unimaginable horror. The entity, amplified by the collective memories and emotions stirred by the festival, would be at its most potent, its influence extending far beyond anything Sarah had yet witnessed. Eleanor's notes had been a desperate cry from the past, a warning delivered across decades.

Now, Sarah was the inheritor of that warning, tasked with a race against time that felt impossibly steep. The archivist had laid the groundwork, providing the theoretical framework and the rudimentary tools, but the execution, the actual creation of a defense, rested on Sarah's shoulders. And the clock was ticking down with brutal efficiency. The festival was not just a celebration; it was a ticking time bomb, and Blackwood's unwitting efforts were winding it tighter. Sarah understood that the upcoming town festival, a gathering meant to celebrate Havenwood's history, might inadvertently provide the entity with a powerful surge of collective emotion and forgotten energy, making it stronger and more dangerous. The correlation was undeniable, a terrifying synergy between the town's communal spirit and the encroaching darkness.

Chapter 5: The Nexus of Fear

Synthesizing the Solution

The sterile chill of the abandoned university laboratory clung to Sarah like a second skin, a stark contrast to the suffocating warmth of fear that had become her constant companion. Eleanor Vance's legacy was no longer a weight in her hands; it was a blueprint etched into her mind, a desperate series of equations and arcane symbols that demanded to be brought to life. The air thrummed with an anxious energy, each shadow in the cavernous room seeming to writhe with unseen intent. Sarah worked with a feverish intensity, her movements precise and economical, born of a desperate urgency that bordered on recklessness.

Eleanor's notes, painstakingly translated and cross-referenced with her own nascent understanding of the entity's unique energy signature, had illuminated a path – a complex, multi-faceted approach that relied on both cutting-edge sonic technology and forgotten esoteric practices. The archivist had theorized that the entity, this parasitic consciousness, was not merely a manifestation of negative energy but a complex waveform, susceptible to disruption through precise sonic frequencies. These frequencies, however, were not achievable with standard equipment. They required a specific modulation, a harmonic resonance that Eleanor had painstakingly calculated through years of observation and experimentation. Sarah found herself poring over schematics that looked more like alchemical diagrams than engineering blueprints, a blend of scientific rigor and ancient mysticism that defied easy categorization.

The first hurdle was the sonic emitter itself. Eleanor had envisioned a device that could generate a focused wave of discordant frequencies, a sonic shield designed to repel the entity. The core component, as Sarah deciphered from the brittle pages, was a 'resonating crystal matrix' – a crystalline structure whose specific molecular arrangement could amplify and refract sound waves in a highly unconventional manner. Sourcing such a crystal was proving to be the most significant challenge. Eleanor's notes hinted at a rare, naturally occurring quartz, found only in specific geological formations known for their unusual energy properties. Sarah had spent the last two days meticulously cross-referencing geological surveys of the region with ancient local folklore, searching for any mention of deposits that matched Eleanor's vague descriptions. The trail led her to a series of disused mining tunnels on the outskirts of Havenwood, tunnels that had been sealed decades ago due to 'unstable seismic activity' – a euphemism, Sarah suspected, for something far more unnatural.

The journey to the old mines was a descent into a different kind of darkness. The air grew heavy, thick with the scent of damp earth and something else, something metallic and faintly acrid that prickled Sarah's nostrils. As she navigated the treacherous, debris-strewn paths, the oppressive silence was broken only by the skittering of unseen creatures and the unsettling groan of timbers protesting against the earth's weight. Each step felt like an intrusion, a trespass into a place that actively resisted her presence. The entity's influence, she felt, was strongest here, in the deep, forgotten places where the earth's own secrets were buried. She clutched the small, heavy toolkit Eleanor had left for her, its contents a strange assortment of specialized probes, sonic oscilloscopes, and a surprisingly primitive-looking tuning fork crafted from an unknown alloy.

The crystalline matrix wasn't just about the physical structure; it was about the energy it could channel. Eleanor's research had delved into the esoteric principles of sympathetic resonance, the idea that objects of similar composition or energetic signature could influence one another. To activate the crystal matrix, Sarah needed to imbue it with a specific energetic charge, a process that involved more than just electrical input. The archivist had detailed a series of ancient symbols, glyphs that predated recorded history, which, when etched into the crystal and activated by a carefully modulated sonic frequency, could theoretically create a 'containment field.' These symbols were not arbitrary; they represented concepts of warding, repelling, and nullification, drawn from obscure texts on geomancy and ancient spirit-lore. Sarah had spent hours sketching them, her hand cramping from the effort, trying to recall their precise forms and their intended placement on the crystal's facets.

Back in the echoing solitude of the laboratory, surrounded by flickering fluorescent lights and the hum of dormant machinery, Sarah began the painstaking process of shaping the crystal. Using specialized diamond-tipped drills and a delicate touch, she meticulously etched the ancient symbols onto the quartz, each line a prayer, each groove a desperate plea against the encroaching darkness. The process was excruciatingly slow, requiring an almost meditative focus. One wrong move, one slip of the hand, and the crystal's integrity could be compromised, rendering the entire endeavor useless.

As she worked, the whispers started. Not the faint, disembodied murmurs she'd heard in the library, but a more insidious, internal dialogue, planting seeds of doubt and despair. They spoke of futility, of the sheer impossibility of her task, of the inevitable triumph of the entity. It was Eleanor's fear, echoed across time, amplified by the very silence Sarah was trying to break. She felt a phantom chill, as if an unseen presence was breathing down her neck, its icy breath a constant reminder of her vulnerability. She could almost feel its hunger, a vast, ancient void yearning to consume.

The next phase involved the sonic frequencies. Eleanor had developed a series of multi-layered sonic pulses, each designed to interact with the crystal matrix and the etched symbols in a specific sequence. The goal was to create a 'feedback loop' that would amplify the repellent effect, turning the crystal into a localized locus of sonic disruption. This required not only the precise frequencies but also a specific waveform modulation, a complex pattern that Eleanor described as a 'harmonic dissonance.' Recreating this modulation was a significant technical challenge. Sarah had to adapt a sonic generator, recalibrating its output and integrating a custom-built amplifier circuit designed to handle the unique energy requirements.

Hours blurred into a relentless cycle of trial and error. Sarah adjusted dials, monitored waveforms on oscilloscopes, and listened intently to the sounds emanating from the modified generator. The frequencies were bizarre, at times almost inaudible, at others rising to a piercing shriek that made her teeth ache. She found herself constantly referring back to Eleanor's faded diagrams, trying to decipher the subtle nuances of the archivist's calculations. The entity seemed to sense her progress, its presence becoming more palpable, more insistent. The shadows in the lab seemed to deepen, coalescing into more defined shapes at the periphery of her vision. A sudden gust of wind, though the windows were sealed shut, sent papers scattering across the floor, a physical manifestation of the unseen forces attempting to disrupt her work.

She remembered Eleanor's cryptic mention of 'sympathetic anchors' – objects or locations within Havenwood that held a particularly strong psychic imprint, points where the entity's influence was amplified. Eleanor had theorized that the repellent field needed to be anchored to these points to be truly effective, creating a network of sonic barriers that would gradually push the entity back. The Founder's Day festival was, unfortunately, a nexus of such points. The town square, the old bandstand, even certain historic buildings designated for tours – all of them were potential amplifiers for the entity, and therefore, crucial points for Sarah's defense.

This meant she couldn't just build one device. Eleanor's research indicated that a distributed network was necessary, a series of smaller, portable emitters strategically placed at these 'resonance points.' The portable emitters would be less powerful than the central device, but their combined effect, synchronized and amplified by the main crystal matrix, could create a significant deterrent. This exponentially increased the complexity of her task. She needed to replicate the crystal matrix and sonic modulator multiple times, using limited resources and under immense pressure.

The materials were another significant constraint. Eleanor's notes alluded to several components that were either obsolete or incredibly rare. One such component was a 'ferrous resonant coil,' described as being wound with a specific alloy found in antique electrical equipment. Sarah had to scour online auction sites and antique shops, sifting through mountains of discarded electronics, searching for the right piece. She finally found a suitable coil within a vintage radio transmitter, its brass casing tarnished but the internal windings remarkably intact. Another component, a 'bifurcated dielectric insulator,' was described as being crafted from a material similar to treated whalebone – a substance that was now ethically impossible and legally prohibitive to obtain. Eleanor had, however, included a desperate alternative: a complex chemical compound that, when applied to a specially treated bone, could mimic the original material's properties. Sarah had to meticulously synthesize this compound in the lab, a dangerous process involving volatile chemicals and precise temperature controls. The risk of explosion was ever-present, a tangible manifestation of the stakes involved.

The ancient symbols, she discovered, weren't just static etchings. Eleanor had devised a method of 'activating' them through a carefully timed sonic pulse, a specific burst of energy that would cause the symbols to resonate and project the repellent field. This required a secondary sonic emitter, smaller and more focused, designed to be keyed to the primary frequency. Sarah found herself needing to build these smaller emitters as well, each one a miniature replica of the core technology, demanding the same meticulous attention to detail.

The race against time intensified with each passing hour. The Founder's Day festival was a mere four days away. Sarah felt the strain in her very bones, the exhaustion gnawing at her resolve. Sleep offered little respite, filled with fragmented nightmares of suffocating darkness and silent screams. Yet, with each minor success – a perfectly calibrated frequency, a successfully etched symbol, a functional coil – a flicker of hope ignited within her. She was not just Sarah anymore; she was the inheritor of Eleanor Vance's desperate fight, a conduit for a legacy of resistance against an unimaginable foe.

She recalled Eleanor's meticulous records of the entity's behavior patterns. The archivist had observed that the entity exhibited a distinct aversion to concentrated 'intentional energy.' This wasn't just about sonic frequencies; it was about directed psychic focus. The ancient symbols, Eleanor believed, acted as conduits for this focused intent, channeling human will and purpose into a tangible force. Sarah found herself practicing simple meditative techniques Eleanor had described, learning to clear her mind, to focus her thoughts with laser-like precision, visualizing the repellent field expanding, pushing back the encroaching darkness. It felt like grasping at smoke, but she was willing to try anything.

The creation of the portable emitters was particularly challenging. They needed to be robust enough to withstand the rigors of being deployed in public spaces without drawing undue attention, yet powerful enough to contribute to the overall defensive network. Sarah adapted her designs, using smaller, more energy-efficient components, and casing them in nondescript metallic boxes that could be easily concealed. She realized that the success of the entire operation hinged on her ability to deploy these devices without raising suspicion, without revealing the true nature of the threat to a town blissfully unaware of the precipice they were teetering on.

The more she delved into Eleanor's research, the more she understood the sheer audacity of the archivist's plan. Eleanor Vance, a quiet librarian, had been a warrior in her own right, armed not with weapons but with intellect and an unshakeable determination. Sarah felt a profound kinship with the woman, a connection forged in the crucible of shared purpose and encroaching dread. Eleanor had faced this threat alone, and now, Sarah was walking in her footsteps, armed with the knowledge she had painstakingly gathered.

The final piece of Eleanor's solution involved a series of 'harmonic amplifiers,' small devices that would boost the signal of the portable emitters and synchronize them into a cohesive network. These amplifiers were essentially miniature versions of the central crystal matrix, designed to create a chain reaction of repellent energy. Building these required the same rare crystals and the same intricate etching process, multiplying the workload and the pressure.

Sarah's hands were raw, her eyes burning from lack of sleep, and her mind a constant whirl of complex calculations and arcane symbols. The laboratory, once a sterile sanctuary of science, had become a battleground, each piece of equipment a weapon, each completed component a small victory. The omnipresent dread of the entity continued to press in, a silent, suffocating weight, but beneath it, a fierce resolve had taken root. She was not just building a device; she was constructing a shield, a desperate bulwark against an unimaginable horror, a testament to the enduring power of human ingenuity and the courage to face the darkness, even when it seemed insurmountable. The whispers in the silence were no longer solely Eleanor's fear, but a growing echo of her own defiance. She would not let Havenwood become the entity's final feast. She would not fail.

Blackwood's Betrayal

The air in the lab crackled with an unspoken tension that had nothing to do with the humming machinery. Sarah watched Blackwood, his posture still unnervingly relaxed, his gaze sweeping over her work with an intensity that felt like a physical touch. His earlier assistance, his seemingly genuine concern, now felt like a carefully constructed facade. The detached observer was too much of an observer, too…knowing. She had painstakingly pieced together Eleanor's legacy, a desperate gamble against an encroaching darkness, and Blackwood's calm presence felt like a ripple in the carefully constructed calm she was trying to maintain.

"You've made remarkable progress, Sarah," Blackwood's voice was smooth, a low baritone that vibrated with a practiced mellifluousness. He gestured to the crystal matrix, its facets glinting under the harsh laboratory lights, the intricate symbols she had painstakingly etched now seeming to pulse with a faint, internal luminescence. "Eleanor's theories were…ambitious. But her understanding of resonant harmonics was unparalleled."

Sarah's eyes narrowed, her grip tightening on a specialized sonic transducer. "You know her work?" The question was sharp, laced with suspicion. Eleanor had been notoriously private, her research buried under layers of academic bureaucracy and personal fear.

How could this man, a relative stranger, have such intimate knowledge of her most guarded secrets?

A flicker of something unreadable crossed Blackwood's face, gone as quickly as it appeared. "My family has a... long-standing interest in the unusual phenomena that plague this region. Eleanor and I corresponded, albeit discreetly. We shared a mutual fascination, a desire to understand what lies beyond the veil."

"Understand?" Sarah scoffed, the sound brittle in the cavernous space. "Eleanor wanted to destroy it. To stop it from feeding." She tapped a finger against the crystal, the faint hum resonating through her glove. "This isn't about fascination; it's about survival."

Blackwood inclined his head, his expression becoming more serious, though the underlying detachment remained. "Survival, yes. But understanding precedes eradication, wouldn't you agree? To truly defeat something, one must first comprehend its nature, its vulnerabilities, its very essence." He stepped closer, his gaze locking with hers, and Sarah felt a prickle of unease crawl up her spine. He wasn't just a witness; he was a participant, albeit a silent one until now. "Eleanor saw it as a parasite. A destructive force to be repelled. She was... thorough, in her methods of containment."

"Containment is just delaying the inevitable if it can break free," Sarah countered, her voice rising with a defensive edge. She remembered the sheer terror in Eleanor's journals, the frantic desperation to find a permanent solution. Containment felt like a temporary measure, a flimsy dam against an unstoppable tide.

"Perhaps," Blackwood conceded, a faint, almost imperceptible smile playing on his lips. "But what if it's not merely a parasite? What if it's something...more? Something that can be guided, its immense energy…redirected?" He gestured towards the complex array of equipment Sarah had assembled. "These sonic frequencies, the resonant crystal matrix… they are designed to disrupt, yes. But they are also designed to resonate, to harmonize. Eleanor understood that resonance can be a pathway, not just a barrier."

Sarah felt a cold dread seep into her bones. His words were like a poisoned dart, twisting her understanding, planting seeds of doubt in the carefully cultivated ground of her resolve. "You're saying… she wanted to control it?"

"Control is a strong word," Blackwood mused, his eyes tracing the intricate patterns of the wiring. "Perhaps 'influence' is more accurate. Or 'harness.' My family's history is… deeply intertwined with this entity, Sarah. We have observed it for generations. We have learned its patterns, its appetites. And we have also learned that it is not an mindless force of chaos. It is… intelligent. And like all intelligent entities, it can be negotiated with. Or, at the very least, understood in a way that allows for its careful management."

The weight of his confession settled heavily in the air, suffocating in its implications. Sarah's carefully constructed world, her singular focus on Eleanor's desperate plan for destruction, began to fracture. Blackwood wasn't just a bystander; he was an inheritor of a different kind of knowledge, a legacy of observation and perhaps, manipulation.

"Your family…" Sarah's voice was barely a whisper, the words catching in her throat. "You've been… studying it? For how long?"

"Longer than you can imagine," he replied, his gaze fixed on the complex machinery. "The whispers you hear, the shadows you perceive... they are but faint echoes of what my ancestors experienced. We have learned to coexist. To carve out a space for ourselves amidst its presence. Eleanor's approach was born of fear, a natural reaction to its raw power. But fear can blind one to possibilities."

"Possibilities of what? Of letting it consume us, piece by piece?" Sarah's voice was tight with a rising anger, a desperate need to cling to the clarity of Eleanor's mission. The archivist's terrifying accounts of the entity's destructive nature were etched into her mind.

"Possibilities of understanding its limitations, its triggers. Of finding a balance," Blackwood insisted, his tone unwavering. "Imagine, Sarah, if instead of simply trying to banish it, we could learn to redirect its energy. To channel it. It is a force of immense power. Power that, in the right hands, could be... beneficial."

The very thought was abhorrent. Beneficial? This...thing that fed on fear, that twisted reality, that drove people to madness? "Beneficial how?" Sarah demanded, her voice sharp. "By letting it feed on someone else? By making sure it doesn't feed on *us*?"

"Not entirely," he corrected, his eyes holding hers. "But by understanding its needs, we can perhaps satiate it without undue destruction. Eleanor's work was a brilliant attempt at a defensive perimeter. But a perimeter, by its very nature, implies a containment *within*. What if the goal should be to manage its existence, to coexist, rather than to eradicate it entirely?"

Sarah felt a surge of adrenaline, a potent mix of fear and defiance. Blackwood's perspective was a horrifying inversion of everything she had come to believe. Eleanor's life had been dedicated to fighting this entity, to creating the means to destroy it.

Now, standing before her, was a man who seemed to view it as a resource, a powerful force to be controlled.

"Coexist?" she repeated, the word tasting like ash in her mouth. "Eleanor saw it as a plague. She dedicated her life to finding a cure, not a treaty."

"And perhaps her dedication was precisely what made her see only one path," Blackwood countered, his voice still calm, unnervingly so. "Fear. Desperation. Those are powerful motivators, but they can also be blinding. My family... we have no such fear. Only a deep, abiding curiosity and a pragmatic approach to survival." He paused, his gaze drifting back to the crystal matrix. "These symbols Eleanor etched, they are wards. But they are also conduits. She understood the power of intent, of focused will. But she focused that will on negation. I believe it can be focused on direction."

Sarah recoiled internally. The idea that Eleanor's meticulous, life-saving work could be twisted, reinterpreted as a means to harness the very thing she sought to destroy, was almost unbearable. It felt like a betrayal of Eleanor's memory, of her sacrifice.

"You're saying you want to *use* this...this device... to control it?" The words were laced with disbelief.

"To study its response," Blackwood corrected, his tone even. "To observe how it interacts with the harmonic dissonance, with the focused intent channeled through these symbols. Eleanor's work is a formidable starting point. But it is incomplete. It is a weapon designed only to repel. I wish to see if it can also be a... leash."

The word 'leash' hung in the air, a chilling testament to his intent. Sarah felt a cold knot tighten in her stomach. She had trusted him, or at least, she had accepted his help without overt suspicion. Now, she saw the truth, a horrifying revelation that sent shivers down her spine. His detachment wasn't mere composure; it was a symptom of a fundamentally different objective.

"And what happens when your 'leash' breaks, Blackwood?" Sarah asked, her voice dangerously low. "What happens when your 'coexistence' turns into its next meal? Eleanor documented its growth, its hunger. It doesn't negotiate. It consumes."

"It consumes what it perceives as a threat, or what it can easily overpower," he replied, his gaze unwavering. "But it also responds to order. To patterns. And to immense, directed power. My family has... managed to hold it at bay, not through outright warfare, but through careful observation and subtle manipulation of its environment. This technology is a more refined tool, a more potent method of achieving what we have always sought: control."

Sarah looked at the array of equipment, the culmination of her desperate efforts. It was meant to be a shield, a weapon of last resort. The thought of it being used for anything else, for some twisted experiment in control, filled her with a profound sense of horror.

"I won't let you," she stated, her voice firm, cutting through the tense silence. "Eleanor's work was about protection, about saving people. Not about playing God with something that has no regard for life."

Blackwood's lips curved into a wry smile, a flicker of amusement in his eyes that Sarah found deeply unsettling.

"Playing God is a dangerous accusation, Sarah. I am merely trying to understand. To find a solution that does not involve a mutually assured destruction. Eleanor's plan is a single-minded pursuit of a singular goal. Mine is… broader. More encompassing. We are allies, yes, but our ultimate aims are diverging."

The realization hit Sarah with the force of a physical blow. The tense alliance she had forged was built on a foundation of misunderstanding, perhaps even deception. Blackwood wasn't just helping her achieve Eleanor's goal; he was trying to co-opt it, to bend it to his own, far more sinister, agenda.

"Diverging?" Sarah stepped back, her hand reaching for a heavy wrench, a primitive defense against this more insidious threat. "My goal is to ensure this thing never hurts anyone again. Your goal seems to be to… bottle lightning. And I don't think you understand how dangerous that truly is."

"Danger is relative," Blackwood said, his gaze sweeping over the laboratory once more, as if assessing its potential, not just as a defense, but as an instrument. "The danger of inaction, of allowing this entity to grow unchecked, is far greater. Eleanor's fear was a understandable reaction to the unknown. But what if the unknown can be… tamed?"

"Tamed?" Sarah's voice was a low growl. "It's not a wild animal, Blackwood. It's something ancient and alien, something that existed before us and will likely exist after. You can't tame it. You can only hope to survive it, or to stop it."

"And I believe Eleanor's method, while valiant, is ultimately flawed in its singular focus," he insisted. "Her solution was a sword. I seek a shield, yes, but also a reins. The power she sought to unleash is immense. To simply discard it, to attempt to obliterate it, might be… wasteful. And ultimately, futile."

Sarah stared at him, the sterile laboratory suddenly feeling like a trap. His words, so calm and reasoned, masked a chilling ambition. He saw the entity not as a horror to be vanquished, but as a force to be mastered, a power to be wielded. His family's history, their generations of observation, had bred a pragmatism that bordered on amorality.

"Wasteful?" she echoed, her voice tight with disbelief. "People's lives are not wasteful, Blackwood. Their sanity is not a resource to be managed."

"And yet, the entity thrives on the very fear and chaos you seek to avoid by direct confrontation," he countered smoothly. "My family has learned that a more subtle approach, a management of its environment, a redirection of its focus, can be far more effective in the long run. Eleanor's sonic emitters, her crystal matrix… they are powerful tools. But their purpose need not be solely destructive."

Sarah felt a profound sense of isolation wash over her. She was alone in her fight, not just against the entity, but against the very people who claimed to understand it. Blackwood's betrayal wasn't one of overt malice, but of fundamental difference in purpose, a chilling divergence that threatened to unravel everything she was working towards. His detached observation was not simply curiosity; it was the calculated assessment of a predator studying its prey, not to destroy it, but to understand its patterns, its vulnerabilities, its potential for… domestication. The Nexus of Fear, it seemed, had many architects, and Blackwood's design was a terrifyingly alien one.

The weight of Blackwood's pronouncements hung heavy in the air, a chilling counterpoint to the sterile hum of the lab. Sarah found herself reeling, her understanding of Eleanor's legacy, her own mission, now a fractured mosaic. The carefully constructed certainty she'd clung to, the singular, unwavering purpose of destroying the entity, had been eroded by Blackwood's unnerving pragmatism. He didn't see a monster to be vanquished, but a force to be... managed. The idea of "taming" such a thing, of wielding its power, sent a fresh wave of dread through her. It was an abhorrent concept, a betrayal of every life claimed by the entity, of Eleanor's very soul.

Her instincts screamed at her to dismiss him, to shut down his insidious theories and reaffirm her commitment to Eleanor's desperate, life-saving plan. Yet, Blackwood's words, delivered with such unnerving calm, carried a disturbing resonance. His family's generations of observation, their learned methods of "subtle manipulation," painted a picture of a different kind of survival, one that didn't necessarily involve the pyrrhic victory of mutual destruction. But at what cost? What moral compromises did such a path entail? The thought of the entity being "redirected," its insatiable hunger merely sated by a different, perhaps more pliable, victim, was a monstrous vision.

With a newfound urgency, Sarah turned away from Blackwood and the humming machinery, her mind racing. If Eleanor's work was a starting point, a weapon of defense, then perhaps the answer lay not solely in replicating her methods, but in understanding the deeper history, the origins of this insidious presence that had woven itself into the fabric of Havenwood.

Blackwood's family might have their own hidden agenda, their own dark history with the entity, but their knowledge, however tainted, was still knowledge. Sarah needed to find a different kind of understanding, one rooted in the town itself, in its very foundations.

Her thoughts immediately turned to the Havenwood Historical Society. It was a quaint, unassuming building on the edge of town, a repository of dusty artifacts and forgotten stories. If anywhere held the secrets of the town's deeper past, it was there. She remembered Eleanor's cryptic notes, references to 'founding pacts' and 'sacrifices made in silence.' These weren't just abstract concepts; they were clues, breadcrumbs leading to the heart of the darkness.

The following morning, as the first tentative rays of dawn pierced the perpetual gloom that seemed to cling to Havenwood, Sarah found herself standing before the weathered oak doors of the Historical Society. The air was thick with the scent of old paper and mildew, a familiar aroma that usually brought her comfort, but today it was tinged with a growing apprehension. Blackwood's words echoed in her mind, a constant whisper of doubt and alternative possibilities. Had Eleanor's fight been a noble, albeit futile, stand against an inevitable force, or had she been merely a pawn in a much larger, older game?

Mrs. Gable, the society's curator, a woman whose sharp eyes missed little despite her diminutive frame, greeted Sarah with a practiced smile. "Back again, dearie? Still digging into the town's... interesting past?" Her tone was laced with a gentle curiosity, but Sarah sensed a deeper awareness, a subtle probing that reminded her of Blackwood's unnerving perceptiveness.

"I'm looking for anything related to the town's founding, Mrs. Gable," Sarah began, her voice carefully modulated. "Specifically, any records concerning the initial settlement and its establishment. I'm particularly interested in the original land deeds and any accounts of the early settlers themselves."

Mrs. Gable's smile didn't waver, but her eyes held a new intensity. "The founding... yes, that's a rather sensitive period, you see. There are... gaps. Not intentionally, of course," she added quickly, as if sensing Sarah's underlying suspicion. "Just the way things are. Time, fires, a general lack of... foresight in preserving everything from so long ago."

Sarah felt a prickle of frustration. "But surely there are some records? Diaries, letters, town council minutes from that era?" She pushed forward, her gaze unwavering. "Eleanor Vance had mentioned some... unusual circumstances surrounding the town's establishment. She believed there was more to the founding than the official histories suggest."

At the mention of Eleanor's name, Mrs. Gable's expression shifted subtly. A flicker of something Sarah couldn't quite decipher – perhaps recognition, perhaps a touch of unease – crossed her face. "Eleanor was a... passionate researcher," she said carefully, her voice taking on a more formal, almost rehearsed, tone. "She delved into many obscure corners of our history. Some might say she delved too deeply."

The implication was clear, and it mirrored Blackwood's own assessment of Eleanor's "fear." Sarah pressed on, determined to unearth whatever truths lay buried beneath the layers of carefully curated history. "I need to see anything related to the original charter, any accounts of the first families who settled here, and any records of land acquisition. I'm particularly interested in any mentions of indigenous populations or pre-settlement land use."

Mrs. Gable led Sarah into a hushed back room, the air thick with the scent of aging paper and leather. Row upon row of meticulously organized files and bound volumes lined the walls, a testament to decades of diligent preservation. Yet, as Mrs. Gable began pulling out folders, Sarah noticed a distinct pattern: the further back they went, the sparser the documentation became. There were beautifully illustrated accounts of the town's growth in the late 19th and early 20th centuries, detailed ledgers of businesses, and heartfelt memoirs of later generations. But the founding period was disturbingly thin.

"As I said, dearie, the early days are quite... patchy," Mrs. Gable murmured, her fingers deftly sifting through brittle pages. "The original settlers, the Blackwoods, the Hawthornes, the Everly-Smiths... they were a hardy bunch, but not overly inclined to elaborate record-keeping. Their focus was on survival, on building a life from nothing."

Sarah scanned the documents Mrs. Gable presented. They were official land grants, sparse, dry accounts of surveyed plots, and basic census data. There were no personal diaries, no letters detailing the anxieties or triumphs of the first arrivals, no accounts of their interactions with the land itself, or with any people who might have been there before them. It was as if the narrative simply *began* with the clearing of the forests and the erection of the first buildings.

"This is all that exists for the founding period?" Sarah asked, her voice tinged with disbelief. "No personal accounts? No journals?"

Mrs. Gable wrung her hands, a gesture that seemed both genuine and, to Sarah's increasingly suspicious mind, a little too practiced. "We have some fragmented town council minutes, mostly concerning property disputes and the establishment of basic infrastructure. But personal narratives? Those seem to have been lost to time. A great shame, really."

Sarah felt a growing unease. This wasn't a natural loss of records; it felt deliberate, a carefully pruned history. She remembered Blackwood's unnerving calmness, his family's "long-standing interest" in the region's unusual phenomena. Could it be that the Blackwood family, the very name associated with the town's founding, was also responsible for its carefully constructed historical amnesia?

"Are there any records that mention why the town was specifically founded in this particular location?" Sarah pressed, her gaze sweeping over the meager collection of founding documents. "Was there something special about this area? Resources, perhaps?"

Mrs. Gable paused, her eyes drifting towards a dimly lit corner of the archives, where a large, intricately carved wooden chest sat, shrouded in dust. "The land was... fertile," she said slowly, her voice dropping to a near whisper. "And there was a certain... energy about the place, even then. The original settlers, as I recall from some later commentaries, felt a strong pull to this valley. A sense of destiny, perhaps."

"Energy?" Sarah seized on the word. "What kind of energy?"

"Oh, just a feeling," Mrs. Gable demurred, waving a dismissive hand. "The kind of feeling you get in ancient places. The kind that makes you feel... observed." She shivered, a subtle, involuntary tremor. "The Blackwoods, particularly, were said to be drawn here. It was their land, originally."

Sarah's mind flashed back to Blackwood's confession: "My family has a... long-standing interest in the unusual phenomena that plague this region." And then, "My family's history is... deeply intertwined with this entity, Sarah. We have observed it for generations." The pieces began to click into place, forming a grim, unsettling picture. The founding families, the Blackwoods at their head, hadn't just settled this land; they had *known* about the entity. They hadn't stumbled upon it; they had been drawn to it, or perhaps, the entity had drawn them.

"What about the chest?" Sarah asked, nodding towards the imposing wooden artifact. "Is that from the founding period?"

Mrs. Gable's eyes widened almost imperceptibly. "That... that is the Founder's Chest," she said, her voice hushed with reverence, and something akin to fear. "It contains some of the original documents, the most vital of them, I'm told. But it's sealed. And the key... the key was lost generations ago."

Sarah felt a surge of adrenaline. The Founder's Chest. The most vital documents. This was it. This was where the truth lay hidden. "Lost? Or hidden?" she murmured, more to herself than to Mrs. Gable. "Are there any records about *why* it was sealed? Or about what might be inside?"

Mrs. Gable shook her head, her gaze fixed on the chest as if it held some terrible power. "There are whispers. Legends. That the chest contains the original charter, the one that laid out the town's purpose. And that it also contains... the agreement. The pact made with the land."

"The pact?" Sarah repeated, her heart pounding in her chest.

"Yes. A pact to ensure the town's prosperity. A... balance struck. The details are shrouded in mystery, of course. The founders were pragmatic men, men who understood the need for... sacrifices, for the greater good. They wanted to create a haven, a place of peace and prosperity. But such things, as we know, often come at a price."

Sarah's mind raced. Eleanor's frantic attempts to destroy the entity, Blackwood's desire to control it. Was the town's prosperity, its manufactured peace, built on a foundation of appeasement? Had the original settlers, faced with a terrifying, inexplicable force, struck a bargain? A bargain that involved feeding it, or perhaps, channeling it, in exchange for its dormancy?

"A price for peace," Sarah whispered, the words tasting like bile. She looked at the sparse documents, the deliberate gaps in the historical record, and the sealed Founder's Chest. It all pointed to a deliberate, systematic suppression of the truth. The entity wasn't just a problem that had *arisen* in Havenwood; it was the very reason for its existence, the dark cornerstone upon which the town was built.

She spent the next few days immersed in the town archives, meticulously piecing together the fragments of information. She cross-referenced land deeds, followed the lineage of the founding families – the Blackwoods, the Hawthornes, the Everly-Smiths – and searched for any oblique references to pre-settlement rituals or beliefs. The picture that slowly emerged was more chilling than she could have imagined. The official histories painted a picture of intrepid pioneers carving a new life out of untamed wilderness. But beneath the surface, in the hushed tones of Mrs. Gable's half-truths and the carefully redacted documents, lay a far more sinister narrative.

Her breakthrough came not from the official records, but from a collection of privately held papers belonging to a long-deceased local historian, a man named Silas Croft, whose meticulous, albeit eccentric, research had been largely dismissed by the mainstream historical society. Croft, it seemed, had been obsessed with the "true founding" of Havenwood, convinced that the official story was a carefully constructed lie. His notes spoke of ancient ley lines, of sacred sites, and of a palpable, unnerving "presence" that had been felt in the valley for centuries, long before the first settlers arrived.

Croft's most damning discovery, painstakingly documented in his journals, was an alleged pre-colonial artifact unearthed during the initial land clearing – a carved stone depicting a swirling, chaotic vortex surrounded by figures in poses of supplication and offering. This artifact, Croft theorized, was not merely a relic; it was evidence that the land itself was intrinsically tied to the entity, a nexus point for its manifestation. The original settlers, primarily the Blackwood family, had not chosen this location by chance. They had known. They had been drawn to it, and in their desperate bid to establish a foothold, they had made a terrible pact.

The pact, according to Croft's interpretations of obscure local folklore and the few cryptic entries he found in what he believed to be a Blackwood family ledger, was not about vanquishing the entity, but about appeasing it. The town of Havenwood, with its outward appearance of serene tranquility, was a carefully maintained façade. The constant, low-level hum of manufactured peace, the suppression of overt emotion, the stifling of dissent – these were not merely cultural quirks. They were the deliberate mechanisms of a long-standing bargain. The settlers had agreed to cultivate an environment of placid harmony, a collective offering of manufactured contentment, in exchange for the entity's relative dormancy. They were, in essence, feeding it a carefully controlled diet of peaceful denial.

Sarah's hands trembled as she read Croft's conclusions. The town's very existence was a testament to a horrifying compromise. The entity wasn't just lurking in the shadows; it was the foundation of Havenwood. It fed on the enforced peace, on the suppressed anxieties, on the manufactured normalcy. And the Blackwoods, with their generations of observation, were the architects of this dark symbiosis. Blackwood's talk of "harnessing" and "coexisting" suddenly took on a terrifying new dimension. He wasn't suggesting a new way to deal with the entity; he was advocating for the continuation, and perhaps the refinement, of the original pact.

She realized with a chilling certainty that Blackwood's interest in Eleanor's work wasn't about destroying the entity, but about ensuring its continued, controlled appeasement. Eleanor, in her desperate pursuit of eradication, had threatened the delicate, ancient balance that had sustained Havenwood for generations. Blackwood, the inheritor of the original pact, saw her as a destabilizing force.

The implications were staggering. The entity wasn't an external threat to be repelled; it was an intrinsic part of Havenwood's identity, a dark force that had been intentionally woven into the town's very fabric. Sarah's mission had shifted dramatically. It was no longer just about stopping the entity; it was about confronting the foundational sin of Havenwood, about exposing the terrible truth that lay beneath its placid surface, a truth that had been deliberately buried and maintained by generations of those who knew. The Founder's Chest, sealed for centuries, held the physical proof of this ancient, horrifying bargain. Unlocking it, and revealing its contents to the town, would undoubtedly shatter the manufactured peace, and likely unleash a fury that Havenwood had been carefully, deliberately, suppressing for centuries. The nexus of fear wasn't just a location; it was a state of being, a collective agreement to deny the darkness that had birthed their haven. And Sarah was about to shatter that agreement.

The Festival Begins

The crisp autumn air, usually a welcome herald of the annual Founder's Day festivities, felt unnaturally chilled this year, carrying a scent that was less of fallen leaves and more of damp earth and something subtly, disturbingly metallic. Sarah stood on the edge of the town square, watching as the final preparations for the festival were made. Bunting, a cheerful cascade of red and gold, was being strung between lampposts, and the central gazebo, usually a beacon of community spirit, was being adorned with an almost frenetic energy. Yet, beneath the veneer of forced festivity, an almost palpable anxiety hummed through the gathered townsfolk.

It was a quiet anxiety, a familiar undercurrent in Havenwood, but today it seemed amplified, almost suffocating. Sarah had spent the last week poring over Silas Croft's journals, each word a chilling confirmation of her worst fears. The town's prosperity, its carefully cultivated tranquility, was a shield, a meticulously constructed lie designed to appease something ancient and terrible. The Founder's Day festival, a celebration of the town's supposed beginnings, was, in reality, a ritualistic perpetuation of that original, horrifying pact.

She watched Mr. Henderson, the baker, a man usually known for his booming laugh and flour-dusted apron, meticulously arranging his artisanal bread on a trestle table. His movements were precise, almost robotic, and his smile, when he offered a greeting to a passing neighbor, didn't quite reach his eyes. Across the square, the mayor, a portly man with a perpetually strained expression, was delivering a speech, his words of community and shared heritage swallowed by the vastness of the sky and the encroaching shadows of the surrounding woods. Even the children, usually a riot of unrestrained joy, seemed subdued, their laughter carrying a brittle, forced quality.

Sarah's gaze drifted towards the dense wall of trees that encircled Havenwood, a dark, brooding presence that seemed to press in on the edges of the town square. The woods had always been a part of Havenwood's charm, a picturesque backdrop. But now, they felt like a cage, the trees themselves appearing to writhe in the deepening twilight, their branches skeletal fingers reaching out. The air grew perceptibly colder as she watched, a stark contrast to the unseasonably warm autumn the rest of the region was experiencing. A shiver, unrelated to the temperature, traced its way down her spine.

As the festival officially commenced, a wave of manufactured merriment swept through the crowd. Music, a jaunty, almost desperate tune, spilled from the gazebo, and townsfolk began to mill about, their movements lacking genuine conviviality. Sarah moved through the throng, her senses on high alert, cataloging the subtle deviations from the norm, the almost imperceptible shifts in behavior that Silas Croft had alluded to in his writings.

She noticed Mrs. Gable, the Historical Society curator, standing near a stall selling handcrafted jams. Her usual sharp, observant gaze seemed clouded, unfocused. She accepted a jar of plum preserves from the vendor with a vacant nod, her lips moving in a silent recitation that Sarah couldn't decipher. It was a small thing, easily dismissed as nerves or preoccupation, but combined with the others, it contributed to the unsettling atmosphere.

Then there was young Timmy Peterson, a boy known for his boundless energy and penchant for mischief. Sarah saw him standing unnaturally still by the carousel, his eyes wide and unblinking, staring at something only he could see in the swirling painted horses. He clutched a brightly colored balloon, but his grip was slack, the string dangling limply. A moment later, he let out a soft, almost mournful cry, and dropped the balloon. It floated upwards, not with the cheerful buoyancy of a child's toy, but with a sluggish, almost reluctant ascent, disappearing into the darkening sky.

Sarah's attention was drawn to the periphery of the square, where the shadows cast by the ancient oaks seemed to deepen and coalesce. She saw fleeting movements within the darkness, shapes that flickered and dissolved before her eyes. Were they tricks of the light, amplified by her heightened state of anxiety? Or were they something more? She remembered Croft's descriptions of the entity's influence on perception, its ability to warp reality, to sow seeds of doubt and unease. The "collective denial" that fueled its dormancy was a fragile thing, easily fractured by genuine observation.

She passed a group of teenagers huddled together, their usual boisterous laughter replaced by hushed whispers and furtive glances towards the woods. One of them, a girl with vibrant pink hair, shivered and pulled her thin jacket tighter, her face pale.

"It's like... the air is watching us," she murmured, her voice barely audible. Her friends nodded in silent agreement, their eyes mirroring her apprehension.

The music from the gazebo faltered, then stuttered to a halt. A collective gasp rippled through the crowd. The Mayor, mid-sentence, his face a mask of forced cheer, seemed to freeze, his eyes widening in sudden terror as he stared past Sarah, towards the treeline. A collective stillness fell over the square, the forced merriment evaporating like mist under a harsh sun. The silence that descended was profound, heavy with unspoken dread.

Sarah followed the Mayor's gaze. The trees seemed to lean in closer, their branches interlacing to form a denser, more impenetrable canopy. The shadows within them writhed, not with the fleeting subtlety of before, but with a more deliberate, menacing dance. A low, guttural hum, barely perceptible at first, began to emanate from the woods, a resonant frequency that seemed to vibrate in Sarah's very bones. It was the sound that Silas Croft had described as the "voice of the land," the low thrum of the entity's ancient awareness.

A few townsfolk began to back away, their movements hesitant, uncertain. Others, trapped by habit and the ingrained instinct for compliance, remained rooted to the spot, their faces etched with a fear they couldn't articulate. Sarah saw Blackwood standing near the gazebo, his posture unnervingly calm amidst the growing panic. His gaze was fixed on the woods, not with the same terror as the others, but with a chillingly detached curiosity, as if observing a fascinating, albeit dangerous, natural phenomenon. His presence, a stark contrast to the palpable fear radiating from everyone else, was a chilling reminder of his family's complicity, their long, dark history intertwined with the very force that was now making its presence known.

The hum intensified, and the ground beneath Sarah's feet seemed to tremble. The laughter and music of moments ago felt like a distant, absurd memory. The forced gaiety had been a thin veil, easily torn. Now, the true face of Havenwood was beginning to show itself – a town built on a foundation of appeasement, its peace maintained by a constant, suffocating denial. The festival, meant to celebrate the town's founding, had instead become an inadvertent offering, a public demonstration of Havenwood's desperate, and ultimately futile, attempts to placate the ancient power that resided within its borders.

Sarah felt a growing certainty that this was not a random surge of the entity's power. This was a response. Perhaps to Eleanor's continued investigation, or perhaps to the subtle erosion of the town's collective denial that had been occurring in the days leading up to the festival. Or perhaps, it was simply time. The ancient pact, demanding its due, was making its presence known. The forced joviality was a fragile shield, and the woods, the source of Havenwood's prosperity and its ultimate terror, were pushing through the cracks.

A young woman near Sarah suddenly let out a choked sob, her eyes darting wildly. "I can't... I can't breathe," she gasped, clutching at her throat. Her companions tried to comfort her, but their touch seemed to agitate her further. Her breath hitched, and her eyes rolled back in her head. Sarah moved towards her, intending to offer assistance, but a sudden, violent tremor shook the ground, throwing everyone off balance.

The carefully arranged stalls toppled, scattering produce and crafts across the cobblestones. The bunting snapped and tore, its cheerful colors now a pathetic mess. The music machine in the gazebo emitted a final, discordant shriek before falling silent.

The hum from the woods swelled, a resonant wave of pure, unadulterated dread that seemed to press in on all sides, threatening to crush the life out of everything. The festival, intended as a celebration of unity and heritage, was devolving into a desperate scramble for survival. The entity was not content with mere appeasement; it was demanding more, and Havenwood, for all its carefully maintained façade, was ill-equipped to provide it. Sarah realized with a sickening lurch that the true cost of Havenwood's peace was about to be collected, and the Founder's Day festival was merely the opening act. The woods were not just surrounding the town; they were encroaching, and the shadows within them held a hunger that had been suppressed for far too long.

A Plea for Awareness

Sarah's heart hammered against her ribs, a frantic drumbeat against the encroaching silence. The tremor had subsided, leaving behind a chilling stillness, a pregnant pause before the storm she knew was coming. The townsfolk, still reeling from the sudden violence, looked around with a mixture of confusion and a dawning, primal fear. This was her chance. This was the moment to shatter the illusion, to wrench them from their slumber of denial.

"It's not just the ground shaking!" Sarah's voice, amplified by desperation, cut through the heavy air. She pushed forward, weaving through the scattered debris, her eyes scanning the faces closest to her. They were a sea of apprehension, of startled uncertainty, but not yet the stark terror that would send them fleeing. "Silas Croft's journals… they warned us. They warned us about this!"

She reached into her jacket, her fingers fumbling slightly as she withdrew the worn leather-bound book. It felt heavy, impossibly so, a conduit to the town's buried history. "This town… Havenwood… it's not built on prosperity. It's built on a pact. A sacrifice. Founder's Day isn't a celebration; it's a continuation of that bargain."

A ripple of unease passed through the crowd, but it was quickly followed by murmurs of dismissal. Heads shook. Eyes flicked towards the mayor and the council members, who were now trying to regain some semblance of control. Their faces were masks of practiced composure, but Sarah could see the tight set of their jaws, the flicker of panic in their eyes when she mentioned Silas Croft.

"Silas Croft was a madman," Mayor Thompson declared, his voice booming, though it lacked its usual confident resonance. He took a step forward, positioning himself between Sarah and the anxious crowd. "He became obsessed with local folklore, with ghost stories. His writings are the product of a disturbed mind, not historical fact."

Sarah brandished the journal. "Disturbed? He documented everything! The disappearances, the unusual harvests, the… the silence of the woods during certain times. He wrote about the 'entity,' the 'silent watcher' that the town founders made a deal with for peace and prosperity. He described the rituals, the offerings… the truth of what Founder's Day truly represents!"

The crowd shifted, a tangible wave of discomfort rolling through them. They were on the precipice of belief, of acknowledging the gnawing unease they had suppressed for so long. But the mayor's words, amplified by the ingrained deference they held for authority, began to anchor them back to their carefully constructed reality.

"Sarah, please," Mrs. Gable, the Historical Society curator, stepped forward, her voice soft but laced with a distinct edge of warning. Her earlier vacant expression had returned, her eyes darting nervously towards the surrounding trees. "You're upsetting people. It's just a… a minor tremor. Happens in this region sometimes."

"Upsetting people?" Sarah's voice rose, cracking with frustration. "Look around you! That hum you heard, that shaking… it's not natural! It's the entity, stirring. It's responding to us! To our denial! Croft wrote about the danger of complacency, of forgetting. He said that the pact had a price, and that price was eternal vigilance, and sometimes… more."

She turned towards the town council, who had gathered near the gazebo, their expressions hardening. Councilman Davies, a man whose family had been in Havenwood for generations, his face a picture of stern disapproval, spoke up. "Sarah, we appreciate your… concern. But this is not the time or place for unsubstantiated accusations. We have a community event to salvage. You are creating unnecessary panic."

"Unnecessary panic?" Sarah repeated, incredulity washing over her. "You're all so focused on appearances, on maintaining this peaceful facade, that you're blind! Croft's journal isn't just ramblings. It's a warning! He provided evidence. Look at this!" She flipped through the brittle pages, her finger landing on a faded sketch. "This is a depiction of the original pact. See the symbols? The same symbols etched into the base of the Founder's

Stone in the old cemetery. The same symbols that appear on the boundary markers of the woods!"

She held the journal aloft, her hand shaking, but her gaze unwavering as she met the eyes of each council member. "These aren't coincidences! This is a pattern! A testament to the truth! The entity is real. It's ancient. And it's demanding payment. This festival, this entire town's existence, is predicated on appeasing it."

Mayor Thompson sighed, a performative gesture of weary patience. "Sarah, we've heard your theories. The council has discussed them. We've reviewed Silas Croft's work, and while it's... colorful, it lacks any verifiable proof. The symbols you're referring to are common agrarian motifs from the period. The 'tremors' are seismic activity, as I said. The 'hum' was likely a localized atmospheric phenomenon."

"Atmospheric phenomenon?" Sarah scoffed. "It vibrated in our bones! It was the sound of something ancient waking up!" She took another step forward, her voice dropping to a more intense, urgent whisper. "Don't you feel it? The wrongness? The way the woods feel... closer? The air is heavy with its attention. It's not just the trees watching us anymore. It's *aware*."

Councilwoman Albright, a woman known for her pragmatism and sharp business acumen, finally spoke, her tone cutting. "Sarah, your distress is evident. Perhaps you should go home. We can arrange for someone to speak with you further, offer some support."

The implication hung heavy in the air: *you're hysterical*. It was a familiar tactic, a way to dismiss inconvenient truths, to label the messenger as unstable, thereby discrediting the message. Sarah felt a cold knot of dread tighten in her stomach.

They weren't just disbelieving; they were actively working to silence her, to preserve their comfortable ignorance.

"Support?" Sarah's voice was tight with a rising tide of despair. "You want to 'support' me? Then listen! Read the journal for yourselves! Go to the cemetery, look at the Founder's Stone! Don't let the comfort of denial blind you! This isn't a story. This is our reality." She thrust the journal towards Davies. "Just read this one passage. Page 47. He describes the 'tithing of shadows.' What do you think that means, Councilman?"

Davies recoiled as if she had offered him a snake. He took a step back, his face paling slightly, but his resolve remained. "I'm not interested in morbid fantasies, Sarah. This conversation is over." He gestured to two burly men who had been loitering near the gazebo, ostensibly for security. "See that she leaves the square. Discreetly."

The men approached, their faces impassive. Sarah felt a surge of adrenaline, but also a profound sense of hopelessness. They wouldn't listen. They *couldn't* listen. The pact, the fear, the denial – it was all too deeply ingrained. The community's complicity was a web, and she was caught in its increasingly tight strands.

As the men reached for her, Sarah looked out at the crowd. Their faces were a mixture of pity, embarrassment, and a stubborn, wilful ignorance. A few looked away, unable to meet her desperate gaze. Others whispered amongst themselves, their hushed tones painting her as the town's resident eccentric, the one who had finally snapped. The fragile facade of normalcy was being reinforced, and she was the one being removed, the aberration that threatened to mar the perfect picture of Havenwood.

"You're all making a terrible mistake," she choked out, her voice barely a whisper as the men guided her away, their hands firm on her arms. "You're choosing ignorance over survival. You're choosing to believe the lie when the truth is screaming at you from the woods." Her eyes, wide with terror and a dawning understanding of the town's collective doom, swept across the square. The music had started again, a hesitant, reedy tune from the gazebo, attempting to drown out the lingering unease. But it was a futile effort. The air still thrummed with the memory of the hum, and the shadows of the woods seemed to deepen, to watch, to wait with an ancient, insatiable patience.

The festival was indeed continuing, but it was no longer a celebration. It was a sacrifice, and she had been the only one brave, or foolish, enough to try and stop it. The price of Havenwood's peace was about to be exacted, and the true horror was not that it was coming, but that the town itself had invited it, year after year, in a silent, terrifying ritual of self-preservation.

Chapter 6: The Night of the Unmaking

The Entity's Manifestation

The last vestiges of daylight bled from the sky, painting the horizon in bruised shades of purple and orange. A chill, entirely unrelated to the autumn air, snaked through Havenwood's town square. The initial tremor, dismissed as a geological anomaly by Mayor Thompson, had left an undercurrent of unease that even the brightly lit stalls and the cheerful, albeit forced, music from the gazebo couldn't entirely dispel. Sarah, having been unceremoniously escorted to the edge of the gathering by the hired 'security,' watched with a sickening certainty as the carefully constructed façade of normalcy began to crumble. The jovial masks the townsfolk wore were thinning, revealing the stark fear that lay beneath.

The entity's presence was no longer subtle. It was a tangible weight pressing down on the square, a silent, suffocating exhalation that seemed to distort the very air. The cheerful lanterns strung between the stalls flickered erratically, their light no longer casting warm glows but rather sharp, dancing shadows that seemed to writhe with a life of their own. The music from the gazebo, which had attempted to reassert a semblance of order, now sounded discordant, the notes snagging and twisting like tormented whispers. Sarah could feel it, a deep, resonant hum vibrating not through the ground this time, but through her very bones, a symphony of suppressed fear and ancient hunger.

It started with the periphery. The crowd, clinging to the illusion of a festival, milled about, some trying to resume their revelry, others casting nervous glances towards the encroaching darkness beyond the square. But the darkness wasn't just an absence of light; it was an active presence. The woods that ringed Havenwood, usually a familiar, comforting presence, now loomed with an unnatural menace. Their silhouettes against the twilight sky seemed to shift and contort, the trees appearing to lean inwards, their branches reaching like skeletal fingers.

Then came the whispers. At first, they were indistinct, a murmur that could be attributed to the nervous chatter of the crowd. But they grew, coalescing into distinct, insidious voices that seemed to echo from within each person's own mind. They spoke of doubts, of regrets, of hidden shames – the suppressed anxieties that the townsfolk had so carefully buried beneath layers of civic pride and manufactured cheerfulness. Sarah saw it in the widening eyes of Mrs. Gable, who suddenly flinched as if struck, her hand flying to her mouth. She saw it in Councilman Davies, who began to nervously pat his pockets, a look of profound disquiet clouding his features.

The illusions began subtly. A child's laughter, momentarily twisted into a guttural sob. A fleeting glimpse of a figure standing at the edge of the crowd, only to vanish when one blinked. The scent of roasting corn was abruptly replaced by the acrid odor of burning flesh, a phantom stench that made stomachs churn and faces blanch. These were not mere tricks of the light or sound; they were visceral assaults on the senses, designed to unravel the fragile grip of reality.

The entity was feeding. Not on flesh or blood, but on the very essence of fear, on the collective weight of unspoken anxieties and the festering resentment that lay dormant beneath Havenwood's placid surface. Sarah recalled Silas Croft's words, scrawled in his spidery hand: *"It thrives on denial, growing stronger with every averted gaze, every stifled scream. Our peace is its sustenance."* The town had offered its peace, its prosperity, its very existence as a perpetual offering, and now, it was being consumed.

The jovial atmosphere had entirely evaporated. The music screeched to a halt, the musician's face a mask of frozen terror as his fingers slipped from the fiddle. A woman screamed, a piercing sound that was quickly swallowed by the growing cacophony of confused shouts and panicked gasps. The lanterns, as if responding to a silent command, flared with blinding intensity, then died, plunging the square into a suffocating, absolute darkness.

In the ensuing blackness, the illusions intensified, becoming more concrete, more terrifying. The ground beneath their feet seemed to pulse, the familiar cobblestones rippling like water. Phantoms flickered into existence – distorted, nightmarish figures born from the deepest fears of those present. Sarah saw her own father, his face contorted in silent accusation, standing just a few feet away, his form shimmering and indistinct. She squeezed her eyes shut, forcing the image away, clinging to the memory of his genuine smile, the one that existed before the pact had taken its silent toll on him, and on all of them.

Panic, raw and untamed, began to spread like a contagion. The carefully maintained order of the festival dissolved into a stampede for the exits, a desperate scramble for safety that was quickly rendered futile. The shadowy figures that had been lurking at the edges of the square now moved inwards, no longer content to merely observe. They were not solid beings, but rather coalescences of the oppressive atmosphere, shifting shapes that glided through the panicked throng, their forms indistinct yet undeniably menacing.

Sarah felt a cold, clammy touch brush against her arm. She recoiled, her breath catching in her throat, but there was nothing there. Only the heavy, cloying darkness. The whispers intensified, now speaking directly to her, her name crooned in a thousand insidious voices, each one promising oblivion, release, or a twisted form of truth. They preyed on her isolation, her desperation, her fear that she had failed, that no one had listened.

Across the square, she could hear screams, not of fear, but of profound, soul-shattering horror. The entity wasn't just generating illusions; it was manifesting physical manifestations of their inner demons. A man, previously standing stoically, was now writhing on the ground, clawing at his own face as if trying to tear away a mask that wasn't there, his cries punctuated by choked sobs of terror. A woman, caught in the eddy of the panicked crowd, stumbled and fell. As others tried to help her up, they recoiled, their screams echoing the chilling realization that she was no longer entirely human. Her skin seemed to stretch and distort, her features elongating into a grotesque caricature of terror, her eyes glowing with an unnatural, malevolent light.

Mayor Thompson's voice, once so authoritative, was now a choked rasp, lost in the rising tide of chaos. "What is happening? What is this... this phenomenon?" His words were drowned out by the guttural roars and unearthly shrieks that now emanated from the very heart of the square. The ground beneath Sarah's feet continued to heave, the pulsing more pronounced, accompanied by a deep, guttural grinding sound, as if the earth itself were being torn asunder.

The central fountain, a symbol of Havenwood's enduring prosperity, began to bubble and churn. The water, instead of its usual clear cascade, turned a murky, viscous black, thick with an unidentifiable residue. Tendrils of darkness, like grasping hands, began to emerge from the water, reaching out, searching, drawing the terrified townsfolk closer. Those who were too slow to react, those caught in the swirling vortex of panic, were pulled towards the fountain, their screams cut short as they were enveloped by the inky blackness, disappearing without a trace.

Sarah watched, her heart a cold, heavy stone in her chest. This was the unmaking Silas Croft had written about. Not a sudden, violent destruction, but a slow, insidious unravelling, a descent into a nightmare reality where their deepest fears clawed their way into existence. The entity wasn't just a force; it was a mirror, reflecting the darkness within the town, amplified a thousandfold.

She looked at the faces around her, or rather, the shapes that had been faces. Terror had stripped away all pretense of civilization, reducing individuals to primal beings consumed by instinct. Some huddled together, their bodies trembling uncontrollably. Others, driven mad by the tormenting whispers, lashed out blindly, attacking perceived threats that existed only in their own fractured minds. The air was thick with the stench of fear, a potent perfume that seemed to invigorate the encroaching darkness.

The boundary markers, those innocuous stones etched with the symbols Sarah had pointed out to the council, began to glow with a faint, sickly luminescence. The hum intensified, a resonant frequency that seemed to vibrate through the very fabric of existence, a song of ancient hunger and insatiable need. The woods, now a solid wall of blackness, seemed to surge forward, the trees themselves contorting, their branches twisting into grotesque, writhing forms that mimicked the agonies of the townsfolk.

Sarah stumbled back, her eyes scanning the square, trying to make sense of the unfolding horror. The town council, their authority utterly nullified, were lost in the pandemonium. Mayor Thompson was on his knees, his face buried in his hands, his body wracked with sobs. Councilman Davies, his earlier disdain replaced by abject terror, was attempting to flee, only to be engulfed by a wave of shadow that seemed to surge from the ground itself. Councilwoman Albright, the pragmatist, was now a shrieking banshee, her screams echoing the primal terror of those around her.

The entity's manifestation was complete. It had shed its subtlety, its veiled threats, and revealed its true, insatiable hunger. It was the sum of all unspoken fears, all suppressed desires, all buried guilt. It was the darkness that had always resided within Havenwood, now given form and voice, and it was consuming its creators. The night of the unmaking had truly begun, and Sarah, the lone voice of warning, could only bear witness to the horrifying spectacle, a chilling testament to the price of a town's carefully guarded peace. The vibrant festival had become a tableau of torment, a festival of the damned, where every illusion was a truth laid bare, and every shadow held an unimaginable horror. The air crackled with the raw energy of fear, a potent fuel that the entity greedily consumed, growing ever more potent, ever more pervasive, in the heart of the doomed town.

Blackwood's Choice

The raw, untamed power radiating from the town square was a spectacle that defied Elias Blackwood's most stringent scientific observations. His initial detachment, the clinical curiosity that had drawn him to Havenwood, was rapidly eroding, replaced by a visceral understanding of the unfolding horror. He had positioned himself on the upper floor of the old clock tower, a vantage point offering an unobstructed, albeit terrifying, view of the pandemonium below. From this height, the screams were a less direct assault on his senses, yet their collective wail still vibrated through the stone, a mournful testament to the entity's unmaking. He had come seeking data, seeking to quantify the unquantifiable, to dissect the impossible with the cold, hard scalpel of logic. Now, logic felt like a flimsy shield against the encroaching chaos.

He watched as the town square, moments ago a tableau of festive celebration, transformed into a theater of absolute desolation. The lights, once merry beacons, flickered erratically, casting long, dancing shadows that writhed like infernal serpents. The very air seemed to thicken, to warp, as if reality itself was being stretched and distorted. He saw figures stumbling, their movements jerky and unnatural, like marionettes controlled by a malevolent puppeteer. The joyous music had indeed been replaced by a cacophony of shrieks and guttural cries, sounds that spoke of shattered minds and souls torn asunder. Elias, ever the observer, noted the patterns, the way the darkness seemed to coalesce and dissipate, the unnatural stillness that would precede a fresh wave of terror. He meticulously logged these observations in his mind, the scientist in him still fighting to maintain a semblance of order amidst the unraveling.

Then his gaze fell upon Sarah. He had seen her earlier, a solitary figure attempting to rally a lost cause, a small, defiant flame against an overwhelming darkness. Now, she was at the edge of the square, near the ancient oak, a place that seemed to be a focal point for the entity's grotesque manipulations. Elias adjusted his binoculars, his breath catching in his throat. He saw her take out the tuning forks, saw the precise, almost reverent way she handled them. He recognized the sigils etched into their metal, symbols he had encountered in his own research, cryptic markings whispered to possess properties that defied conventional physics. He remembered Silas Croft, the recluse whose fragmented notes Elias had so readily dismissed as the ramblings of a madman. Now, those ramblings seemed to echo with a chilling prescience.

Sarah struck the first fork. The sound, pure and clear, was a beacon in the oppressive din. Elias watched, his scientific skepticism warring with a burgeoning sense of awe, as the shadows around her seemed to recoil. The tendrils of darkness that had been creeping with predatory intent paused, their progress momentarily arrested. He observed a subtle shift in the atmospheric pressure, a ripple effect that his instruments, if he had them with him, would have surely registered. He saw the fear in her eyes, a raw, palpable emotion, yet it was tempered by a grim determination. He saw her take out the sonic emitter, the crude device Silas had clearly poured his desperate ingenuity into.

When Sarah activated the emitter, a beam of light, impossibly pure, pierced the swirling blackness. Elias felt a jolt, a primal recognition of something ancient and powerful being invoked. The symbols materialized on the corrupted fountain, burning themselves into the night. He could almost *feel* the energy emanating from them, a counter-frequency that vibrated against the entity's oppressive hum. He saw the possessed figures falter, their unnatural movements momentarily disrupted. It was a tangible effect, a defiance that Elias, the man of science, could not deny. He understood then that Silas had not been mad; he had been terrified, and he had been right.

The entity retaliated. Elias witnessed the wave of psychic energy that slammed into Sarah, a force so potent that it sent her staggering. He saw the tuning forks fall, the sonic emitter flicker. The whispers, he inferred, must have intensified, preying on her deepest fears. He saw her vulnerability, the way the darkness seemed to claw at her resolve. His mind raced. He knew the theoretical underpinnings of what Silas had been attempting, the concept of sympathetic resonance, of introducing discordant frequencies to disrupt an established pattern. He had dismissed it as speculative, bordering on pseudoscience, but now, he saw it in action.

He thought of his own research, the hours spent studying the subtle energetic signatures of consciousness, the anomalies that hinted at forces beyond his current understanding. He had collected data, cataloged phenomena, but he had never truly *faced* anything like this. He had remained a detached observer, an academician studying a specimen. But watching Sarah, seeing her courage in the face of such overwhelming power, something shifted within him. The responsibility that Silas had felt, the burden of knowledge that had driven him to his death, began to weigh on Elias. He was no longer just an observer; he was a witness, and a witness had a responsibility.

He knew, with a certainty that chilled him to the bone, that Sarah was outmatched, at least in terms of the raw power she could currently wield. The sonic emitter was failing, and while the tuning forks were potent, they were too isolated, too sporadic in their effect. He thought of his own collection, the unique devices he had brought with him, instruments designed to measure and, in some cases, to *manipulate* subtle energies. He had a device, a personal resonant amplifier, designed to detect and amplify specific sonic frequencies. It was experimental, highly unstable, but if calibrated correctly, it could potentially amplify Sarah's efforts tenfold, creating a sustained wave of disruption.

The decision, when it came, was swift, almost instinctive. It was a departure from his lifelong dedication to objective observation, a leap into the messy, terrifying realm of direct intervention. He couldn't stand by and watch this entity unmake an entire town, and he couldn't bear to see Sarah, her bravery so starkly evident, fall. He made his choice.

He scrambled from the clock tower, his descent a blur of adrenaline and calculated risk. He navigated the deserted, shadow-drenched streets, the screams and disembodied cries now a more immediate, tangible threat. The air grew colder, heavier, as he approached the town square. The lingering scent of Silas's description, a phantom rot, was undeniably present, a subtle perfume of decay that clung to everything. He moved with a newfound urgency, his scientific mind now focused on a singular, critical task: reaching Sarah and deploying his own contribution to this desperate battle.

As he neared the square, he saw Sarah circling the oak, striking the tuning forks with renewed vigor. The symbols on them pulsed, a fragile network of light against the encroaching darkness. The entity's whispers were a furious storm in his own mind, a disorienting barrage of doubt and fear. He could feel the pressure building, the air crackling with an almost unbearable tension. He ignored it, his focus locked on Sarah, on the small circle of resistance she was desperately trying to maintain.

He reached the edge of the square, the cacophony of the unmaking washing over him in full force. He saw Sarah stumble, her movements becoming less precise as the entity's influence pressed in. The whispers were now audible to him too, insidious suggestions worming their way into his thoughts, sowing seeds of doubt about his own actions, his own sanity. *"You are a fool, Elias,"* they hissed, their voices like dry leaves skittering across cold stone. *"Interfering will only bring you into our embrace. You cannot escape the inevitable."*

Elias ignored them. He reached into his satchel, his fingers closing around the resonant amplifier. It was a sleek, metallic device, far more sophisticated than Silas's emitter, but its purpose was similar: to project and amplify specific frequencies. He had designed it to detect and mimic the unique bio-acoustic signatures of certain rare fungi, a project that had led him down a rabbit hole of esoteric sonic research. He knew, with a certainty born of desperation, that the frequencies Silas had identified, and amplified through the tuning forks, were key.

He saw Sarah's struggle, the way she was barely holding her ground. He knew he had to act, and he had to act now. He took out the amplifier, its polished surface reflecting the distorted, flickering lights of the square. He quickly accessed his research data, pulling up the sonic patterns Silas had painstakingly documented, the specific frequencies that were designed to disrupt the entity's cohesive song. He selected a sequence, his fingers flying across the device's interface.

The amplifier hummed to life, a low, resonant thrum that began to build. Elias raised the device, aiming it towards the heart of the chaos, towards the corrupted fountain where the entity's presence was most concentrated. He activated the amplification sequence, and a beam of pure, resonant sound erupted from the device.

It wasn't just noise; it was a complex wave of harmonically charged vibrations, a carefully constructed sonic disruption designed to shatter the entity's hold.

The effect was immediate and profound. The pure tones from Sarah's tuning forks, which had been struggling to maintain their integrity, suddenly surged with renewed power, their frequencies amplified and sustained by Elias's device. The discordant symphony Sarah had begun now swelled into a powerful, sustained wave of disruption. The oppressive hum of the entity faltered, replaced by a grating, tearing sound, as if its very structure was being ripped apart.

The shadowy figures convulsed, their unnatural movements becoming more erratic, more violent, as if the anchor holding them in the entity's thrall was being violently severed. The whispers in Elias's mind, and undoubtedly in Sarah's, intensified, becoming a furious, discordant roar of pain and rage. He saw Sarah's expression shift, a flicker of surprise and renewed hope igniting in her eyes. She met his gaze across the chaotic square, a silent acknowledgment passing between them.

Elias continued to maintain the amplification, his scientific discipline now serving a higher purpose. He adjusted the frequencies, fine-tuning the output to match the subtle shifts in the entity's own chaotic resonance. He was no longer just an observer; he was an active participant, his knowledge and technology now allied with Sarah's courage and Silas's legacy. He watched as the symbols projected by Sarah's emitter, now bolstered by his amplifier, burned brighter, their forms becoming sharper, more defined. The darkness around them seemed to shrink back, unable to withstand the combined assault of ancient wards and modern technology, orchestrated by two unlikely allies.

The battle was far from over, but Elias Blackwood had made his choice. He had stepped out of the shadows of detached observation and into the terrifying, exhilarating light of action. He had seen the unmaking, and he had decided to fight it. And in doing so, he had found a purpose that transcended even his most ambitious scientific endeavors. He had found a cause worth fighting for, a battle worth waging, a fight for the very essence of reality itself. He was no longer Elias Blackwood, the detached scientist. He was Elias Blackwood, the intervener, standing shoulder to shoulder, albeit separated by a maelstrom of horror, with Sarah, in the heart of Havenwood's unmaking. The scientific pursuit had led him to the precipice of the impossible, and now, he was taking the leap.

The Town's Forgotten Past Awakens

The unmaking wasn't merely an external assault; it was an internal excavation, a violent exhumation of Havenwood's festering past. Elias, his resonant amplifier now a steady hum in his hands, felt the shift keenly. It was as if the very foundations of reality, already strained by the entity's presence, were groaning under the weight of resurrected trauma. The spectral chaos in the town square, once a manifestation of pure, unfettered malevolence, now began to coalesce into more specific, agonizing forms. These were not random phantoms; they were echoes, the psychic detritus of generations, given terrifying substance by the entity's insatiable hunger.

He saw it first near the old general store, a place where, in his research, he'd uncovered records of a brutal lynching during the town's early days. A spectral figure, gaunt and ragged, materialized from the swirling darkness, its form indistinct but its suffering palpable. Elias recognized the outline of a man, his spectral hands clawing at an unseen rope, his silent scream a silent agony that seemed to pierce through the auditory din. It was accompanied by a chorus of spectral voices, whispers of accusation and condemnation, voices that Elias realized were not just the entity's but the collective, unresolved anger of those who had participated in, or at least allowed, such an atrocity. The air around this apparition grew heavy with a phantom stench of fear and decay, a scent Elias had noted in Silas Croft's frantic journal entries, a smell that clung to places where profound human cruelty had taken root.

Then, a cluster of figures near the town hall began to writhe. Elias recognized the location as the site of a devastating fire decades ago, a blaze that had claimed the lives of several families, a tragedy the town had largely compartmentalized, attributing it to faulty wiring and bad luck. Now, those same families, their spectral forms shimmering with phantom flames, were replaying their final moments. He saw a mother shielding her child, her spectral eyes wide with terror as the spectral inferno consumed them. He heard the phantom crackle of burning timber, the desperate cries of those trapped, their pleas for help echoing through the amplified sonic landscape. The heat, though not physical, was a chilling sensation, a psychic residue of agonizing death. The townsfolk who had gathered for the town's centennial celebration, many of whom had previously scoffed at Sarah's dire warnings, were now face-to-face with the very history they had tried to bury. Their initial terror, born of the general unmaking, morphed into a profound, personal horror as these specific, undeniable manifestations of Havenwood's darkest moments converged upon them.

Elias watched, his scientific objectivity struggling against a rising tide of empathy and horror, as a former councilman, a man who had publicly dismissed Sarah as a hysterically overwrought woman, stumbled backward, his face a mask of pure terror. The councilman was staring at a spectral vision of himself, standing amidst the spectral flames of the town hall fire, his younger self seemingly ineffectual, paralyzed by inaction as the tragedy unfolded. The spectral entity's whispers, laced with the councilman's own buried guilt, now seemed to mock him. *"You stood by,"* the whispers insinuated, a chilling echo of his own inner voice. *"You let them burn. You let them die."* The councilman cried out, a raw, guttural sound that was instantly swallowed by the prevailing din. He clawed at his own face, his denial crumbling like dry earth under the force of these resurrected specters.

Further into the square, near the ancient oak that had been Sarah's anchor, new apparitions began to form. These were subtler, more insidious. Elias saw the spectral forms of children, their faces etched with a profound, unnatural sadness. They were remnants of a forgotten orphanage that had once stood on the outskirts of town, a place whispered to have been a site of neglect and quiet cruelty. These spectral children didn't scream or writhe; they simply stood, their translucent forms radiating an aura of profound desolation, their silent tears falling like phantom rain. Some reached out with spectral hands, their touch a phantom chill that caused the living townsfolk to flinch and recoil. The entity was weaving a tapestry of collective guilt, each thread a repressed memory, a forgotten wrong, a buried trauma.

Sarah, meanwhile, was fighting a different kind of battle. Her focus was on maintaining the sonic anchor, the pure frequencies that Elias's amplifier was bolstering. But the newly manifested specters, imbued with the raw emotion of their past lives, were a powerful distraction, a potent psychological weapon aimed directly at the minds of the townsfolk, and by extension, at Sarah herself. Elias saw her falter for a moment, her grip on the tuning forks loosening as a spectral vision of her own father, a man lost to a tragic accident years ago, materialized before her, his spectral form wreathed in the phantom scent of damp earth and pine needles, a scent that always clung to him. The entity's whispers, sensing her vulnerability, zeroed in. *"He wouldn't want this, Sarah,"* they hissed, their voices mimicking her father's gentle tone. *"He wouldn't want you to suffer. Give up. Let go."*

Elias felt a surge of protective instinct, a feeling alien to his detached scientific nature. He adjusted the amplifier, shifting its resonance to create a localized field of pure, stabilizing sound around Sarah, a subtle sonic shield designed to counter the more invasive psychic whispers. He knew the tuning forks alone weren't enough to ward off these deeply personal specters; they were designed to disrupt the entity's overarching cohesive hum, not to dispel the individual manifestations of trauma. His amplifier, however, could be modulated to target specific frequencies, and he was now attempting to create a harmonically disruptive counter-frequency to the spectral manifestations themselves, a sonic dissonance that might, at least momentarily, push them back.

The townsfolk, stripped of their denial and confronted with their own buried histories, reacted in a myriad of ways. Some, like the former councilman, succumbed to immediate, incapacitating terror. Others, however, seemed to draw a strange, defiant strength from the visceral reality of the manifestations. Elias saw an elderly woman, her face etched with the lines of a life lived through hardship, approach a spectral apparition of a child from the forgotten orphanage. Instead of recoiling, she reached out with a trembling hand, not to touch, but to offer a spectral comfort. "I see you," she whispered, her voice a fragile thread in the cacophony, but one that carried a profound weight of recognition. "We didn't forget you. Not all of us." The spectral child seemed to flicker, its form momentarily less defined, as if a sliver of peace had pierced through its endless sorrow.

This was the crux of it, Elias realized. The entity fed on repressed energy, on unacknowledged pain. By bringing these buried traumas to the surface, by forcing the townsfolk to confront the specters of their past, it was both tormenting them and, paradoxically, creating an opening for their release. The collective denial that had held Havenwood together, like a brittle shell, was shattering. And within that shattering, there was a nascent possibility of healing, of acknowledgement, of a true reckoning with their forgotten past.

Elias, his mind working at a feverish pace, began to analyze the sonic signatures of the individual specters. He noticed that the apparitions tied to acts of overt violence, like the lynching, produced a more dissonant, chaotic frequency, while those linked to neglect and passive suffering emitted a more mournful, resonant hum. This information was crucial. Silas's theories, he now understood, were not just about disrupting a singular alien entity, but about addressing the underlying energetic disharmony within the town itself, a disharmony amplified and weaponized by the entity.

He began to fine-tune his amplifier, not just to amplify Sarah's sonic anchor, but to introduce specific, counter-resonances targeted at the individual spectral manifestations. He focused on the lynching apparition first. The raw, ragged frequency it emitted was almost unbearable, a sonic embodiment of injustice and rage. Elias projected a complex series of harmonically opposing frequencies, attempting to introduce a discordant note into the specter's very being, a sonic paradox designed to unravel its manifestation. The spectral figure recoiled, its form flickering violently, as if struck by an invisible force. The accompanying whispers of accusation intensified, becoming a shrieking chorus of protest.

Then, he turned his attention to the spectral victims of the town hall fire. Their spectral cries, carrying the agony of their deaths, were laced with a frequency of profound loss and despair. Elias adjusted his amplifier again, this time projecting a sequence designed to resonate with empathy and remembrance. He was essentially trying to amplify the unexpressed grief of the living, to offer a sonic balm to the spectral wounds. He saw a spectral child, clutching a phantom doll, look towards him, its translucent eyes seeming to hold a flicker of recognition, a momentary cessation of its tormented replay.

The air crackled with a new kind of energy, a complex interplay of the entity's malevolent influence, Sarah's unwavering sonic defiance, and Elias's calculated intervention. The chaos hadn't diminished, but it had transformed. It was no longer just an external invasion; it was a collective reckoning, a purging of the psychic impurities that had festered in Havenwood for generations. The townsfolk, caught in the crossfire of their own resurrected past, were experiencing a terrifying, transformative ordeal. Many were still paralyzed by fear, their screams echoing the spectral wails around them. But a few, like the elderly woman, were finding a nascent strength, an unexpected resilience in the face of their spectral tormentors.

Elias knew this was only the beginning. The entity was powerful, and the depth of Havenwood's buried past was vast. He had brought his scientific acumen to bear on a problem that had previously seemed insurmountable, and in doing so, he had stepped into a role he had never anticipated. He was no longer just an observer. He was a participant, a conductor of a chaotic orchestra of spectral memories and sonic frequencies, a reluctant ally to Sarah, and a witness to the terrifying, undeniable awakening of Havenwood's forgotten past. The unmaking was not just about destroying the present; it was about reclaiming the past, about forcing the town to finally confront the ghosts it had so diligently tried to ignore. And as the night wore on, Elias understood that this confrontation, however horrifying, was the only path to salvation. He watched Sarah, her face streaked with sweat and tears, her resolve unwavering, and he felt a profound sense of shared purpose. They were both fighting the same battle, a battle against the darkness that resided not just in the supernatural realm, but within the very fabric of human history, within the unspoken traumas and unacknowledged sins that could, when awakened, tear reality itself asunder. The town's forgotten past had not just awoken; it had arrived, demanding its due, and Elias and Sarah were now its unwilling, yet determined, arbiters.

A Battle of Wills

The resonant hum of Elias's amplifier had become a tangible pressure in the air, a counter-frequency to the encroaching psychic discord. Sarah, her knuckles white where she gripped the finely tuned tuning forks, met his gaze across the spectral chaos. Her eyes, though strained, held a flicker of grim determination, a silent acknowledgment of the escalating war. The entity, sensing their coordinated resistance, redoubled its assault. The spectral manifestations weren't merely echoes anymore; they were actively shaping the immediate environment, bending the very air to their will. The phantom flames of the town hall fire seemed to lick closer, casting an eerie, flickering light on the terrified faces of the remaining townsfolk. The spectral lynched man, no longer confined to his original manifestation, began to drift, his silent agony now emanating a chilling aura that warped the ground beneath his feet, making it appear as if it were dissolving into nothingness.

Elias felt the drain acutely. Maintaining the broad-spectrum amplification and simultaneously attempting to isolate and counter specific spectral frequencies was like trying to juggle molten lead. Each individual manifestation, fueled by generations of buried trauma, possessed its own unique, agonizing resonance. The lynching specter, a vortex of pure rage and injustice, screamed a silent, sonic accusation that Elias felt vibrating in his very bones. He countered with a wave of disruptive frequencies, attempting to unravel its cohesive form, to introduce a paradoxical silence into its deafening torment. The result was a violent shudder that ran through the apparition, a momentary distortion, like a bad reception on an old television, before it snapped back into its horrific focus. The whispers, now a chorus of the lynching victims' tormentors, intensified, laced with Elias's own suppressed anxieties about his past failures, about the times he had stood by and done nothing. *"Coward,"* they hissed, their voices echoing his deepest insecurities. *"You are no different."*

Sarah, meanwhile, was wrestling with the spectral image of her father. The gentle mockery in the entity's imitation of his voice was a precisely aimed dart, seeking to pierce the armor of her resolve. *"Let them suffer, Sarah,"* the phantom father whispered, his spectral hand reaching out as if to comfort her. *"This is not your fight. You can't save them."* Sarah faltered, her breath hitching. Elias saw the subtle shift, the momentary crack in her unwavering focus. He immediately adjusted the amplifier, broadcasting a focused sonic wave, a pure, unadulterated frequency of remembrance – not of loss, but of the strength her father had always encouraged in her. He amplified the memory of his laughter, of his unwavering belief in her capabilities. It was a gamble, a desperate attempt to inoculate her against the entity's insidious manipulation. The spectral father flickered, the imitation faltering as the genuine echo of Sarah's memory began to assert itself.

The townsfolk were no longer passive observers; they were active participants, their fear and confusion a potent fuel for the entity. A woman who had lost her child in the town hall fire earlier in her life, now found herself confronted by the spectral form of her daughter, her tiny spectral hand outstretched, not in accusation, but in a desperate plea for a comfort she could no longer provide. The woman, initially paralyzed, let out a raw, primal scream, not of terror, but of agonizing grief and regret. This scream, laden with unprocessed sorrow, resonated with the spectral child, causing it to shimmer, its form wavering as if caught between the entity's influence and the raw outpouring of maternal love. Elias recognized this as a critical juncture. The entity thrived on repression. Direct confrontation, raw emotion, even pain, when acknowledged, could disrupt its hold. He focused a harmonic frequency tuned to empathy towards the grieving mother, attempting to amplify her grief, to validate it, to help her transmute it from a source of pain into a conduit of release.

Blackwood, his face a mask of grim concentration, was working with an almost instinctual understanding of the entity's machinations. He hadn't yet fully grasped the technical nuances of Elias's amplifier, but he understood the spiritual and psychological underpinnings of the entity's power. He moved with a fluid grace through the spectral chaos, his presence a steadying force, a beacon of focused intent.

He wasn't broadcasting sonic waves; he was projecting something far more primal – his own unwavering will, his refusal to succumb to fear. He would occasionally touch a spectral manifestation, not to dispel it, but to acknowledge it, to imbue it with a sense of understanding, a silent promise that its suffering would not be in vain. Each touch seemed to momentarily disrupt the entity's control, causing ripples of dissonance to spread through its pervasive influence.

Elias's internal monologue was a rapid-fire analysis of the sonic signatures. The lynching specter pulsed with a sharp, jagged frequency, laced with static – the raw sound of an unjust end. The fire victims emanated a sustained, mournful hum, punctuated by bursts of high-pitched distress. The forgotten orphanage children, those subtle and heartbreaking specters, produced a low, melancholic drone, a sound so profound in its sadness it threatened to drown out all other sensations. He began to realize that Silas's theories about Havenwood's intrinsic energetic disharmony were intrinsically linked to the entity's ability to manifest these specific traumas. The town was not just a victim; it was a fertile ground, its past a repository of unresolved emotional energy that the entity was now exploiting.

He recalibrated the amplifier, shifting its output to target the orphanage children's drone. He couldn't produce joy, but he could introduce a frequency of gentle remembrance, of quiet dignity, attempting to offer a sonic counterpart to their endless sorrow. He imagined it as weaving a counter-melody, a song of solace to their silent lament. As the new frequencies pulsed out, he saw one of the spectral children pause in its slow, aimless wandering, its head tilting as if listening. A faint, almost imperceptible shift occurred, a softening of its spectral edges. It was a fleeting moment, but it was a testament to the possibility of influence, of disrupting the entity's absolute dominion.

The strain on Elias was immense. His vision began to blur at the edges, and a dull ache throbbed behind his eyes. The constant barrage of spectral noise, amplified by his own equipment, was a form of sensory overload, pushing his physical and mental endurance to its limits. He risked temporal displacement if he overloaded his systems, a concept he had previously only theorized about. The line between scientific experimentation and outright survival was rapidly dissolving. He glanced at Sarah, her face illuminated by the spectral glow, and saw that she too was faltering, her breathing shallow.

The entity, a master of psychological warfare, was exploiting this fatigue. The spectral manifestations began to converge, their individual torments merging into a single, overwhelming wave of despair. The lynching specter's rage combined with the fire victims' agony, creating a cacophony of pure suffering that seemed to press in from all sides. Elias felt the familiar tendrils of doubt creeping into his mind. Was he capable of this? Had he underestimated the sheer, unadulterated malevolence of this entity? *"You are not strong enough,"* the whispers insinuated, now laced with the collective doubt of all the townsfolk who had ever felt inadequate, who had ever feared failure. *"You are just a scientist, playing with forces you don't understand."*

He forced himself to focus, to push back against the encroaching negativity. His scientific training, his years of rigorous study, were not mere academic exercises; they were his weapons. He remembered Silas's meticulous notes, the almost intuitive understanding Silas had possessed of these energies. He began to cross-reference the spectral frequencies he was detecting with Silas's theoretical models, searching for a pattern, a weakness, a specific sonic vulnerability. He realized that while the entity fed on fear and despair, it was also inherently chaotic.

Its power lay in its ability to manipulate existing discord. Therefore, the key wasn't just to counter its influence, but to introduce a higher order of complexity, a controlled dissonance that would destabilize its very structure.

Sarah, sensing Elias's struggle, took a deep, steadying breath. She shifted her stance, adjusting the angle of the tuning forks, and began to hum, a low, resonant note that seemed to vibrate with an ancient power. It wasn't the pure, amplified tone Elias was producing, but something more organic, more grounded in the earth, in the very soul of Havenwood. This hum acted as a subtle anchor, a connection to the natural world that the entity seemed to find antithetically disruptive. Elias recognized the sonic signature of the earth's own resonant frequency, a fundamental vibration that pulsed beneath all terrestrial life. He began to amplify Sarah's hum, blending it with his own technological output, creating a synthesized resonance that was both raw and refined, ancient and cutting-edge.

This new, combined frequency seemed to cause a visible tremor in the spectral manifestations. The interwoven tapestry of torment began to fray at the edges. The lynching specter recoiled, its form flickering violently, as if being torn apart by opposing forces. The spectral fire victims' cries lessened in intensity, their phantom flames dimming. The entity's pervasive whispers, once a unified chorus of malevolence, began to fragment, losing their coherence. It was a battle of wills played out on a sonic battlefield, a desperate struggle where the very fabric of reality strained under the supernatural assault. The outcome hung precariously in the balance, a testament to the raw, untamed power of the entity and the desperate, unyielding courage of those who stood against it. Elias, his mind a whirlwind of data and analysis, felt a profound sense of the precariousness of their situation. Every decision, every frequency adjustment, could mean the difference between survival and utter annihilation. He pushed harder, channeling every ounce of his scientific knowledge and his growing sense of responsibility into the amplifier, fighting for every sliver of coherence in the face of overwhelming chaos.

Chapter 7: The Aftermath and the Echoes

The Entity's Retreat

The combined resonance, a symphony of Sarah's grounding hum and Elias's technological amplification, struck the spectral chaos like a physical blow. The entity, its grip on Havenwood loosening with every pulse of this new, synthesized frequency, buckled. The spectral manifestations, no longer held in a cohesive, terrifying tableau, began to fray, their forms flickering erratically. The phantom flames of the town hall fire sputtered and died, leaving behind only wisps of cold smoke. The spectral lynched man, his silent agony amplified into a deafening dissonance, thrashed as if caught in an invisible current, his form stretching and distorting before snapping back into a more localized, less aggressive state. The whispers that had plagued Elias and Sarah, once a unified chorus of despair and accusation, now devolved into a cacophony of individual, panicked murmurs, each voice losing its borrowed strength and clarity.

Sarah felt the shift immediately. The oppressive weight that had been pressing down on her spirit, the suffocating despair the entity had so meticulously cultivated, began to recede. It was like the first breath of fresh air after being submerged for too long.

Her humming, which had been a strain against the entity's pervasive influence, now flowed with a newfound ease, the resonance deepening and expanding, carrying with it the quiet strength of the earth, a testament to life's persistent tenacity. She saw Elias, his face etched with exhaustion but his eyes blazing with a renewed focus, meticulously adjusting the sonic emitters, fine-tuning the frequencies to exploit the growing disarray within the entity. He was no longer just defending; he was orchestrating a deliberate expulsion.

Blackwood, sensing the opportune moment, moved with a silent purpose. He had been the anchor, the steadfast presence amidst the spectral tempest. Now, as the entity recoiled, he became the conductor of its retreat. He didn't need Elias's precise calculations; he understood the ebb and flow of spiritual energy, the undeniable push and pull of will. He began to trace intricate, glowing symbols in the air with his fingers, symbols that seemed to shimmer with an internal light, resonating with the very ground beneath their feet. These weren't mere sigils; they were pathways, conduits designed to guide the disrupted spectral energies away from Havenwood, back towards whatever dimensional nexus had birthed them. Each movement was deliberate, a focused expulsion, a silent command for the darkness to depart.

The effect was palpable. The spectral figures, once solid enough to induce terror, now appeared translucent, their tormenting energies dissipating like morning mist under a rising sun. The overwhelming psychic pressure that had suffocated the town began to lift, leaving behind an unnerving stillness. The townsfolk, who had huddled in fear, their faces a mixture of horror and disbelief, slowly began to stir. The phantom visions that had tormented them, the echoes of their deepest losses and regrets, flickered and faded, leaving only the raw, exposed reality of their trauma. They were still here, in the ruined town hall, in the lingering scent of ozone and the palpable absence of the malevolent presence, but they were no longer trapped in the entity's curated nightmare.

Elias felt the drain, a profound exhaustion that settled deep into his bones. His vision swam for a moment as the constant stream of spectral data abruptly ceased, leaving a void that felt almost as disorienting as the onslaught. The hum of his amplifier, which had been a lifeline, now seemed to fade into a gentle thrum, a lullaby to his spent nervous system. He lowered his hands from the controls, his muscles screaming in protest. He risked a glance at Sarah, her shoulders slumped with relief, her eyes reflecting the faint, dawning light that was beginning to filter through the shattered windows of the town hall. They had done it. They had pushed back the darkness.

"It's... it's gone?" a hesitant voice broke the silence. It was Mrs. Gable, her face pale, her eyes wide as she cautiously peered out from behind a fallen beam. Other voices joined hers, tentative, disbelieving. The fear hadn't evaporated entirely; it had simply receded, leaving behind a deep, cavernous dread. The experience had been too visceral, too real, to be simply forgotten. The specters had been manifestations of their own pain, their own history, and while the external source of that torment had retreated, the scars remained etched upon their psyches.

Sarah moved towards the townsfolk, her movements slow and deliberate, offering a comforting presence without pushing too hard. Her father's spectral voice, so recently a weapon wielded by the entity, was now just a distant memory, a fading echo of betrayal that her own strength had overcome. She met the gaze of those around her, offering a silent reassurance that the immediate danger had passed. Elias, meanwhile, began the arduous process of powering down his equipment, each movement slow and controlled, ensuring no residual energies remained to inadvertently prolong the disquiet. The silence that descended was heavy, not with dread, but with the weight of shared experience, with the raw, exposed nerves of a community that had faced its deepest fears and survived.

Blackwood stood by the shattered doorway, his gaze sweeping across the devastated hall. He saw the lingering spectral residue, faint traces of the entity's presence clinging to the emotional debris of the town. He knew this wasn't an end, but a reprieve. The nexus from which the entity had emerged remained, a wound in the fabric of reality, and it would undoubtedly attempt to breach the veil again. But for now, Havenwood was safe. The oppressive psychic atmosphere had lifted, replaced by the stark reality of the aftermath. The townsfolk were shaken, their faith in the ordinary shattered, but they were alive. They had witnessed the impossible, and in doing so, had been irrevocably changed.

The entity's retreat was not a sudden, cataclysmic vanishing act. Instead, it was a gradual unfurling, a slow withdrawal of its pervasive influence. The spectral apparitions, which had seemed so solid and menacing moments before, began to lose their definition, their outlines blurring as if viewed through rippling water. The cacophony of spectral voices, a terrifying chorus of torment that had threatened to shatter Elias's sanity, fractured into a million disjointed whispers, each one fading into the pervasive silence that followed. The oppressive weight that had settled over Havenwood, a psychic suffocation that had made every breath a struggle, began to lift, not with a sudden rush, but with a slow, agonizing exhale.

Elias felt the change as a physical sensation. The vise that had been tightening around his temples finally loosened, and the dull ache behind his eyes receded, replaced by a profound, bone-deep exhaustion. He could feel the subtle shifts in the ambient energy, the retreat of the malevolent frequency that had saturated the very air. He observed through the amplified visual feeds how the spectral flames of the town hall fire, which had burned with an unnatural intensity, now flickered and died, leaving behind only wisps of cold, spectral smoke that dissipated into nothingness. The phantom figure of the lynched man, no longer a towering embodiment of injustice, began to shrink, his spectral form becoming less defined, his silent screams replaced by a mournful, fading wail that was quickly swallowed by the returning quiet.

Sarah, her body trembling with the residual adrenaline and the immense strain of maintaining her focus, felt the shift in a more intuitive, visceral way. The psychic connection she had forged with the entity, a connection that had felt like a venomous tendril wrapped around her soul, began to retract. It was a painful, wrenching sensation, like tearing away diseased flesh, but with it came a surge of relief so potent it made her knees weak. She saw the spectral imitation of her father, his mocking words still echoing in the recesses of her mind, flicker and fade, the illusion finally broken. The strength her father had instilled in her, the resilience he had always encouraged, was now the force that propelled her forward, a bulwark against the encroaching emptiness left by the entity's departure.

Blackwood, his movements economical and precise, saw the subtle cues that Elias's technology confirmed. The intricate, glowing symbols he had etched into the very fabric of the town hall's spectral residue were acting as conduits, drawing the dissipating energies away from the physical plane. He saw the spectral manifestations, now weakened and disjointed, being pulled into these ethereal currents, their forms dissolving as they were guided towards the dimensional nexus from which they had originated. It wasn't a forceful expulsion, but a guided retreat, a redirection of the negative energy that the entity had so desperately sought to exploit. He felt the entity's residual anger, a cold, resentful fury at its forced withdrawal, but it was a fading echo, its power broken, its focus disrupted.

The townsfolk, witnessing the slow, almost reluctant disintegration of the spectral horrors that had tormented them, began to emerge from their terrified stupor. A collective gasp rippled through the assembled survivors as the palpable sense of dread finally lifted, leaving behind an eerie silence that was almost as unsettling as the earlier onslaught. The terror had left an indelible mark, a deep-seated unease that would undoubtedly linger, but the immediate, suffocating presence of the entity was gone. They looked at each other, their faces etched with a mixture of disbelief and dawning realization, the shared horror forging a silent, unbreakable bond between them. The spectral fires were out, the spectral screams had faded, and the spectral tormentors were retreating into the shadows from which they had emerged.

Elias lowered his hands from the amplifier, his arms feeling like lead. The feedback loop of spectral data had ceased, leaving him with a profound sense of disorientation. He looked around the damaged town hall, the debris strewn everywhere, the air thick with the lingering scent of ozone and something indefinable, something ancient and cold. He saw Sarah, her breath coming in ragged gasps, her eyes meeting his with a shared understanding of the immense struggle they had just endured. Blackwood stood by the doorway, his silhouette framed against the pale light of dawn, a silent sentinel who had guided them through the storm.

The oppressive atmosphere, a suffocating blanket of psychic dread, had finally lifted. It wasn't a triumphant victory, not the kind that ended with cheers and celebrations. It was a quiet, weary survival. The entity had been forced to retreat, its manifestation in

Havenwood fractured and weakened. The sonic frequencies Elias had generated, combined with Sarah's grounding resonance and Blackwood's symbolic anchors, had created a localized backlash, a disruptive interference pattern that the entity could not sustain. It had been forced back into its own dimension, its attempt to fester and feed on the town's collective trauma thwarted.

Sarah felt the withdrawal like a physical release. The tendrils of fear and despair that had gripped her heart began to loosen, the psychic chains that bound her to the entity's will snapping one by one. She looked at Elias, his face streaked with grime and exhaustion, but his eyes held a flicker of triumph, a testament to his scientific resolve. He had managed to create a sonic counter-frequency, a discordant harmony that had ripped through the entity's cohesive manifestation, sowing chaos within its carefully constructed dominion.

Blackwood, his gaze sweeping across the remnants of the spectral onslaught, felt the last vestiges of the entity's presence dissipate. The symbols he had drawn on the ravaged floorboards and the shattered walls were now glowing with a faint, residual energy, acting as a final deterrent, a promise that Havenwood was not an easy target. He had channeled an ancient form of spiritual defense, a force that predated Elias's technology, yet worked in perfect, albeit volatile, synergy with it. The entity had recoiled, its psychic energy disrupted by the combined assault of technology and primal will.

The silence that descended upon the town hall was profound. It was a silence born of shock, of disbelief, and of the sheer, overwhelming exhaustion that followed such a harrowing experience. The townsfolk, huddled together, their faces pale and drawn, slowly began to stir. They looked around, their eyes wide with a mixture of terror and dawning comprehension.

The spectral manifestations that had tormented them just moments before were gone, replaced by the stark, brutal reality of the damaged building and the lingering scent of something ancient and malevolent.

A woman, who had been confronted by the spectral image of her lost child, let out a shaky sob, not of fear this time, but of profound, grief-laden relief. The phantom child had faded, its spectral form dissolving like smoke, leaving only the raw, agonizing memory of loss. Her grief, no longer weaponized by the entity, was now her own, a burden she could begin to process, to carry, rather than be crushed by.

Elias watched as the last of the spectral residue dissipated. His equipment hummed softly, a testament to its resilience. He knew the entity was not destroyed, merely repelled. It had been forced back into its dimensional nexus, wounded and weakened, but capable of returning. The equilibrium had been shattered, and the attempt to restore it had come at a terrible cost, both physically and emotionally, for everyone involved.

Sarah moved towards the surviving townsfolk, her presence a calm anchor in the midst of their shattered reality. Her father's spectral voice, once a potent weapon of psychological warfare, was now just a painful memory, a phantom echo that her own inner strength had finally silenced. She offered a quiet word of reassurance, her voice raspy but steady, acknowledging their shared ordeal and the tentative hope of survival.

Blackwood walked through the debris, his gaze impassive. He knew the fight was far from over. The entity had retreated, but the door through which it had entered remained ajar. Havenwood had been a crucible, and it had forged something new within its survivors – a grim resilience, a newfound understanding of the unseen forces that could shape their lives. The immediate threat had passed, but the echoes of the entity's presence would resonate in the hearts and minds of Havenwood's people for a long time to come. The oppressive atmosphere had lifted, leaving behind the stark, unvarnished aftermath of a battle waged against an enemy that defied comprehension, an enemy that had been forced to retreat, leaving behind a stunned silence and a community forever changed.

Counting the Cost

The aftermath was a canvas of chaos, painted with the debris of merriment and the stark, brutal strokes of terror. The festival grounds, once vibrant with the promise of shared joy and community spirit, now lay in ruins. Tattered banners hung like mournful flags from splintered poles, the remnants of festive stalls lay overturned, their wares scattered and broken. The air, still thick with the acrid tang of ozone and the phantom scent of decay, clung to everything, a constant, nauseating reminder of the night's unspeakable events. Laughter had been replaced by the rasp of choked sobs, the scent of popcorn and roasted nuts by the metallic tang of fear and the faint, unsettling aroma of something ancient and wrong.

Sarah moved through the wreckage, her heart a heavy stone in her chest. The adrenaline that had fueled her through the ordeal was slowly ebbing, leaving behind a gnawing exhaustion that settled deep into her bones. Her hands, still faintly trembling, were slick with a mixture of sweat and something else – something warm and sticky that she tried not to identify. She knelt beside a young woman, no older than herself, her eyes wide and unseeing, staring into the middle distance as if still trapped in the spectral horrors that had manifested. The woman's breath came in shallow, ragged gasps, and a low, guttural keening escaped her lips. Sarah's father's voice, once a comforting sound, had been twisted into a weapon, a conduit for the entity's insidious whispers, and she could only imagine the personal hell this woman must have endured, her own deepest fears and losses weaponized against her. "It's okay," Sarah murmured, her voice hoarse, reaching out a tentative hand to rest on the woman's shoulder. "It's over. You're safe now." But the words felt hollow, inadequate against the chasm of trauma that had opened within the woman's mind.

Blackwood, his usual stoic demeanor etched with a weariness that seemed to penetrate his very being, was tending to a man who had suffered a deep gash on his arm, likely from a falling piece of debris. He worked with practiced efficiency, his movements surprisingly gentle as he cleaned the wound and applied a makeshift bandage torn from a discarded tablecloth. His eyes, however, held a grim recognition of the deeper wounds inflicted. This wasn't just physical damage; it was a psychic evisceration. He had seen the vacant stares, the uncontrollable tremors, the utter devastation that the entity had wrought upon the minds of those it had directly confronted. The carefully constructed normalcy of Havenwood, a fragile edifice built on years of quiet routine and shared history, had been not just chipped away at, but irrevocably shattered. The shared trauma was a new, unwelcome foundation, binding them together in a way no festival ever could.

The lingering psychic residue was a tangible weight, a suffocating blanket that pressed down on Sarah's senses. She could feel it clinging to the shattered remnants of the stage, to the upturned tables, to the very air itself. It was a subtle, insidious presence, a discordant hum beneath the silence, a whisper of the darkness that had been forced to retreat but not destroyed.

Her own psychic equilibrium, though bolstered by Elias's technology and Blackwood's ancient protections, felt precarious, like a glass about to shatter. The echoes of her father's betrayal, amplified and weaponized by the entity, still reverberated in the deepest recesses of her mind. She had fought against them, used them as fuel for her own resilience, but the memory, the raw wound of it, remained.

Elias, his face smudged with grease and sweat, was methodically dismantling his equipment, his movements slow and deliberate. The exhaustion was profound, a leaden weight that made each action feel like a Herculean effort. He powered down the sonic emitters, their intricate arrays now inert, silent witnesses to the battle that had raged. The hum of his technology, once a shield and a weapon, now faded into a quiet whir, a mournful dirge for the energy expended. He had pushed his systems to their absolute limits, wrestling with frequencies that defied conventional understanding. The mental strain of processing the entity's spectral data, of constantly adapting and counteracting its psychic onslaught, had been immense. He felt a deep, unsettling emptiness where the constant stream of information had been, a void that was both a relief and a disquieting reminder of the unseen war that had taken place.

"We need to start assessing the full extent of the damage," Elias said, his voice rough with fatigue, as he carefully packed away a delicate sensor. "Not just the physical, but... the others." He gestured vaguely towards the townsfolk, many of whom were still huddled together, wrapped in shock blankets and the comforting arms of others who, though equally traumatized, were functioning with a slightly more intact sense of reality. The word "others" hung in the air, a euphemism for the psychological devastation that was only just beginning to reveal itself.

Sarah nodded, her gaze sweeping across the faces of her neighbors, friends, and family. She saw the blank stares, the trembling hands, the sudden, unprovoked bursts of weeping. She saw the eyes that darted nervously at shadows, the bodies that flinched at sudden movements. The fear had been a tangible thing, a suffocating presence, and its sudden absence had left a vacuum that was being filled by a deep, pervasive dread. The carefully constructed façade of normalcy, the unspoken agreement to pretend that the strange occurrences of Havenwood were merely local legends and exaggerated tales, had been ripped away. They had all seen the impossible, and the knowledge of it was a burden that could never be shed.

Blackwood approached them, his gaze sharp and assessing. He carried no technology, no visible tools, yet he exuded an aura of ancient wisdom and immense strength. "The immediate threat has passed," he stated, his voice calm and steady, a much-needed anchor in the swirling chaos of emotions. "But the scars remain. They will need time to heal." He looked at Sarah and Elias. "Your combined efforts saved them. But this… this is only the beginning of the reckoning."

The "reckoning" Blackwood spoke of was already manifesting. A man, Mr. Abernathy, who had been a jovial presence at every town gathering, was now rocking back and forth on the ground, his hands clamped over his ears as if trying to block out phantom screams. He was muttering incoherently, his words a jumbled mess of accusations and pleas. Sarah had seen him earlier, his face contorted in terror as a spectral figure, mirroring his own estranged son, had loomed over him, whispering poison into his mind. Now, the spectral figure was gone, but the poison had already seeped in, its corrosive effects evident in his shattered psyche. Sarah felt a pang of guilt, a familiar sting that she had felt so often in the aftermath of her father's manipulations.

She had learned to compartmentalize, to separate her own pain from the suffering of others, but witnessing it so directly, so acutely, was still a bitter pill to swallow.

"We need to get them somewhere safe," Sarah said, her gaze fixed on Mr. Abernathy. "Somewhere quiet. They need… comfort."

"Comfort is a luxury we can afford them now, Sarah," Elias replied, his voice devoid of its usual scientific detachment. "But it won't erase what they've witnessed. The entity's influence, even in its retreat, has left a psychic residue, a contamination of the mind. It's like a virus." He rubbed his temples, the dull ache returning. "My equipment could detect and disrupt its primary frequencies, but the subtle, insidious corruption of the subconscious… that's a different matter entirely."

Blackwood nodded in agreement. "The mind, when exposed to such profound existential dread, can fracture. It is vulnerable, its defenses lowered. The entity preyed on those vulnerabilities, amplifying existing fears, twisting memories, creating personalized nightmares. For those directly confronted, the echoes will be profound. They will need more than just rest."

The words hung in the air, heavy with the unspoken understanding of the profound psychological toll the night had taken. The physical damage to the festival grounds, while significant, was superficial compared to the insidious damage wrought upon the minds and souls of the people of Havenwood. The carefully constructed normalcy that had always defined their lives was a casualty of the night's horrors, replaced by a shared trauma that would forever bind them, a constant reminder of the darkness that lurked just beyond the veil of their everyday existence. The communal experience, once a source of strength and unity, had now become a crucible, forging a new, unsettling identity for the town – one shaped by fear, resilience, and the chilling knowledge of the impossible. The cost of survival was not just physical, but deeply, irrevocably psychological.

The fractured state of the community was evident in the hushed, trembling conversations that had begun to replace the initial stunned silence. Neighbors who had known each other for decades now looked at one another with a new, wary understanding, their shared experience having laid bare the deepest vulnerabilities. Mrs. Gable, whose home had been a focal point for some of the spectral manifestations, clutched a worn rosary, her lips moving in silent prayer, her eyes still wide with a terror that no amount of reassurance could fully dispel. She had seen her deceased husband, not as the loving man she remembered, but as a spectral, accusatory figure, his ethereal form radiating an overwhelming sense of disappointment. The entity had not only conjured specters but had twisted the very fabric of their memories, turning cherished recollections into instruments of torment.

Sarah knelt beside her, offering a soft smile that didn't quite reach her own weary eyes. "We're all going to be alright, Mrs. Gable," she said, her voice a gentle balm. "We're here. We're together." But even as she spoke the words, she knew they were a fragile shield against the storm that raged within the older woman. The comfort she offered was genuine, born of her own deep empathy, but it was the comfort of a fellow survivor, not a healer. She, too, was still grappling with the echoes of her father's spectral voice, the chilling clarity of his betrayal, now amplified and weaponized by an otherworldly force.

Elias, having secured his equipment, began to move among the injured, his scientific mind now focused on a more immediate, tangible problem: triage. He helped carry those who couldn't walk, his lean frame surprisingly strong. He directed others who were more mobile, instructing them on how to tend to the less severe injuries, his voice calm and authoritative, a stark contrast to the emotional turmoil that he himself was undoubtedly experiencing. His mastery of technology had allowed them to fight back, to repel the entity, but the consequences of that fight were now laid bare for all to see. The psychic wounds were not something his equipment could directly mend, and that realization weighed heavily on him.

"We need to establish a temporary medical station here, at the town hall," Elias announced, his gaze sweeping over the scene. "We'll need to gather any available supplies – bandages, antiseptic, anything we can find." He looked at Sarah, a silent question in his eyes. "Do you think we can rally them?"

Sarah met his gaze, a flicker of her inherent strength igniting within her. "We have to," she said, her voice firm. "We've already faced the worst. We can't let this break us." She glanced at Blackwood, who had remained a silent, observant presence, his aura of quiet resolve a steadying influence.

Blackwood finally spoke, his voice carrying an authority that resonated with an ancient power. "The physical wounds can be mended with time and care. The mental wounds, however, are a different matter. They require understanding, patience, and a refusal to let the darkness define them." He turned his gaze towards the scattered remnants of the festival, the broken stalls and overturned seating. "This place," he said, his voice low and resonant, "was meant for celebration. Now, it is a testament to survival. The memories that will forever be tied to this ground are no longer of joy, but of terror. This is the cost."

The cost was not just measured in the splintered wood and torn fabric. It was measured in the haunted eyes, the trembling hands, the profound disconnect from reality that Sarah witnessed in so many of her neighbors. It was in the knowledge that their innocence, their belief in a safe and predictable world, had been irrevocably shattered. The entity had been a manifestation of fear, and it had fed on that fear, growing stronger, more invasive, until it had breached the very fabric of their lives. While Elias's technology and Sarah's intuitive connection had managed to disrupt and repel it, the lingering effects were a chilling testament to its power.

A young boy, no older than ten, was sobbing uncontrollably, pointing a trembling finger at the dark, shadowed corner of the partially collapsed bandstand. "He was there," the boy choked out, his voice cracking with terror. "He was right there. He looked at me." Sarah knew the entity had a particular knack for preying on the most vulnerable, for twisting innocent fantasies into nightmarish encounters. This boy, likely having imagined a friendly ghost or a playful spirit, had instead been confronted with something ancient and malevolent, something that had whispered promises of oblivion.

Sarah hurried over to him, her own heart aching with a fierce protectiveness. She sat beside him, not touching him, but offering a silent, steady presence. "It's alright," she said softly, her voice laced with a compassion that transcended her own weariness. "That was the bad thing. It's gone now. You're safe here." She met his wide, terrified eyes, trying to convey a strength she herself was only just rediscovering.

Elias joined them, his scientific brain already trying to find a practical solution. "We need to create a secure perimeter," he declared, his voice a little too loud in the hushed atmosphere.

"Make sure everyone is accounted for and moved to a safer location. The town hall, with its reinforced structure, is the most logical place." He looked at Blackwood, seeking his counsel.

Blackwood nodded slowly. "The emotional landscape of this place is still volatile. Any sudden movements, any loud noises, could trigger further distress in those who are still susceptible. We must proceed with the utmost care." His gaze lingered on the shattered remnants of the festival's vibrant decorations, a stark visual metaphor for the shattered lives of the townsfolk. "The illusion of normalcy is broken. Now, we must face the truth, however painful it may be."

The truth was a grim one. The cost of Elias's technological brilliance and Sarah's intuitive connection was the burden of knowledge, the terrifying understanding of a reality far more complex and dangerous than they had ever imagined. They had pushed back the darkness, but in doing so, they had also exposed Havenwood to its chilling reality. The festival grounds, once a symbol of community spirit, had become a stark monument to their collective trauma, a grim reminder of the night the veil between worlds had thinned, and the true cost of survival had been paid in the currency of shattered minds and lingering fear. The carefully constructed façade of their everyday lives had crumbled, leaving them exposed to a reality they could no longer ignore. The echoes of the entity's presence would resonate in the quiet moments, in the hushed whispers, in the haunted glances exchanged between neighbors, a constant, chilling reminder of what they had endured, and what they had lost. The communal trauma was not just an event; it was a new way of being.

Blackwood's Reckoning

Blackwood stood amidst the wreckage, the acrid scent of ozone and something more ancient, something like decay and fear, clinging to his worn leather jacket. His gaze, usually sharp and assessing, held a profound weariness, a weight that settled deeper than mere physical exhaustion. He had played a crucial role in repelling the entity, his knowledge of ancient wards and forgotten incantations proving invaluable. Yet, as he watched the traumatized townsfolk, their faces etched with a horror that would likely never fade, a gnawing emptiness bloomed within him. His actions, while saving lives, felt insufficient, tainted by a deeper, more complex truth that he had kept buried for too long.

Sarah approached him, her own exhaustion evident, but her eyes held a steady resolve, a quiet strength that had emerged from the crucible of the night's events. "You did good, Blackwood," she said, her voice raspy but sincere. "You saved a lot of people."

Blackwood offered a faint, almost imperceptible nod, his gaze drifting towards the shattered remnants of the festival stage, the splintered wood and torn banners a grim testament to the violence that had erupted. "Saving them from the immediate threat," he conceded, his voice a low rumble, "is a temporary measure. The true reckoning, the one that truly matters, is only just beginning." He turned to face her, his expression unreadable, yet charged with a gravity that made Sarah instinctively brace herself. "My methods, my knowledge… it all comes with a price, Sarah. A price I've been paying for a very long time, and one that Havenwood has now been forced to share."

He paused, as if gathering the courage to articulate truths that had been locked away for generations. "You see me as a protector, a guardian of ancient lore. And in a way, I am. But my family's involvement with... *this*... predates your town's founding. We are not merely observers, Sarah. We are... chroniclers. Custodians of secrets that should have remained buried."

Sarah felt a prickle of unease. Blackwood's stoicism had always masked a profound depth, but this was different. This was a confession, heavy with the weight of inherited burdens. "What do you mean?" she asked, her voice barely a whisper.

"My lineage," Blackwood began, his gaze sweeping over the devastation, "is tied to the study of entities like the one that visited us last night. Not to fight them, necessarily, but to understand them. To document their patterns, their methods of ingress, their effects on the mortal plane. My ancestors were... researchers. Scholars of the esoteric, drawn to the fringes of reality, to the places where the veil between worlds is thin."

He ran a hand over his grizzled beard, his eyes reflecting a distant, haunted past. "For generations, we have tracked these phenomena, noting their appearances, their durations, the patterns of psychic disruption they leave in their wake. It's a dangerous obsession, a dangerous inheritance. We are drawn to the abyss, and in doing so, we often find ourselves standing precariously close to its edge."

The implication was chilling. His presence in Havenwood, his seemingly fortuitous arrival just as things began to spiral out of control, wasn't mere coincidence. It was a pattern, a culmination of years of observation, perhaps even anticipation.

"You knew," Sarah stated, the realization dawning with a sickening clarity. "You knew something like this could happen."

Blackwood's silence was his answer. "My family has encountered similar manifestations throughout history," he admitted, his voice devoid of any attempt to soften the blow. "We've developed methods, not to banish, but to... contain. To mitigate the damage. My technologies, Elias's innovations, they are extensions of that ancient knowledge, adapted to a modern era. But understanding the nature of such beings also means understanding their power. And their potential for destruction is... immense."

He recounted tales of his forebears, of dusty journals filled with cryptic symbols and chilling accounts of spectral incursions that had decimated villages and driven communities to madness. He spoke of the allure of forbidden knowledge, the constant struggle between the desire to comprehend and the imperative to protect. His family had dedicated their lives to this macabre pursuit, their existence defined by the study of the very forces that preyed on humanity.

"The entity that manifested here," Blackwood continued, his voice taking on a graver tone, "is a parasitic consciousness. It feeds on fear, on despair, on the fractured psyches of those it targets. My family's research has shown that such entities are drawn to places where strong emotions have been amplified, where the fabric of collective belief is susceptible to manipulation. The festival, with its heightened sense of communal joy and shared experience, created a fertile ground."

He looked at Sarah, his expression a complex mixture of regret and grim acceptance. "My initial intentions were, perhaps, less altruistic than they appeared. I came here not just to observe, but to... test. To see if the ancient wards, passed down through my family, would hold against this particular strain of manifestation. My father, and his father before him, always emphasized the importance of empirical data. And in this line of work, Sarah, the cost of data is often measured in suffering."

Sarah recoiled slightly. The thought that he had, in some way, allowed this to happen, even for the sake of knowledge, was difficult to process. "You experimented on us?" she asked, her voice trembling with a mixture of anger and hurt.

"Not experimented," Blackwood corrected, his tone firm but not defensive. "Observed. And intervened when the risk of complete annihilation became too great. My family's mandate is to document, not to cause suffering. But the line between observation and consequence is often blurred when dealing with forces beyond our comprehension. I saw an opportunity to gather invaluable information, to refine our understanding of these entities, and yes, to test the efficacy of our defenses. I admit, my focus was on the 'what if,' the academic pursuit, perhaps more than the immediate human cost."

He admitted to the carefully orchestrated nature of his presence, the subtle nudges he had given Elias, the guidance on how to best deploy his technology, all in service of a larger, generational study. He spoke of the intricate network of observations his family maintained, a silent watch over the world's hidden vulnerabilities. He had been drawn to Havenwood because of its history, its subtle anomalies, the whispers of unexplained occurrences that had been dismissed as local folklore. His family had cataloged similar incidents across the globe, recognizing the tell-tale signs of psychic interference.

"My father," Blackwood said, his voice low and heavy, "was lost to this pursuit. He became too engrossed in the data, too detached from the reality of the dangers. He believed he could control it, outwit it. He was wrong. The entity he was studying consumed him, leaving behind nothing but a void and a legacy of fear." He looked at Sarah, his eyes holding a newfound respect, a stark contrast to the detached academic he had seemed before. "You, however... you possess an intuitive connection, a natural resilience that I have only read about in the most ancient texts. Your presence here, your ability to withstand the entity's influence and even to channel your own psychic energy to disrupt it, that was... unexpected. And deeply significant."

He confessed that his family's 'observations' often involved a degree of calculated risk. They would seek out locations where such phenomena were known to occur, not to eradicate them, but to document their manifestations. It was a dangerous, often lonely existence, a burden passed down through generations, a pact with a knowledge that promised enlightenment but delivered only peril. He had come to Havenwood with a pre-existing knowledge of its potential, an understanding that this seemingly idyllic town sat upon a nexus of unseen energies.

"My family believed that by understanding these entities, we could find a way to coexist with them, or at least to predict and mitigate their impact," Blackwood explained. "It is a desperate hope, born from a century of observing destruction. We are the librarians of nightmares, Sarah, cataloging the creatures that haunt the shadows, documenting their every move. But the act of cataloging does not inherently make us immune to their power."

The weight of his confession settled upon Sarah. His actions, while ultimately beneficial, were born from a place of calculated detachment, a professional curiosity that had almost cost them everything. He had been a guardian, yes, but also a scientist, and the boundaries between those roles had become dangerously blurred.

"I cannot stay here," Blackwood declared, his voice resonating with a newfound resolve. "My family's work... it attracts attention. Not just from the entities themselves, but from others who seek to exploit this knowledge for their own purposes. The knowledge I possess, the secrets I carry, they are a dangerous burden. Havenwood has weathered this storm, but for it to truly heal, it needs to return to its own quiet rhythm, unburdened by the echoes of my family's past."

He looked at the dazed faces of the townsfolk, the lingering fear in their eyes. "I have seen too much," he admitted, his voice almost a whisper. "My family has seen too much. The potential for destruction inherent in the unknown, in the forces we seek to understand... it is a humbling, terrifying realization. I have spent my life studying the abyss, and last night, the abyss stared back. And it showed me a glimpse of its true power."

He straightened, his weariness momentarily replaced by a steely resolve. "I will leave Havenwood. I will carry the burden of my family's legacy, and the knowledge I have gained here, with me. The world is far more complex and dangerous than most people imagine. And sometimes, the greatest act of protection is to remove oneself from the equation, to allow those who are untouched by this darkness to find their own path to healing."

He met Sarah's gaze, a flicker of genuine respect in his eyes. "You have a strength, Sarah, that I admire. You have faced the impossible and emerged not unscathed, but unbroken. Elias's technology, my knowledge... they are tools. But true resilience comes from within. Never forget that."

With that, Blackwood turned and walked away, disappearing into the pre-dawn gloom. He left behind a town in ruins, a community fractured by trauma, and Sarah with a deeper, more complex understanding of the unseen forces that shaped their world, and the equally complex, often dangerous, motivations of those who sought to understand them. His departure was not an abandonment, but a necessary act of preservation, a recognition that some battles, once fought, left behind scars that were best left to heal in solitude. The echoes of his family's ancient pursuit, and his own ambivalent role in Havenwood's ordeal, would forever linger in the quiet corners of the town, a stark reminder of the night the veil had thinned, and the true cost of knowledge had been laid bare. He carried with him the weight of generations, a lone sentinel moving back into the shadows, forever bound to the dangerous dance with the unknown.

The Truth Revealed

The dawn painted the sky in bruised hues of purple and grey, mirroring the desolation that clung to Havenwood like a shroud. The air, still thick with the metallic tang of ozone and the pervasive scent of fear, felt heavier than the physical debris scattered across the town square. Blackwood was gone, a phantom who had materialized from the shadows, orchestrated a terrifying symphony of survival, and then melted back into the anonymity from which he'd emerged. His departure, abrupt and decisive, had left a vacuum, a profound silence that screamed louder than the lingering screams of the night before.

Sarah stood where he had left her, the weight of his confessions settling upon her shoulders with the crushing finality of a tombstone. His revelation – that his family were not saviors, but chroniclers, researchers of the very forces that had descended upon Havenwood, that *he* had come not just to protect, but to observe, to test – churned in her gut. The word "experiment" had been thrown around, then retracted, replaced with a more palatable "observation," but the implication remained. Her town, her neighbors, had been part of a grand, generational experiment, their suffering a data point in an ancient, esoteric study.

The townsfolk, those who could still stand, were a testament to the night's horrors. Their faces, pale and etched with a terror that no amount of sleep would erase, were turned towards her, no longer with the dismissive glances of yesterday, but with a fearful, almost reverent, awe. The skepticism that had once met her theories, her fears, had been shattered, replaced by a stark, undeniable reality. They had seen. They had experienced. And in their eyes, Sarah saw a reluctant acceptance, a dawning comprehension that the quiet, seemingly ordinary existence of Havenwood had been a carefully constructed illusion, a fragile dam holding back an unfathomable tide.

Mayor Thompson, his usual bluster replaced by a profound, shaking weariness, approached her hesitantly. His formal attire was torn and stained, a stark contrast to the dignity he usually exuded. "Sarah," he began, his voice hoarse, barely audible above the rustling of debris. He stopped, his gaze sweeping over the wreckage, the shattered remnants of what had been a vibrant festival. "What… what do we do now?"

Sarah looked at the broken landscape, the faces of her community etched with disbelief and despair. Blackwood's words echoed in her mind: *"My methods, my knowledge… it all comes with a price,*

Sarah. A price I've been paying for a very long time, and one that Havenwood has now been forced to share." He had spoken of his family's legacy, of ancient wards and forgotten pacts, of a darkness that predated the town's founding. He had spoken of his father, consumed by the very pursuit that had nearly consumed them all. The truth, raw and devastating, was that Havenwood's peace had never been natural; it had been a carefully maintained equilibrium, a debt paid in secret for generations.

"We... we have to understand," Sarah said, her voice surprisingly steady, carrying the authority that Blackwood's departure had inadvertently thrust upon her. "What happened here wasn't random. It was... connected. To the history of this place. To things we've always ignored, or explained away." She thought of her own research, the dismissed theories, the whispers of the town's elders, the fragmented stories that had always seemed like mere folklore. They were not folklore. They were fragments of a truth too terrifying to confront.

The surviving elders, those who had managed to evade the entity's direct assault, gathered around, their faces a mixture of fear and a dawning, terrible recognition. Mrs. Gable, her usually stern features softened by shock, clutched a tattered shawl around her shoulders. "The old stories," she murmured, her voice trembling. "The ones my grandmother told me. About the 'Whispering Hollow,' and the... the appeasement."

Mr. Henderson, his hands shaking as he tried to light a cigarette, nodded grimly. "My grandfather... he was one of the original settlers. He spoke of a... a bargain. To keep the 'shadows' at bay. He always said it was just superstition, but..." He trailed off, his eyes wide with the memory of the night's horrors.

Sarah realized then that the weight of Blackwood's knowledge was now her burden. He had been the custodian of a secret history, and with his departure, that mantle had fallen to her. The carefully guarded secrets of Havenwood, the pacts made in hushed tones by generations past, were no longer buried. They were exposed, laid bare by the terrifying reality of the entity's manifestation. This was not just about survival; it was about confronting the very foundation of their town, the hidden truths that had shaped its destiny.

The process of communal healing would be a long and arduous one. How do you heal a town when the very ground beneath it is riddled with secrets, when its peace was bought with a currency of fear and appeasement? Sarah knew that the immediate task was to address the immediate trauma, to comfort the grieving, to tend to the wounded. But beneath the surface, a deeper wound festered, a wound that needed to be exposed to the light before it could begin to mend.

The following days were a blur of activity. Search and rescue efforts continued, though the hope of finding any more survivors dwindled with each passing hour. The makeshift infirmary overflowed with the injured, their physical wounds attended to by the few remaining doctors and volunteers, but their psychological scars ran far deeper. Sarah found herself at the center of it all, not by choice, but by necessity. The townsfolk looked to her, not for answers, but for some semblance of understanding, some guidance through the bewildering aftermath.

Mayor Thompson, regaining some of his composure, convened a town meeting, not in the shattered remnants of the festival hall, but in the more subdued setting of the community center. The air was thick with unspoken grief and a palpable sense of unease. The faces of the survivors were a testament to the horrors they had endured, their eyes haunted, their spirits battered. Skepticism had been replaced by a grim acceptance, a fearful acknowledgement of the supernatural forces that had ravaged their home.

"We... we owe it to ourselves," Mayor Thompson began, his voice wavering slightly, "to understand what has happened here. Sarah has... Sarah has been instrumental in uncovering certain truths about our town's past. Truths that... that may shed light on this tragedy." He looked at Sarah, his gaze conveying a mixture of reliance and apprehension.

Sarah stood, the weight of their collective gaze pressing down on her. She began to speak, her voice amplified by the microphone, echoing in the hushed room. She spoke of Blackwood's revelations, not in their entirety, but enough to convey the essence of his family's involvement, of their role as chroniclers of the arcane. She spoke of the entity as a manifestation of something ancient, something tied to the very land Havenwood occupied.

"Our town," she explained, her voice gaining strength with each word, "was founded on a place of... significance. A place where the veil between worlds is thin. The founders, in their wisdom, or perhaps their fear, made a pact. A pact to appease something that resided here, something powerful and ancient, to ensure their safety, their prosperity." She saw the flicker of recognition in the eyes of the older townsfolk, the confirmation of stories they had long dismissed.

She spoke of the "Whispering Hollow," not as a place of legend, but as a focal point, a nexus of energy. She described the appeasement ritual, a sacrifice, a symbolic offering that had been performed for generations, a silent debt paid to keep the darkness at bay. The entity that had manifested was not just an anomaly; it was a consequence, a debt called due when the ritual had been disrupted by the festival's unforeseen energies, amplified by the collective emotions of the crowd.

The silence that followed her words was profound, broken only by the stifled sobs of a few individuals. The carefully constructed reality of Havenwood had been irrevocably dismantled, replaced by a truth that was both terrifying and undeniably compelling. The dismissive glances were gone, replaced by a shared understanding, a communal trauma that bound them together.

"My family," Sarah continued, her voice softening, "has always been... sensitive to the town's history. We've kept records, fragments of the past. We knew there were... unusual occurrences, but we never fully grasped the extent of it until now." She spoke of her own research, the clues she had found, the dismissals she had faced. "The festival," she stated plainly, "was the catalyst. The amplified emotions, the disruption of the ancient patterns... it opened the door."

Mayor Thompson stepped forward again, his face etched with a newfound resolve. "This is... difficult to accept. But we cannot deny what we have seen. We cannot ignore the evidence. We have been living a lie, a comfortable ignorance, and the price for that ignorance has been devastating." He looked around the room, his gaze meeting the eyes of his constituents. "We must now face this truth, however painful it may be. We must understand the pact our ancestors made, and we must decide, as a community, how we move forward."

The days that followed were filled with hushed conversations, with the rediscovery of forgotten traditions, with the piecing together of a fragmented history. The surviving elders, emboldened by Sarah's forthrightness and their own harrowing experiences, began to share their fragmented knowledge.

They spoke of specific locations, of ancient symbols etched into stones hidden deep within the surrounding woods, of the cyclical nature of the entity's presence, tied to lunar phases and celestial alignments.

Sarah, with her newfound respect and her own extensive research, became the reluctant keeper of Havenwood's true history. She meticulously documented the accounts, cross-referencing them with the fragmented journals and oral histories passed down through her own family line. The narrative that emerged was not one of simple folklore, but of a deliberate, generational effort to maintain a precarious balance, a hidden pact that had kept Havenwood safe for decades, perhaps centuries.

The rituals, long relegated to the realm of superstition, were re-examined with a desperate intensity. Sarah, guided by the elders and the sparse, cryptic notes left by Blackwood's predecessors, began to understand the intricacies of the appeasement. It wasn't merely a sacrifice of goods or livestock; it was a ritual that involved specific incantations, the burning of particular herbs, and the channeling of collective intent. The entity, it seemed, fed on a specific emotional resonance, a vibration that was both primal and deeply spiritual.

The core of the pact, Sarah discovered, was not just to appease, but to *contain*. The entity was a powerful, parasitic consciousness, drawn to emotional turmoil. The rituals were designed to create a counter-resonance, a calming, grounding energy that effectively dampened its ability to manifest, to feed. The disruption of the festival had been a catastrophic failure of this containment, a sudden, overwhelming surge of amplified emotion that the ancient wards could not withstand.

The process of communal healing was inextricably linked to confronting this buried past. It was a painful excavation, unearthing secrets that had been deliberately hidden, truths that had been deemed too dangerous to acknowledge. But as the fragments of the past were pieced together, a sense of shared purpose began to emerge from the ruins. The townsfolk, humbled and terrified, started to understand that their survival was not a matter of luck, but a consequence of the careful, often fearful, stewardship of those who had come before them.

"My great-grandmother," old Mrs. Gable confided to Sarah, her voice raspy with age and emotion, "she was the one who kept the 'whispering stone' safe. She said it hummed with a... a deep sadness. She would sit by it, singing the old songs, to soothe it." Sarah realized that these weren't just quaint local customs; they were vital components of a long-forgotten defense system.

The community began to work together, not just to rebuild the physical structures of their town, but to rebuild their understanding of their own history. The whispers of the past were no longer dismissed as mere stories; they were treated as vital clues, pieces of a puzzle that held the key to their future. The elders, once marginalized by their adherence to tradition, found their voices amplified, their knowledge sought after with a desperate urgency.

There were still moments of profound grief, of raw, unadulterated fear. The memory of the entity's chilling presence, its insidious whispers, the sheer terror it had evoked, would forever be etched into the collective consciousness of Havenwood. But alongside that fear, a new emotion began to bloom: a sense of agency, of responsibility. They were no longer passive victims of unseen forces; they were inheritors of a legacy, inheritors of a duty to protect their home, not just from external threats, but from the echoes of their own buried past.

The communal healing was a process of acknowledging the debt, of understanding the sacrifice, and of embracing the responsibility. It was about accepting that the peace they had enjoyed was a fragile, carefully maintained state, a testament to the sacrifices of generations who had understood the true nature of the darkness that lurked just beyond the veil. Sarah, no longer an eccentric historian but a vital link to a forgotten truth, found herself guiding them through this painful, yet ultimately liberating, process. The raw, unfiltered truth had been revealed, and in its stark, terrifying clarity, Havenwood had found the first, tentative steps towards a genuine, and hard-won, recovery. The echoes of the past were no longer whispers of fear, but lessons in resilience, guiding them towards a future where understanding, not ignorance, would be their shield.

Lingering Shadows

The silence that descended upon Havenwood after Blackwood's departure was not the gentle hush of peace, but a taut, brittle quiet, laced with the lingering scent of fear and something far more ancient. The dawn, which had once promised a fresh start, now felt like a temporary reprieve, a brief pause in an ongoing, unseen war. Sarah walked through the debris-strewn streets, each step crunching on shattered glass and splintered wood, the ghosts of the previous night's terror clinging to her like cobwebs. The townsfolk, their faces etched with a weariness that no amount of sleep could erase, moved with a somber purpose, tending to the wounded, clearing the wreckage, and avoiding each other's eyes, as if the shared trauma was too raw to acknowledge directly.

The woods, a familiar, comforting presence for so long, now loomed with an alien menace. The dense canopy, once a source of shade and dappled sunlight, seemed to press down on the town, the shadows within deepening, stretching, and warping into shapes that played tricks on the eye. The usual symphony of birdsong was absent, replaced by an unnerving stillness, a watchful quiet that suggested the forest itself held its breath. Sarah found herself instinctively scanning the tree line, a phantom sense of being observed prickling at her skin. She knew, with a certainty that chilled her to the bone, that the entity wasn't gone. It had retreated, perhaps, drawn back into the primordial depths from which it had emerged, but it had not been vanquished. The pact, the rituals, the appeasement – these were not abstract concepts anymore; they were the fragile bulwarks that kept a monstrous reality at bay. And if Havenwood, or any of its inhabitants, forgot the price of their continued existence, the 'guile of night' would surely resurface.

The weight of this knowledge was a constant, heavy cloak Sarah wore. Blackwood had gifted her with the burden of understanding, and with that understanding came the unending responsibility of vigilance. Her research, once a solitary pursuit fueled by a nagging curiosity, was now a desperate endeavor, a race against the tide of communal amnesia. She meticulously cataloged the surviving elders' accounts, cross-referencing them with her own family's cryptic journals, trying to decipher the nuances of the appeasement rituals, the specific energies that attracted the entity, and the precise methods of its containment. It was like piecing together a shattered mirror, each shard reflecting a distorted piece of the truth, and only by assembling them all could she hope to see the full, terrifying image.

The communal gatherings, held in the still-reeling aftermath, were a strange mix of shared grief and hesitant hope. Mayor Thompson, his initial attempts at normalcy overshadowed by the palpable fear that gripped the town, struggled to steer the conversation. He spoke of rebuilding, of resilience, but his words often faltered as the specter of the entity loomed in the collective consciousness. Sarah, now the reluctant authority on Havenwood's hidden history, found herself stepping forward, her voice steady despite the tremor in her hands. She explained, in measured tones, the cyclical nature of the entity's presence, the importance of maintaining the wards, and the necessity of adhering to the ancient pacts.

"It's not just about appeasing something," she explained to a hushed crowd in the community center, the lingering smell of antiseptic doing little to mask the underlying fear. "It's about balance. The entity is drawn to emotional dissonance, to chaos. Our ancestors understood that. They created a counter-harmony, a steady hum of communal intent that kept it dormant." She gestured towards the woods, a silent accusation. "The festival, with its amplified emotions, its sudden disruption of the established patterns... it was a siren song, an invitation they couldn't refuse."

The older generation listened with a solemn understanding, their own fragmented memories aligning with Sarah's findings. Mrs. Gable, her eyes sharp despite her age, spoke of the 'singing stones' hidden deep in the woods, stones that, according to her grandmother, vibrated with a mournful energy, and were meant to be soothed with ancient chants. Mr. Henderson recounted how his father, a man of few words and even fewer beliefs in the supernatural, had always insisted on performing a small, private ritual on the eve of significant celestial events, a ritual he'd dismissed as a harmless eccentricity. Now, Sarah understood it as a desperate, personal act of warding, an individual's attempt to maintain the failing balance.

The challenge wasn't just in understanding the past, but in ensuring it wouldn't be forgotten. The human tendency towards selective memory, the desire to return to normalcy, was a dangerous current Sarah had to fight against. She organized informal gatherings, encouraging the elders to share their stories, to teach the younger generations the songs, the symbols, the specific ways of observing the subtle shifts in the natural world that signaled the entity's proximity. Her own home, once a sanctuary of quiet study, became a repository of this rediscovered lore, filled with maps marked with ancient glyphs, shelves overflowing with yellowed texts, and the faint, ever-present aroma of dried herbs used in protective incense.

The woods remained a constant source of unease. There were reports of strange occurrences, fleeting shadows glimpsed at the edge of vision, an unnatural cold that descended even on warm days, and the unsettling feeling of being watched that no amount of rationalization could dispel. A group of teenagers, emboldened by a bravado born of denial, ventured too deep into the shadowed trees and returned hours later, pale and shaken, speaking of disembodied whispers that seemed to emanate from the very air, of branches that moved without wind, and a suffocating sense of despair that had almost overwhelmed them. They were met not with disbelief, but with a grim understanding. Sarah, hearing their fragmented accounts, felt a cold dread bloom in her chest. The entity was testing the boundaries, probing for weaknesses, reminding them of its persistent, lurking presence.

The concept of 'home' had irrevocably changed for the people of Havenwood. It was no longer just a collection of houses and streets, but a place intrinsically linked to a dangerous, unseen force. The town square, once a vibrant hub of activity, now felt exposed, vulnerable. The festival hall, its structure partially repaired, stood as a stark reminder of the night the illusion of safety shattered. Sarah found herself drawn to the edge of town, to the boundary where the manicured lawns gave way to the untamed wilderness. She would stand there, listening to the unnerving silence, feeling the subtle shift in the air, a constant, low-level hum of apprehension that had become as familiar as her own heartbeat.

Blackwood's words echoed in her mind: *"My methods, my knowledge… it all comes with a price, Sarah. A price I've been paying for a very long time, and one that Havenwood has now been forced to share."* He had left her with the knowledge, but also with the chilling awareness of the ongoing struggle. The pact was not a one-time negotiation; it was a perpetual engagement, a constant negotiation with forces that defied easy understanding. The price was vigilance. The price was memory. The price was the willingness to confront the darkness, not just in the woods, but within themselves, the capacity for fear and despair that the entity fed upon.

The task of education was arduous. Not everyone was receptive to the notion of a generations-old pact with a malevolent entity. Some clung to the hope that it was a singular, albeit terrifying, event, a bizarre anomaly that would fade with time. Others, traumatized into a state of denial, simply refused to speak of it, their silence a fragile shield against the returning terror. Sarah understood their resistance, the desperate need for normalcy, but she also saw the danger in their willful ignorance. A single lapse, a single moment of forgetting, could invite disaster back into their lives.

She began to weave the historical narrative into the fabric of their everyday lives. She organized community gardening projects that subtly incorporated the planting of specific herbs known for their protective properties. She introduced storytelling sessions for children, carefully curated tales that, while not overtly terrifying, emphasized the importance of respect for nature, of listening to the unseen, and of remembering the lessons of the past. She sought out any physical remnants of the pact – ancient carvings on stones, weathered markers in the woods, forgotten artifacts in the town archives – and brought them into the light, using them as tangible evidence of the enduring truth.

The lingering shadows were not merely metaphorical. The woods seemed to hold a physical manifestation of the entity's presence, a palpable miasma that clung to the air. Animals behaved erratically near the treeline, their movements skittish, their calls often replaced by an unnerving silence. Hikers reported feeling an oppressive weight, a sense of being herded or guided away from certain areas. Sarah found herself spending more and more time in the very woods that now represented Havenwood's greatest vulnerability, studying the subtle changes in flora, the unusual patterns of decay, the unnerving stillness that pervaded certain groves. She was charting the entity's territory, trying to understand its boundaries, its habits, its vulnerabilities.

The memory of Blackwood's final warning, his gaze intense as he spoke of his family's legacy and the constant struggle, played on repeat in her mind. *"They are not gone. They merely sleep. And the sleep of such things is rarely peaceful."* This was not an end, she knew. It was a new beginning, a new phase of existence for Havenwood, one defined by a constant, quiet war waged not with weapons, but with memory, with understanding, and with the unwavering commitment to the forgotten pact. The weight of vigilance was hers to bear, and the echoes of the past, she realized, were not just warnings, but the very foundation of their continued survival. She was the guardian of their forgotten history, the keeper of the flame that kept the encroaching darkness at bay, and the ever-watchful eye on the edge of the woods, listening for the first subtle stirrings of the ancient, slumbering threat. The town had survived the immediate onslaught, but the true battle, the battle for remembrance, had only just begun.

Chapter 8: The Vigil and the Scar

Sarah's New Role

The silence that followed Blackwood's departure was a heavy, suffocating blanket, far more oppressive than the aftermath of the initial terror. Havenwood, once a picturesque haven, now felt like a hollowed-out shell, its inhabitants moving with a phantom limb, forever sensing a loss that was still very much present. Sarah found herself walking these familiar, yet now alien, streets, the crunch of debris underfoot a constant, jarring reminder of the night the veil had been irrevocably torn. The scent of damp earth and pine, once a comforting embrace, now carried an undercurrent of ancient dread, a whisper of what lurked just beyond the tangible world. The townsfolk, their eyes hollowed by sleepless nights and the stark realization of their precarious existence, moved with a quiet solemnity, tending to the immediate needs of survival while the unspoken question of 'what next?' hung heavy in the air.

The woods, the silent, brooding sentinels of Havenwood, had transformed in Sarah's perception. The dense canopy, once a welcoming shield against the sun's glare, now felt like a suffocating shroud, the shadows within deepening, stretching, and contorting into shapes that danced at the periphery of her vision. The usual symphony of birdsong had been replaced by an unnerving stillness, a watchful silence that seemed to indicate the very trees held their breath. An instinct, honed by Blackwood's cryptic warnings and her own burgeoning understanding, kept her scanning the tree line, a persistent, prickling sensation on her skin that suggested she was perpetually observed. The entity was not gone. It had merely receded, drawn back into the primeval depths from which it had emerged, but it had not been defeated. The pact, the rituals, the appeasement – these were no longer abstract concepts of folklore; they were the fragile bulwarks against a terrifying, encroaching reality. And if Havenwood, or any of its inhabitants, dared to forget the price of their continued existence, the 'guile of night' would surely awaken once more.

The weight of this knowledge settled upon Sarah like a physical cloak. Blackwood had bestowed upon her the unenviable gift of understanding, and with it came the unending, crushing burden of vigilance. Her research, once a solitary pursuit driven by an insatiable curiosity, had transformed into a desperate, frantic endeavor, a relentless race against the tide of communal amnesia. She meticulously documented the accounts of the surviving elders, cross-referencing them with her family's cryptic journals, striving to decipher the intricate nuances of the appeasement rituals, the specific energies that acted as a siren song to the entity, and the precise methods of its containment. It was akin to assembling a shattered mirror, each shard reflecting a distorted fragment of the truth, and only by painstakingly piecing them all together could she hope to grasp the full, terrifying image.

The communal gatherings, held in the raw, fractured aftermath, were a disquieting blend of shared grief and a fragile, desperate hope. Mayor Thompson, his initial attempts at projecting normalcy drowned out by the palpable fear that gripped the town, struggled to steer the narrative. He spoke of rebuilding, of resilience, but his words often faltered, dissolving into the unspoken acknowledgment of the entity's lingering presence in their collective consciousness. Sarah, now the reluctant oracle of Havenwood's hidden history, found herself stepping forward, her voice surprisingly steady despite the tremor in her hands. She explained, in measured, precise tones, the cyclical nature of the entity's presence, the critical importance of maintaining the ancient wards, and the absolute necessity of adhering to the pacts forged in ages past.

"It's not simply about appeasing a force," she explained to a hushed, attentive crowd gathered in the still-reeling community center, the faint scent of antiseptic doing little to mask the underlying current of fear. "It's about maintaining a delicate balance. The entity is drawn to emotional dissonance, to chaos. Our ancestors understood this profoundly. They created a counter-harmony, a steady, resonant hum of communal intent that served to keep it dormant." She gestured towards the dense, foreboding line of trees at the edge of town, a silent accusation. "The festival, with its amplified emotions, its sudden, jarring disruption of the established patterns... it acted as a siren song, an irresistible invitation they couldn't refuse."

The older generation listened with a solemn, almost reverent understanding, their own fragmented memories coalescing with Sarah's meticulous findings. Mrs. Gable, her eyes still sharp and piercing despite her advanced age, spoke of the 'singing stones' reputedly hidden deep within the woods, stones that, according to her grandmother's whispered tales, vibrated with a mournful, resonant energy and were meant to be soothed with ancient, forgotten chants. Mr. Henderson recounted how his father, a man of few words and even fewer beliefs in the supernatural, had always insisted on performing a small, private ritual on the eve of significant celestial events, a ritual he had always dismissed as a harmless, if peculiar, eccentricity. Now, Sarah understood it for what it truly was: a desperate, personal act of warding, a lone individual's valiant attempt to maintain the failing cosmic balance.

The true challenge, Sarah realized, lay not merely in uncovering the past, but in ensuring that its vital lessons would not be swallowed by the sands of time. The inherent human tendency towards selective memory, the deep-seated desire to return to a perceived normalcy, was a powerful, dangerous current that Sarah found herself battling constantly. She began organizing informal gatherings, actively encouraging the elders to share their stories, to impart their knowledge to the younger generations, teaching them the songs, the symbols, and the specific, subtle ways of observing the natural world that served as early indicators of the entity's proximity. Her own home, once a sanctuary of quiet, introspective study, gradually transformed into a veritable repository of this rediscovered lore. It became a space filled with hand-drawn maps marked with ancient, enigmatic glyphs, shelves overflowing with fragile, yellowed texts, and the faint, ever-present aroma of dried herbs used in protective incenses, a testament to the new custodianship she had willingly embraced.

The woods remained a constant, pervasive source of unease, a palpable manifestation of the lingering threat. Reports of strange occurrences began to trickle in, fleeting shadows glimpsed at the very edge of vision, an unnatural cold that descended even on the warmest days, and the unsettling, persistent feeling of being watched that no amount of rationalization could dispel. A group of teenagers, their bravado a flimsy shield against their underlying fear, ventured too deep into the shadowed embrace of the trees and returned hours later, pale, shaken, and speaking in hushed, fragmented whispers of disembodied voices that seemed to emanate from the very air, of branches that moved with no discernible wind, and of a suffocating, all-encompassing sense of despair that had almost claimed them. They were met not with disbelief, but with a grim, collective understanding. Sarah, listening to their broken accounts, felt a cold dread bloom in her chest. The entity was testing the boundaries, probing for weaknesses, a stark reminder of its persistent, lurking, and patient presence.

The very concept of 'home' had irrevocably shifted for the inhabitants of Havenwood. It was no longer merely a collection of houses, streets, and familiar landmarks; it was a place intrinsically, and terrifyingly, linked to a dangerous, unseen force. The town square, once a vibrant hub of communal activity and everyday life, now felt exposed, vulnerable, a stage upon which the horrors of the past had played out. The festival hall, its structure partially repaired, stood as a stark, enduring monument to the night the illusion of safety had shattered into a million irreparable pieces. Sarah found herself increasingly drawn to the edge of town, to the liminal space where the manicured lawns of civilization gave way to the wild, untamed expanse of the wilderness. She would stand there for hours, listening to the unnerving silence, feeling the subtle, almost imperceptible shifts in the air, a constant, low-level hum of apprehension that had become as familiar and ingrained as her own heartbeat.

Blackwood's final words echoed incessantly in her mind, his gaze intense, his voice heavy with the burden of a legacy he had carried for so long: *"My methods, my knowledge… it all comes with a price, Sarah. A price I've been paying for a very long time, and one that Havenwood has now been forced to share."* He had left her with the raw knowledge, but also with the chilling awareness of an ongoing, protracted struggle. The pact was not a single, decisive negotiation; it was a perpetual engagement, a constant, delicate negotiation with forces that defied easy comprehension. The price, she understood now with grim clarity, was vigilance. The price was remembrance. The price was the unwavering willingness to confront the encroaching darkness, not just in the silent depths of the woods, but within the very fabric of their own being, acknowledging the capacity for fear and despair that the entity so readily exploited.

The task of educating the town was arduous, a painstaking process of chipping away at ingrained disbelief and ingrained normalcy. Not everyone was readily receptive to the notion of a generations-old pact with a malevolent, ancient entity. Some desperately clung to the hope that the recent events were a singular, albeit terrifying, anomaly, a bizarre aberration that would fade with the passage of time. Others, traumatized into a state of profound denial, simply refused to speak of the entity, their silence a fragile, inadequate shield against the encroaching terror. Sarah understood their resistance, the desperate, primal need for the comforting illusion of normalcy, but she also recognized the inherent danger in their willful ignorance. A single lapse, a solitary moment of forgetting, could, and likely would, invite disaster back into their lives with devastating consequences.

She began to weave the fragmented historical narrative into the very fabric of their everyday lives, subtly at first, then with increasing deliberation. She organized community gardening projects, projects that subtly incorporated the planting of specific herbs known for their ancient protective properties. She introduced storytelling sessions for children, carefully curated tales that, while not overtly terrifying, emphasized the profound importance of respect for nature, the necessity of listening to the unseen, and the enduring value of remembering the hard-won lessons of the past. She actively sought out any physical remnants of the pact – ancient carvings etched into weathered stones, forgotten markers hidden deep within the woods, overlooked artifacts buried within the dusty archives of the town – and brought them into the light, using them as tangible, irrefutable evidence of the enduring truth that lay beneath the veneer of their everyday lives.

The lingering shadows were not merely metaphorical constructs. The woods seemed to hold a physical manifestation of the entity's insidious presence, a palpable miasma that clung to the air, chilling it to the bone. Animals began to behave erratically near the treeline, their movements skittish and unnatural, their usual calls often replaced by an unnerving, absolute silence. Hikers reported experiencing an oppressive weight, a disorienting sense of being herded or subtly guided away from certain, ill-defined areas. Sarah found herself spending an increasing amount of her time in the very woods that now represented Havenwood's greatest vulnerability, meticulously studying the subtle, almost imperceptible changes in the flora, the unusual patterns of decay, the unnerving stillness that pervaded certain, specific groves. She was charting the entity's territory, attempting to understand its boundaries, its habits, its potential weaknesses, her knowledge growing with each passing, anxious day.

The memory of Blackwood's final, urgent warning, his gaze burning with a desperate intensity as he spoke of his family's burdensome legacy and the constant, unrelenting struggle, played on repeat in her mind like a broken record. *"They are not gone. They merely sleep. And the sleep of such things is rarely peaceful."* This was not an end, she knew with a chilling certainty. It was a new beginning, a new, terrifying phase of existence for Havenwood, one defined by a constant, quiet war waged not with conventional weapons, but with the fragile, yet potent, forces of memory, understanding, and the unwavering commitment to the forgotten pact. The heavy weight of vigilance was now hers to bear, and the echoes of the past, she realized with a dawning, grim comprehension, were not merely warnings; they were the very bedrock upon which their continued survival depended. She was the guardian of their forgotten history, the keeper of the flickering flame that held the encroaching darkness at bay, and the ever-watchful eye positioned on the edge of the woods, perpetually listening for the first subtle, chilling stirrings of the ancient, slumbering threat. The town had survived the immediate, brutal onslaught, but the true battle, the critical battle for remembrance, had only just begun, a silent war waged in the hearts and minds of every inhabitant. Her new role was not one of choice, but of stark, terrifying necessity.

Sarah made the conscious decision to remain in Havenwood. The thought of leaving, of abandoning the town to its fate or to the inevitable tide of forgetfulness, was an unbearable one. Blackwood had entrusted her with a legacy, a burden of knowledge that had become as much a part of her as her own DNA. She was no longer just Sarah, the quiet historian; she was Sarah, the protector, the keeper of the flame, the guardian against the 'guile of night'. Her small, unassuming cottage on the edge of town, with its overgrown garden and slightly askew porch, felt less like a home and more like a command center. The library, once a sanctuary of quiet contemplation, was now transformed into the epicenter of her new existence. Shelves that had once held novels and poetry now groaned under the weight of ancient tomes, meticulously copied journals, and her own burgeoning collection of notes and observations.

She dedicated herself to the singular, overwhelming task of ensuring that Havenwood would never again fall prey to complacency. The memory of the recent horror, the visceral terror of the entity's presence, was already beginning to fade for some, a natural human response to overwhelming trauma, but a dangerous one. Sarah worked tirelessly to preserve that memory, not to inflict fear, but to instill a deep, abiding respect for the forces they were now irrevocably bound to. Every anomaly, no matter how small or seemingly insignificant – an unexplained cold spot, an unnatural stillness in the woods, a fleeting shadow caught at the corner of an eye – was meticulously documented, cross-referenced, and analyzed. Her research wasn't just academic; it was a vital, ongoing effort to map the entity's patterns, to understand its rhythms, and to identify any potential weaknesses or triggers.

The library became her sanctuary and her battlefield. The scent of old paper and drying ink was now mingled with the pungent aroma of protective herbs she burned nightly, their smoke curling towards the ceiling like a silent prayer. She pored over her family's journals, deciphering the cryptic annotations that spoke of generations dedicated to this very struggle, finding solace in the knowledge that she was not alone in this fight, even if she was the only one actively engaged in it. The entries spoke of specific lunar cycles that amplified the entity's influence, of certain natural occurrences that acted as harbingers of its approach, and of ancient rituals that, while not entirely eradicating the threat, could dampen its power and push it back into the shadows.

She began to meticulously recreate these rituals, starting with the simpler ones. The creation of protective amulets, infused with the energy of specific herbs and whispered incantations, became a daily practice. She learned to prepare sacred oils, their ingredients gathered with reverence and caution from the very woods that harbored the danger. Her hands, once accustomed to the delicate turning of pages, now became adept at mixing poultices and binding charms. The process was not without its risks. There were moments when the air in the library grew heavy, charged with an unseen energy, when the shadows seemed to deepen and writhe, and when the whispers from the woods seemed to press against the very windows of her cottage. During these times, she would redouble her efforts, her voice steady as she recited the ancient words, her focus unwavering.

Sarah also understood that active deterrence was as crucial as passive protection. She began researching methods of creating localized wards, small pockets of protective energy that could be placed around homes and public spaces. This involved a deeper dive into the symbology of the pact, the geometric patterns and glyphs that, according to her ancestors, held inherent power. She spent hours sketching these symbols, painstakingly transferring them onto pieces of treated wood and stone, imbuing each one with her intention, her will, her fierce determination to safeguard Havenwood. The process was slow, demanding, and often mentally exhausting, but the stakes were too high for anything less than her absolute commitment.

She recognized the inherent danger of relying solely on her own efforts. Havenwood needed to be actively involved, not just as passive recipients of her protection, but as active participants in their own survival. This meant educating the town, not with fear-mongering tactics, but with a clear, concise understanding of the reality they faced. She started by approaching the town council, presenting them with her findings, her research, and her proposed solutions. The initial reaction was, as expected, a mixture of skepticism and disbelief. Mayor Thompson, while acknowledging the undeniable events of the previous weeks, still struggled to reconcile them with his understanding of the world.

"Sarah," he'd said, his voice strained, "we appreciate your dedication. Truly. But these are... extraordinary claims. We've never dealt with anything like this before."

"And that is precisely why we must deal with it now, Mayor," Sarah had replied, her voice firm, her gaze direct. "Ignoring it will not make it disappear. It will only make us more vulnerable when it returns. My research, the journals, the testimonies... they all point to a pattern, a cycle. We have a chance, a brief window, to prepare. To arm ourselves not with weapons, but with knowledge and the right precautions."

Slowly, painstakingly, she began to win them over. The undeniable evidence of the entity's presence, the lingering fear that still permeated the town, provided a fertile ground for her message. She organized public informational sessions, sharing her research in a digestible, accessible format. She explained the concept of the pact, the delicate balance that had been maintained for centuries, and the catastrophic consequences of its disruption. She didn't shy away from the darker aspects, but framed them within the context of preservation and remembrance.

"The entity is not a monster to be slain," she explained during one such session, her voice resonating with quiet conviction. "It is a part of the natural order, a force that exists alongside us, drawn to certain energies. Our ancestors understood this. They didn't fight it; they acknowledged it. They appeased it. They built a symbiotic relationship, a fragile coexistence, based on mutual respect and understanding. That is the pact we must now relearn."

She began to teach the townsfolk the basics of warding, simple techniques that could be incorporated into their daily lives. She showed them how to properly cleanse their homes, how to create small, personal protective amulets, and how to recognize the subtle signs of the entity's presence. She organized workshops on identifying and cultivating the herbs that held protective properties, transforming their gardens into subtle bastions of resistance. It was a slow, arduous process, but gradually, a new sense of purpose began to emerge within the community. The fear was still present, a quiet undercurrent, but it was now tempered with a sense of agency, of proactive defense.

Sarah's dedication was unwavering. She spent her days immersed in research, her nights preparing for the next day's teachings and rituals. She became the town's historian, its protector, and its guiding light, a solitary beacon in the encroaching darkness. The weight of this responsibility was immense, a constant pressure that threatened to crush her, but she bore it with a quiet resolve. She knew that the survival of Havenwood depended on her ability to keep the past alive, to ensure that the lessons learned in terror were never forgotten, that the memory of the 'guile of night' remained a potent force, a constant reminder of the delicate balance they had to maintain. Her new role was a solemn vow, a lifelong commitment to guarding the fragile peace of Havenwood.

The Community Rebuilds

The festival grounds, once a vibrant heart of celebration, were now a stark testament to the night's devastation. The cheerful bunting lay in tatters, interwoven with the splintered remnants of stalls and the lingering scent of ozone and something far more ancient, far more primal. The collective will of Havenwood, however, was not to let the physical scars define them entirely. Under Sarah's quiet guidance and with the hesitant but growing support of the town council, a new kind of rebuilding began. This wasn't about simply restoring what was lost; it was about integrating the experience, the terror, and the hard-won understanding into the very fabric of their lives. The task was monumental. Every broken plank, every scorched patch of earth, every overturned cart served as a visceral reminder, a haunting echo of the entity's brief, brutal reign.

Mayor Thompson, his usual robust demeanor now tinged with a profound weariness, found himself overseeing a different kind of civic duty. The initial days were consumed by practicalities: the grim task of clearing the debris, attending to the injured, and providing a semblance of order in the face of overwhelming chaos. But beneath the surface-level reconstruction, a deeper, more intricate process was underway. Sarah, working closely with the council members – Mrs. Gable, Mr. Henderson, and a few others who had visibly aged overnight – began to formulate strategies not for eradication, but for coexistence. The idea of vanquishing the entity entirely was, as Sarah had come to understand, a naive delusion. Their ancestors had learned this lesson through generations of cautious engagement, and now Havenwood had been violently reminded.

"We can't simply pretend it didn't happen," Sarah stated during one of their hushed, often late-night meetings in the less-damaged section of the town hall. The air was thick with the smell of dust and desperation, a potent cocktail that had become the prevailing atmosphere of Havenwood. "Ignoring it will be our downfall. We need to acknowledge it, understand it, and build our defenses accordingly. Not defenses of stone and mortar, but defenses of awareness, of tradition, of memory."

The festival grounds became a focal point for this new approach. Instead of a hurried, unceremonious cleanup, Sarah proposed a communal ritual of remembrance. It was a departure from the townsfolk's natural inclination to forget, to sweep the unpleasantness under the rug, but the sheer magnitude of what had occurred had shattered that inclination for many. On a designated Saturday, the surviving townsfolk gathered, not with somber faces, but with a quiet determination. They didn't rebuild the festival stalls as they had been; instead, they repurposed the cleared space. Certain areas were designated for the planting of specific herbs, chosen for their ancient protective properties – rosemary for remembrance, lavender for purification, and vervain, which Sarah's grandmother's journals described as a conduit for spiritual clarity.

Mr. Henderson, who had been notoriously skeptical of anything beyond the tangible world, found himself meticulously placing smooth, river-worn stones around the perimeter of these herb gardens. Each stone was inscribed with a single, potent glyph, carefully copied from Sarah's research into the protective markings used by the town's earliest settlers. The act of carving each symbol, of imbuing it with his focused intent, seemed to ground him, to give him a tangible stake in the town's collective vigilance. He spoke little, but his actions were loud, his commitment evident in the precise lines he etched and the careful placement of each stone.

Mrs. Gable, her usually sharp tongue softened by a newfound gentleness, took charge of organizing the younger generations. She gathered them around her, not to recount the horrors in graphic detail, but to impart the wisdom of their ancestors. She taught them the ancient songs, not the joyous melodies of festivals past, but the haunting, resonant chants that were meant to soothe and harmonize with the natural energies of the land. These were not songs of fear, but of respect, of understanding that even the darkest forces had their place, and that harmony, not conflict, was the key to survival. The children, wide-eyed and attentive, learned to hum the low, guttural tones, their small voices weaving a delicate tapestry of sound that seemed to push back against the oppressive silence that had settled over Havenwood.

Sarah's role evolved from historian to architect of this new equilibrium. She worked with the town council to establish a series of protocols. These weren't rules designed to incite panic, but rather gentle guidelines for fostering a heightened state of awareness. One of the most significant developments was the establishment of a 'vigil rota.' This wasn't a watch for an immediate threat, but a commitment to observing the subtle shifts in their environment. Members of the community were assigned rotating periods to simply *observe*. They were tasked with noting unusual animal behavior, sudden drops in temperature, inexplicable silences in the woods, or any persistent feeling of unease that couldn't be attributed to mundane causes. These observations were meticulously recorded in a new town log, housed in the library, serving as a living, breathing chronicle of the entity's presence and its subtle ebb and flow.

"Think of it not as looking for danger," Sarah explained to the first group of volunteers, their faces a mixture of apprehension and quiet resolve, "but as listening to the whispers of the world around us. Our ancestors were attuned to these whispers. They understood that the veil between our world and theirs was thin, and that a constant, respectful attention was necessary to maintain the balance. We are not spies; we are listeners."

This fostered a sense of shared responsibility. The fear that had previously isolated individuals was slowly being replaced by a communal understanding, a shared purpose. It was a delicate balance, indeed. The aim was not to live in perpetual terror, but to cultivate a state of cautious, informed vigilance – a resilience born not from ignorance, but from a deep, abiding respect for the forces that had, and could again, impact their lives. The festival grounds, once a symbol of their vulnerability, were slowly transforming into a testament to their nascent strength. The herb gardens, tended with care, began to bloom, their fragrant presence a subtle, yet potent, counterpoint to the lingering shadows. The stone inscriptions, weathering the elements, served as a constant reminder of their ancestral wisdom.

The community's approach to remembrance was particularly noteworthy. Rather than attempting to sanitize the memory of the festival tragedy, they chose to honor it. A simple, unadorned stone was erected in the center of the newly designated vigil garden. It bore no names, no dates, only a single, powerful inscription: *"In Remembrance, We Remain."* This acted as a focal point, a place for quiet reflection. During the weekly vigil meetings, participants would gather at the stone, sharing their observations and reinforcing their commitment to the ongoing process of understanding. It was a somber acknowledgment, but also a powerful statement of defiance against the forces that had sought to shatter their community.

Sarah understood that the mental and emotional landscape of Havenwood was as scarred as the physical one. The immediate aftermath had been a period of shock, of disbelief, and then of raw, unadulterated terror. Now, as the town began to tentatively rebuild, she recognized the danger of this trauma calcifying into a persistent, debilitating fear. Her efforts were therefore geared not just towards practical measures, but towards fostering a sense of agency and control. By involving the community in the vigil, in the tending of the herb gardens, and in the learning of the ancestral songs, she was actively empowering them, shifting the narrative from victimhood to resilience.

The council meetings, once dominated by discussions of immediate damage control, now increasingly focused on long-term strategies. They debated the placement of the protective wards Sarah had been developing, the scheduling of the vigil rotas, and the integration of the ancestral teachings into the town's educational framework. There was a palpable shift in the council's dynamic. Mayor Thompson, initially hesitant, now leaned heavily on Sarah's knowledge, his respect for her growing with each passing day. He saw that her understanding of Havenwood's hidden history was not mere academic curiosity, but a vital, life-saving resource.

"We need to make this 'vigil' a part of our identity now, Sarah," Mayor Thompson said, his voice resonating with a newfound conviction during one of these sessions. "It's not just about watching out for... for what's out there. It's about remembering who we are, and what we are capable of protecting. It's about building a community that is not just safe, but strong, in its awareness."

The idea of 'new traditions' was not merely symbolic. It was a deliberate, conscious effort to redefine Havenwood. The annual Harvest Moon festival, once the catalyst for disaster, would be reimagined. Instead of a raucous celebration of abundance, it would become a time for communal introspection and reaffirmation of their pact. The music would be subtler, the gatherings smaller and more focused on shared stories and the passing down of knowledge. The dances would be less about abandon and more about measured, harmonious movements that echoed the ancient chants.

Sarah's own home, once a quiet refuge, was now a hub of activity. Townsfolk would visit regularly, seeking clarification on a particular glyph, advice on a garden's placement, or simply a reassuring word. The scent of protective herbs had become a comforting, familiar aroma that permeated her cottage, a tangible sign of their collective effort. She spent hours meticulously cross-referencing the records from the vigil rota with the historical accounts, looking for any discernible patterns, any correlation between specific environmental cues and the entity's perceived activity. It was a painstaking process, but one that she undertook with an unwavering dedication, driven by the knowledge that every piece of information gleaned was a step towards securing Havenwood's future.

The woods, though still a source of unease, were no longer solely perceived as a place of inherent danger. They were becoming a landscape to be understood, a territory with its own subtle language. The townsfolk, through the vigil rota, were slowly learning to interpret this language, to distinguish between the natural rustling of leaves and the unnatural stillness, between the call of a familiar bird and the unsettling silence that often preceded a more ominous presence. This growing attunement was, in itself, a form of rebuilding, a restoration of a lost connection between the town and its environment, a connection that had been severed by generations of complacency.

The scars remained, a testament to what had transpired, but they were no longer viewed as purely negative. The damaged festival grounds, the unadorned memorial stone, the carefully planted herb gardens – these were becoming symbols of their resilience, of their ability to adapt and to learn. Havenwood was not erasing its past; it was integrating it, weaving the threads of terror and survival into a new tapestry of community. Sarah, the reluctant oracle, the keeper of forgotten lore, found a quiet satisfaction in witnessing this transformation. The path ahead was long and undoubtedly fraught with its own unique challenges, but for the first time since the night the veil had been torn, Havenwood was not merely surviving; it was beginning to truly rebuild, not just its structures, but its very soul. The vigilance was now a conscious choice, a communal commitment, a new way of life, and in that commitment lay the seeds of enduring strength. The entity was still a presence, a shadow at the edge of their awareness, but the fear it inspired was slowly, steadily, being transmuted into a potent, protective vigilance.

A Letter from Blackwood

The crisp autumn air carried a different kind of chill now, one that had nothing to do with the approaching winter and everything to do with the subtle, persistent hum of vigilance that had become Havenwood's new normal. Months had passed since the festival's devastation, and the town, though outwardly healed, bore the indelible marks of its brush with the primal. The herb gardens flourished, their fragrant tendrils a quiet defiance against the encroaching darkness, and the vigil rota, a meticulously maintained tapestry of townspeople's observations, had become as integral to their lives as the changing of seasons. Sarah, whose small cottage had become a sanctuary of lore and a hub of communal effort, found a measure of peace in the routine, a fragile calm built on the bedrock of shared purpose. Yet, the echoes of that night never truly faded; they merely receded, becoming a low thrum beneath the surface of everyday life, a constant reminder of the thinness of the veil.

It was on a Tuesday, a day as ordinary as any other, that a letter arrived, its envelope an unassuming cream parchment bearing a postmark from a distant, unfamiliar city. The handwriting was precise, almost unnervingly neat, a stark contrast to the frantic scrawls or hurried notes Sarah had grown accustomed to.

Unfolding it, she recognized the name immediately – Blackwood. The man she had encountered only briefly, a spectral presence at the fringes of that terrible night, now reaching out from the void. His words, when she began to read, were like a key unlocking a vast, unseen world, confirming her deepest fears and, paradoxically, offering a strange kind of solace in shared knowledge.

"My Dearest Sarah," the letter began, the salutation itself possessing a formality that felt both antique and intensely modern. "I write to you with a measure of urgency, having followed the whispers that reached me concerning Havenwood. Your resilience in the face of… *that*, does not surprise me, though it commands my profound admiration. The patterns, you see, are universal." Sarah's breath caught in her throat. Universal. The word resonated with a chilling finality. She had suspected, had desperately hoped, that Havenwood's ordeal was not a singular, monstrous anomaly. Blackwood's confirmation was a cold, hard truth that both validated her instincts and expanded the terrifying scope of their struggle.

He elaborated on his ongoing research, a global endeavor to document and understand similar phenomena, occurrences that defied rational explanation and left swathes of humanity grappling with the unfathomable. He spoke of isolated incidents, of communities that had inexplicably collapsed, of strange atmospheric disturbances, of collective bouts of madness that mirrored the subtle, insidious grip she had witnessed firsthand. His research, he explained, spanned decades, a meticulous collection of anecdotal evidence, fragmented historical accounts, and the hushed testimonies of those who had glimpsed the edges of a reality far more complex and terrifying than most dared to imagine. He described his own encounters, veiled in careful language that hinted at immense personal risk, at a relentless pursuit of understanding that had consumed his life. It painted a picture of a world perpetually teetering on the precipice, with Havenwood merely one of many towns to have felt the seismic shift.

"Your town," Blackwood continued, his script becoming slightly more animated, "is not unique, Sarah. Far from it. What you experienced was a manifestation, a powerful, aggressive surge of an ancient, pervasive influence. I have spent years tracing its tendrils, its subtle incursions into the fabric of human society. The echoes of its presence can be found in the folklore of disparate cultures, in the whispered legends of shadow-dwellers and spirit-haunters, in the recurring motifs of dread and fascination that pervade our collective unconscious." He cited examples – a remote village in the Himalayas that had fallen silent generations ago, its inhabitants vanishing without a trace; a coastal town in the Pacific Northwest that had been plagued by a pervasive melancholia, leading to widespread despair and societal breakdown; even fleeting references in obscure historical texts to entire cities that had seemingly blinked out of existence, leaving behind only the wind to whisper their stories. Each mention was a pinprick of light in the vast darkness of her ignorance, illuminating the scale of the threat and the sheer, overwhelming magnitude of what they were up against.

"You spoke of the entity as an 'invader'," he wrote, his pen seeming to pause for emphasis. "And in a way, you are correct. But it is not a physical invasion in the way we typically understand it. Its strength lies not in brute force, but in its capacity for insidious infiltration. It does not conquer; it corrupts. It does not destroy; it erodes." This was a concept Sarah had begun to grasp, a truth she had tried to convey to the council in those early, desperate days. The true danger wasn't the visible destruction, but the invisible decay, the subtle poisoning of the mind, the erosion of will. Blackwood's words gave her research a terrifying validation.

"The entity," he went on, "and I use the term loosely, for its nature is far more amorphous than a single 'being', is adept at exploiting the vulnerabilities of the human psyche. It thrives on fear, yes, but more insidiously, it feeds on doubt, on despair, on the erosion of self-belief. It can manifest not just as external phenomena, but as internal whispers, as amplified anxieties, as the subtle twisting of perception that leads individuals to question their own sanity. Havenwood's tragedy, I suspect, was born of a moment when this subtle influence broke through the barriers of everyday consciousness, amplified by whatever energies were present during your festival."

He detailed his own methodology, the painstaking process of sifting through the detritus of human history and belief, searching for the recurring signatures of this pervasive influence. He spoke of the psychological toll, the constant battle against the creeping paranoia that threatened to engulf anyone who delved too deeply into such matters. He himself admitted to periods of profound isolation, of questioning his own grip on reality, of the agonizing loneliness that came with knowing things that others could not, or would not, comprehend.

"Your ancestors, Sarah, understood this implicitly," Blackwood stated, his writing taking on a more focused intensity. "Their rituals, their protective symbols, their careful observance of natural cycles – these were not mere superstitions. They were sophisticated defenses, honed over generations, against a force that sought to unravel the very fabric of their existence. They knew that vigilance was not a passive state, but an active engagement. They understood that the entity's power was magnified by ignorance and amplified by fear.

Your efforts to reintroduce these practices, to foster a sense of communal awareness – these are the correct, indeed the *only*, path forward."

He then addressed her courage directly, a rare moment of overt praise that made Sarah's cheeks flush with a warmth that had nothing to do with shame or fear. "I must express my profound gratitude for your courage, Sarah. You stepped into the heart of the storm, not with a weapon, but with knowledge and a deep respect for the forces at play. You recognized that true strength lies not in defiance, but in understanding and adaptation. It is a wisdom that is tragically rare."

Blackwood then delivered a warning, a stark reminder of the ongoing danger that sent a shiver down her spine. "However," he continued, his tone shifting, becoming grave, "you must not underestimate its persistence. The entity's influence, once established, can subtly permeate even the most mundane aspects of life. It can find purchase in the smallest cracks, in the most overlooked corners of our daily existence. A casual remark, a fleeting thought, a moment of unguarded doubt – these can be the entry points for its influence. It does not always roar; often, it merely whispers, and its whispers can be more devastating than any shout."

He elaborated on this insidious nature, detailing how the entity could subtly alter perceptions, sow discord within communities, and erode trust through seemingly innocuous means. He spoke of how it could exploit existing societal tensions, magnifying them until they erupted into open conflict. It could foster an atmosphere of suspicion, turning neighbor against neighbor, friend against friend, all under the guise of legitimate concern or righteous indignation. The goal, he posted, was not necessarily immediate annihilation, but a slow, agonizing breakdown of social cohesion, leaving individuals isolated and vulnerable, ripe for further manipulation.

"Consider the subtle shifts in human behavior," Blackwood advised. "The amplification of minor grievances, the tendency towards suspicion, the erosion of empathy. These are not always natural human failings; sometimes, they are echoes of its presence, subtle nudges that guide us towards self-destruction. The vigilance you have instilled in Havenwood is crucial not just for recognizing external threats, but for guarding against this internal erosion. You must remain aware of the psychological battlefield, Sarah. The most dangerous enemy is often the one that convinces you that you are your own worst enemy."

He stressed the importance of maintaining open communication, of actively fostering empathy and understanding within the community, and of being acutely aware of how fear and uncertainty could be weaponized. He urged Sarah to continue her work, to deepen her understanding of the entity's methods, and to remain a steadfast guardian of Havenwood's collective consciousness. His letter was a stark reminder that the battle was far from over; it had merely shifted from the immediate, visceral terror of the festival night to a more protracted, nuanced struggle for the very soul of the town.

"Do not become complacent," he implored. "The entity is patient. It learns. It adapts. And it waits for moments of weakness, for cracks in the armor of vigilance. Continue to cultivate the practices that anchor your community – the observation, the remembrance, the shared knowledge. These are your bulwarks against its insidious advance. And remember, Sarah, you are not alone in this fight. There are others who understand, others who are watching, others who are fighting their own battles against this same pervasive shadow."

The letter ended with a promise of further communication, of sharing resources and insights as their respective endeavors progressed. Sarah carefully refolded the parchment, her mind a whirlwind of dread and determination. Blackwood's words had confirmed her worst fears, painted a grimly accurate picture of the vast, unseen war they were now a part of. Havenwood was not an isolated incident; it was a ripple in a much larger, more terrifying tide. But in that realization, there was also a sliver of hope. She was not alone. The knowledge she had painstakingly gathered, the traditions she had revived, were not just for Havenwood; they were part of a global effort, a fight for the very sanity of humanity. The vigil in Havenwood was no longer just a local safeguard; it was a crucial outpost in a war waged in the shadows, a war fought not with steel, but with awareness, with knowledge, and with an unwavering commitment to holding back the encroaching darkness, one watchful moment at a time. The scent of lavender and rosemary from her window box seemed to deepen, a subtle perfume of defiance in the face of an invisible, ever-present threat.

The Whispers Persist

The air in Sarah's cottage, usually redolent with the comforting scents of dried herbs and beeswax, seemed to hold a new, almost imperceptible undertone. It was a scent that couldn't quite be placed, a faint dissonance in the otherwise harmonious blend of her sanctuary. On nights when the moon hid its face, and the ancient oaks surrounding Havenwood cast elongated, skeletal shadows, Sarah sometimes felt it. A whisper, not of sound, but of a sensation – a prickling on the back of her neck, a fleeting glimpse of movement at the edge of her vision, like a moth flitting through the periphery of lamplight. These were not the overt terrors of the

253

festival, the visceral dread that had gripped the town in its icy fist. These were subtler, far more insidious. They were the lingering tendrils of an influence that refused to be entirely banished, a chilling reminder that the veil, though strengthened, remained perilously thin.

She would find herself staring into the deepest shadows of her room, her breath catching, her heart giving a sudden, erratic lurch. A flicker of movement, a distortion in the familiar pattern of the wood grain on her table, a sense of being watched by unseen eyes. These moments were rare, often dismissed as fatigue or the tricks of an overactive imagination. Yet, they persisted, a persistent hum beneath the surface of her regained calm. They were the whispers Blackwood had warned her about, the insidious infiltrations that sought to erode the foundations of sanity and security. She'd recall his words: *"It does not always roar; often, it merely whispers, and its whispers can be more devastating than any shout."*

These whispers were not auditory in the conventional sense. They were more akin to a psychic residue, a faint tremor in the fabric of reality that only those attuned to its frequency could perceive. Sarah, with her deepened understanding and her constant vigilance, was undeniably attuned. She found that during periods of stress, when the weight of her responsibilities pressed down, these phantom sensations intensified. A difficult conversation with the council about the dwindling supplies for the observatory, a late-night session poring over her research notes, the gnawing worry about the approaching winter and its potential to isolate the town further – any such strain seemed to act as a beacon, drawing the whispers closer.

One particularly unnerving evening, while cataloging a new batch of herbs that had been painstakingly gathered from the dew-kissed meadows, she felt a distinct chill settle over her.

It was as if an unseen hand had brushed past her, leaving a trail of icy air in its wake. She turned, her senses on high alert, expecting to see a draft from the ill-fitting window. But the window was shut tight, the latch firmly secured. Then, out of the corner of her eye, she saw it – a fleeting shadow, darker than the ambient gloom, dart across the floorboards. It was gone as quickly as it appeared, leaving no tangible trace, yet the sensation of its passing lingered, a phantom touch that made her skin crawl.

She remembered a passage from one of the ancient texts she had acquired from an antiquarian bookseller in a distant town, a text that spoke of "after-echoes," residual energies left behind by significant events. It had been dismissed by some as mere folklore, but Sarah knew better. She understood that the festival, and the entity's intrusion, had left an imprint on Havenwood, a scar that, while not visible to the naked eye, was deeply etched into the spiritual and psychological landscape of the town. These whispers were the reverberations of that scar, a constant reminder that the wound had never truly healed, only begun to scab over.

The vigil rota, a meticulously updated document detailing every observed anomaly, every strange occurrence, no matter how minor, became her anchor in these moments of unsettling perception. She would note down these fleeting sensations, these whispers of the unseen, not as proof of the entity's return, but as confirmation of her continued connection to its presence, a connection she had to actively manage. She wrote: "*Observed a fleeting shadow in cottage, accompanied by a distinct drop in ambient temperature. No apparent environmental cause. Sensation of being watched. Dismissed as residual paranoia, but noted for ongoing vigilance.*" It was a ritual of acknowledgment, a way of pinning down the ephemeral, of refusing to let the whispers dissolve into the realm of the subconscious, where they could fester and grow.

There were times, particularly during the long, silent nights, when the weight of her knowledge felt almost unbearable. She would lie awake, listening to the rustling of leaves outside her window, to the creaks and groans of the old cottage settling, and her mind would invariably drift back to the entity. She would try to recall its essence, its alien nature, and in those moments, the whispers would seem to intensify, almost as if they were drawn to her contemplation. It was a delicate balance, this constant awareness, this need to remember without succumbing to the fear that Blackwood had so eloquently described as its primary sustenance.

The townspeople, for the most part, seemed to have found a measure of peace. The overt manifestations had ceased, and the pervasive fear had receded, replaced by a quiet determination. They attended the vigil meetings, they tended their gardens, they lived their lives with a newfound appreciation for the ordinary. Yet, Sarah sensed a subtle undercurrent of unease, a collective awareness that the world was not as solid and predictable as it once seemed. She saw it in the way people sometimes glanced over their shoulders, in the hushed conversations that ceased when she approached, in the almost desperate normalcy they sought to cultivate.

Even in the brightest daylight, when the sun cast long, golden shafts through the ancient trees, Sarah could sometimes feel it. A flicker at the edge of her sight, a moment of disorienting déjà vu, a sudden, inexplicable sense of melancholic dread. It was as if the entity had woven itself into the very fabric of Havenwood, a subtle stain that even the most vibrant sunlight could not entirely erase. These were the whispers, the soft encroachments that reminded her that true peace was not a destination to be reached, but a continuous, conscious effort. It was a vigilance that extended beyond the night, beyond the vigil meetings, into the very marrow of her being.

She found herself becoming more attuned to the emotional currents within the town. Blackwood's insights into the entity's ability to exploit psychological vulnerabilities had made her acutely aware of any discord or heightened negativity. A heated argument in the market square, a rumour that spread like wildfire, a moment of collective anxiety about the impending winter – these were the potential cracks, the places where the whispers might find purchase. Sarah made it her mission to address these subtle shifts, to foster understanding and empathy, to counter any burgeoning fear with reason and shared experience.

One afternoon, she overheard a group of children playing near the edge of the woods. Their laughter, usually a joyous sound, was tinged with a peculiar edge, a competitive roughness that seemed out of character. Then, one of the children, a boy named Thomas, suddenly stopped, his eyes wide, staring into the dense undergrowth. He let out a small gasp, and then, as if something had snapped him out of a trance, he shook his head and ran off, the other children quickly following, their earlier merriment forgotten. Sarah approached the spot where he had stood, her heart pounding. She saw nothing, heard nothing, but the air felt heavy, charged with an unseen presence. She knew, with a chilling certainty, that Thomas had felt a whisper.

She sought him out later that day, finding him sitting alone by the riverbank, skipping stones with a listless expression. She sat beside him, offering a gentle smile. "Did you see something in the woods today, Thomas?" she asked softly. The boy flinched, his eyes darting towards her, then away. He shook his head, but his lower lip trembled. Sarah didn't press. Instead, she spoke of the beauty of the river, of the strength of the ancient trees, of the importance of looking for the light, even in the deepest shadows. She spoke of courage, of how sometimes, the bravest thing we can do is to acknowledge a fear, and then to choose to stand tall anyway. She saw a flicker of understanding in his eyes, a nascent resilience. She knew that nurturing this nascent strength in the town's youngest inhabitants was as vital as any ritual or observation.

The whispers were not just external sensations; they were internal. They were the moments of doubt that crept into Sarah's own mind, the insidious thoughts that questioned her path, her sanity, her ability to protect Havenwood. *Was she imagining it all? Was Blackwood simply a man driven by delusion? Was the town truly safe, or was she merely deluding herself, clinging to a fragile illusion of security?* These were the whispers of her own psyche, amplified, distorted. She fought them by returning to her research, by consulting her notes, by speaking with the other vigil members, grounding herself in the tangible evidence of their shared experience.

The responsibility weighed heavily. While the townspeople had entrusted her with a newfound sense of direction, they also looked to her for reassurance. She couldn't afford to succumb to the whispers, to let them erode her own resolve. She had to be the unwavering beacon, even when her own light flickered. This was the true burden of vigilance – not just to observe, but to maintain the strength to act, to lead, even when the unseen forces sought to undermine her from within.

She began to notice how these whispers could subtly manifest in the interactions between townsfolk. A misunderstanding that escalated disproportionately, a minor offense that festered into resentment, a shared anxiety that morphed into suspicion.

These were not necessarily the direct actions of the entity, but rather the fertile ground it cultivated, the subtle shifts in the collective emotional landscape that made the town more susceptible to its influence. Sarah found herself mediating more often, encouraging open communication, gently steering conversations away from speculation and towards understanding. She advocated for communal activities that fostered connection and shared purpose, simple gatherings that reaffirmed their unity and bolstered their collective spirit.

During the monthly vigil meetings, she began to introduce a new element to their discussions. Beyond the usual reports of strange lights or unsettling sounds, she encouraged members to share instances of heightened anxiety, of unusual irritability, or any personal experiences that felt subtly "off." This was met with some initial hesitation, as it skirted the edge of the tangible, but Sarah's calm, reasoned approach gradually encouraged openness. She framed these personal experiences not as weaknesses, but as vital data points, indicators of the entity's continued, albeit subtle, presence.

One of the older members, Mrs. Gable, a woman known for her quiet stoicism, hesitantly shared a story. "I... I've been having trouble sleeping," she admitted, her voice barely above a whisper. "Not nightmares, exactly. Just... an unease. A feeling that something is just outside my window, even when I know nothing is there. And yesterday, I found myself being unnecessarily sharp with young Timmy from the bakery. He's always been such a good boy, but for a moment, I just... I felt a surge of irritation. It wasn't like me."

Sarah nodded, her gaze meeting Mrs. Gable's with understanding. "Thank you for sharing that, Mrs. Gable. These are the subtle manifestations we must be aware of. It's not about succumbing to

259

fear, but about acknowledging these shifts, understanding that our resilience requires constant tending." She then drew a parallel to the ancient practices, explaining how their ancestors had recognized the importance of maintaining inner harmony as a defense against external influences.

The whispers, Sarah understood, were a constant test. A test of their collective memory, of their strength of will, of their ability to discern the subtle from the significant. They were the silent harbingers of a struggle that demanded not just outward vigilance, but an internal fortification. The battle for Havenwood was not a single, decisive confrontation, but a continuous, intricate dance with a force that thrived in the shadows, in the overlooked corners of everyday life, and in the quietest whispers of the human heart. And Sarah knew, with a profound and unsettling clarity, that the dance had only just begun. The scar remained, a silent testament to what they had endured, and a perpetual reminder that true peace was earned, not given, and that the whispers, though faint, would always persist, a subtle yet insistent call to arms.

The Unending Watch

The moon, a sliver of bone against the velvet of the night sky, cast long, skeletal fingers across the sleeping town of Havenwood. Sarah stood at the precipice where the ancient woods kissed the cultivated fields, the familiar scent of damp earth and decaying leaves filling her lungs. It was a place of transition, a threshold between the known and the unknown, and tonight, it felt like her permanent station. The chill in the air was more than just the late autumn bite; it was the lingering phantom of a presence that, though banished, had etched itself into the very soul of this place.

She looked out at the cluster of cottages, their windows dark and silent, each a small ember of warmth and life against the encroaching darkness. Havenwood. Her Havenwood. It was a name that had once conjured images of rustic charm and peaceful isolation. Now, it resonated with a deeper, more profound meaning, a sanctuary she was bound to protect, a secret she was fated to keep. The whispered anxieties that had once plagued her had solidified into a quiet certainty, a profound understanding of her role. She was not merely a resident, a herbalist, or a scholar; she was the guardian, the sentinel standing against the tide that had once threatened to drown them all.

The scar, the invisible, agonizing wound left by the entity's intrusion, was still present. Not a physical mark, but a deep-seated awareness, a constant hum beneath the surface of normalcy. It was in the way the wind sighed through the pines, carrying echoes of ancient, unsettling truths. It was in the unnerving stillness that sometimes fell upon the forest, a silence that felt too deliberate, too watchful. And it was within her, a permanent alteration of her own being, a constant vigilance woven into the very fabric of her existence. She carried it with her, not as a burden, but as a testament to what they had endured, and to the strength she had discovered in the crucible of fear.

She remembered the terror, the visceral, soul-shattering dread that had gripped Havenwood. The whispers had then been a deafening roar, a cacophony of fear that had threatened to shatter the collective sanity of the town. But they had faced it. They had endured. And in the aftermath, a new kind of silence had fallen – not the absence of sound, but the stillness of a held breath, the quiet resolve of those who had stared into the abyss and refused to be consumed. Sarah had been at the heart of that resistance, and in doing so, she had been irrevocably changed.

Her nights were now a tapestry of watchful stillness. Sleep, when it came, was a shallow, easily disturbed thing. Her senses remained sharp, attuned to the subtlest shifts in the night's symphony. The hoot of an owl, the rustle of a nocturnal creature in the undergrowth – these ordinary sounds were now filtered through the lens of her unique understanding, each potentially a signal, a clue, or simply the natural world asserting its presence. But the memory of the entity's unnatural intrusions had left an indelible mark. She could no longer afford the luxury of blissful ignorance.

The townsfolk had returned to their routines, their lives slowly, tentatively rebuilding themselves. They spoke of the events of the festival with a hushed reverence, a collective trauma that had forged a new bond between them. But beneath the surface of their regained normalcy, Sarah sensed a residual tremor, a subtle awareness that the world was not as stable as it once appeared. It was in the way they sometimes paused, their gazes drifting towards the shadows of the woods, a fleeting expression of unease crossing their faces before being quickly masked by a forced smile. They trusted her, yes, but they also understood, on some primal level, that her vigilance was their shield.

She, however, carried the heavier burden. For while they could retreat into the comfort of their homes, of their routines, her watch was unending. It extended beyond the formal meetings of the vigil, beyond the meticulous cataloging of anomalies. It was a state of being, a constant, conscious effort to maintain the fragile peace they had won. She had to remember everything – the scent of ozone that preceded a significant event, the peculiar way shadows seemed to deepen and coalesce, the unsettling sensation of being observed by eyes that did not exist. These memories were not mere recollections; they were the tools of her trade, the keys to understanding the lingering threats.

She ran a hand over the rough bark of an ancient oak, its gnarled branches reaching towards the sky like supplicating arms. This tree had stood here long before Havenwood, a silent witness to centuries of change. It, too, bore the scars of time, of storms and harsh winters. It was a symbol of resilience, and Sarah drew strength from its enduring presence. She had learned that true strength was not the absence of fear, but the courage to act in its presence, to stand firm even when the ground beneath you felt like it was shifting.

The 'guile of night,' as Blackwood had once described the entity's insidious nature, was not a force that could be entirely destroyed, not in the way one might defeat a physical foe. It was more akin to a persistent shadow, a stain that, once imprinted, could never be fully scrubbed away. It could be contained, diminished, held at bay, but its potential for resurgence was an ever-present reality. And Sarah was the bulwark against that resurgence.

Her cottage, once a sanctuary of quiet study and healing, had become the nerve center of this ongoing defense. The shelves laden with herbs and tinctures now also held worn leather-bound journals filled with her meticulous observations, diagrams of celestial alignments, and intricate notations on the subtle energetic shifts she perceived. Her life, once defined by the rhythms of nature and the needs of her patients, was now inextricably linked to the unseen currents that flowed through Havenwood.

She recalled the conversations with Blackwood, his cryptic warnings and his unwavering conviction. He had seen something in her, an innate sensitivity that he had helped to hone, a quiet strength that had resonated with his own deep understanding of the forces at play. He had passed the mantle to her, not through a formal ceremony, but through shared knowledge, through the silent acknowledgment of her readiness. And now, she understood the weight of that inheritance.

There were moments, particularly on nights like this, when the sheer magnitude of her responsibility pressed down on her. The isolation could be profound. While the townsfolk found solace in their shared experience, her unique position set her apart. She was the one who had to remain ever-alert, the one who could not afford to falter. The whispers, though muted, still found their way into her own thoughts, probing for weakness, sowing seeds of doubt. *Was she truly making a difference? Or was she merely a solitary figure engaged in a futile struggle against an unstoppable tide?*

But then she would feel the steady thrum of life from the town, the quiet resilience of the people she protected. She would remember the faces of those she had helped, the laughter of children playing in the sunlight, the shared moments of quiet contentment. These were the anchors that kept her grounded, the tangible proof that her vigil was not in vain. The scar was a reminder of their vulnerability, but it was also a testament to their survival, to their enduring capacity for hope.

She turned her gaze back towards the dark expanse of the woods. The trees stood like silent sentinels, their branches etched against the moonlight. Within their depths lay mysteries, ancient energies, and the ever-present possibility of the unknown. She felt a connection to this wild, untamed place, a kinship forged in shared experience. It was a place that had tested her, that had revealed her own hidden depths, and that now, in a strange and profound way, felt like a part of her own being.

The guile of night was a patient adversary. It did not always manifest in dramatic displays of power. More often, it worked through subtlety, through insidious suggestion, through the slow erosion of resolve. It fed on fear, on doubt, on discord. And Sarah's primary weapon was her unwavering commitment to vigilance, her refusal to let the whispers take root in her own heart, or in the hearts of the people she served.

She had learned to listen not just with her ears, but with her entire being. She felt the subtle shifts in the town's collective mood, the currents of anxiety or unease that could signal the entity's attention. She had become adept at diffusing tension, at fostering understanding, at reminding people of the strength they possessed when they stood together. Her herbal remedies, while still potent for physical ailments, were now also imbued with a deeper purpose – to soothe troubled minds, to bolster faltering spirits, to remind those who felt lost of their own inner light.

She thought of the future, of the seasons that would turn, of the new generations that would grow up in Havenwood. Would they ever know the true extent of what had transpired? Perhaps not. And perhaps that was for the best. Her duty was not to inflict the trauma of the past upon them, but to ensure that they would never have to experience it. Her vigilance was a silent promise, a whispered vow spoken in the language of the stars and the rustling leaves.

As the moon climbed higher, bathing the landscape in its ethereal glow, Sarah felt a sense of profound peace settle over her. It was not the peace of complacency, but the hard-won tranquility of acceptance. She understood her place in the intricate tapestry of Havenwood. She was the thread that held it together, the unwavering watch that ensured its continued existence.

The scar was a part of her, a testament to her journey, and a constant reminder of the vigilance required. The guile of night might persist, it might whisper and probe, but Sarah, the guardian of Havenwood, would forever be watchful, her resolve as enduring as the ancient oaks that stood sentinel beside her.

Her vigil was not a task; it was her fate, and in embracing it, she had found her true strength.

ACKNOWLEDGMENTS

My deepest gratitude goes to the quiet strength of those who find solace in the shadowed corners of their own lives, the unsung guardians who stand watch when the world sleeps. To the readers who brave the darkness with me, thank you for your courage.

APPENDIX

The Havenwood Almanac: A Chronological Account of Anomalies and Observations

The following appendix details significant, recorded events and perceived energetic shifts within the Havenwood region, compiled by Sarah, Guardian of Havenwood. This is a selective compilation, focusing on events that correlate with the heightened "**Guile of Night**" phenomena.

Year of the Whispering Wind (Observed Anomaly: Auditory Hallucinations, Increased Nocturnal Activity): Early signs of atmospheric disturbances noted. Instances of shared auditory phenomena among select residents.
Year of the Shadow Bloom (Observed Anomaly: Peculiar Flora Growth, Distorted Light Patterns): Unnatural growth patterns observed in the Eldoria Woods. Reports of shadows behaving independently of their source.
Year of the Festival of Veils (Key Event: The Entity's Manifestation): The period of most intense activity, culminating in the near-catastrophic manifestation. Detailed accounts are held in Sarah's personal journals, detailing the sensory overload and energetic disruptions.
The Stillness (Period of Observation: Post-Manifestation): A period of relative quiet following the entity's expulsion. Noteworthy for a profound, almost tangible stillness that settled over Havenwood, interpreted as a residual energetic imprint.
The Resurgence (Observed Anomaly: Subtle Energetic Oscillations, Heightened Vigilance): The current period, characterized by subtle, cyclical energetic shifts. Residents report a general increase in unease, though the overt manifestations have been significantly curtailed due to ongoing vigilance.

Further detailed observations, including meteorological correlations and specific energetic signature readings, are contained within Sarah's personal research archives.

GLOSSARY

Guile of Night: A metaphorical term used to describe the insidious, pervasive nature of the entity's influence, characterized by subtlety, manipulation, and a tendency to exploit fear and doubt.

Havenwood: The fictional town at the center of the narrative, a place once idyllic but now perpetually under subtle, unseen threat.

The Entity: The nameless, formless malevolent force that sought to infiltrate and corrupt Havenwood. Its nature is described as a pervasive darkness rather than a distinct physical being.

Guardian of Havenwood: The designated protector and sentinel of the town, tasked with monitoring and mitigating the influence of the "guile of night." This role is currently held by Sarah.

Energetic Imprint: The lingering residual influence or trace left behind by significant events or powerful entities.

The Stillness: A period of profound quiet following a major energetic event, interpreted as a sign of the entity's diminished but not extinguished presence.

BIOGRAPHY

Dr. A. Romani is an indie author and inspirational storyteller who's made waves in the literary world with his unique voice and compelling narratives. Armed with a doctorate that sharpened his research and communication skills, he's built a diverse portfolio spanning multiple genres—each infused with his signature blend of inspiration and insight. What sets **Dr. Romani** apart is his commitment to the transformative power of stories. He doesn't just put books out there; he creates movements of positivity and encouragement. Through his Indie Author works, he connects directly with readers seeking both entertainment and enlightenment. His books consistently resonate with audiences worldwide, offering comfort and motivation to those navigating their own life stories. **Dr. Romani** believes every story has the potential to change lives, and he's dedicated to being that beacon of hope— one book, one story at a time.

www.ingramcontent.com/pod-product-compliance
Lightning Source LLC
Chambersburg PA
CBHW031214020726
47499CB00002B/582